3/20 written by my friend -
Enjoyed the story. Easy read
Ann

JB

BIG BEAUTIFUL COW

BIG BEAUTIFUL COW

Dear Ann -
Thank you so
much & please
enjoy! ♡ Jillian

BY

JILLIAN NAVARRO

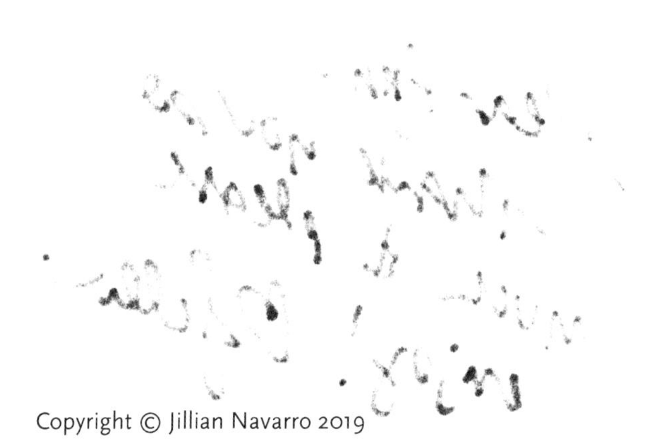

ISBN: 978-1-7336842-0-0 (paperback)

BIG BEAUTIFUL COW

To the world you may be just one person; but to one person you may be the world. ~ Anonymous

1

At first the chirp was part of her dream. Chirp. Pause. Pause. Chirp. Pause. Pause. The dream was an unlikely mismatch involving her father and a blonde, possibly illegitimate son - *interesting, no brothers she was aware of* - arguing about turkey. Her dad insisted on a blast of heat at the beginning for optimum browning; and then roasting low and slow until the meat was succulent and juicy. The blondie remained adamant that deep frying was the way to go. Creating crackling skin and a moist interior, the modern method, he insisted, was clearly superior. Chirp. Pause. Pause. Chirp. Pause. Pause. Were her dream father and his newly discovered offspring listening to some sort of techno? On Thanksgiving? Chirp. Pause. Pause. Chirp. Pause. Pause. Joanna fuzzily opened one eye. Her father and blondie floated away. The chirp kept chirping. The digital clock read 3:17am. Joanna groaned.

"What the hell *is* that?" She mumbled.

Joanna was not a good sleeper. Never had been. Her mother, Lily continues to tell anyone who will listen, "May would never go to sleep and Joanna, you could never wake up. I used to have to wake that girl up on Christmas morning." They were Jewish, but Lily thought Christmas should be everyone's holiday, "it's just about presents and a jolly old guy and those reindeer. How are these things religious?" She had a point. "I used to have to wake that girl up to watch Sesame Street!" Joanna's mother did not understand it is not the quantity of sleep, but the quality of sleep that provided rest. Joanna could not recall ever really feeling "rested" upon wakening, not even as a small child. Never invigorated and ready to face the day. And never had that movie-moment stretch, with the morning sun streaming through the window and the bird chirping on the windowsill. Chirp. Pause. Pause. Chirp. Pause. Pause.

Joanna was now awake enough to realize the chirp was here to stay unless she got up and dealt with it. Whatever it was. She swung her legs out of the massive bed, so large it was the only piece of furniture that fit in the bedroom. Diego had insisted on a California King. "*I need a lot of space, baby!*", despite the small rooms in their apartment. The bed was so large they had to forgo the matching night stands and instead purchased tiny pedestal tables that barely contained the requisite clock/I-product/radio contraption and bedside lamp. Joanna gingerly reached her toes for the floor. Inevitably there would be a book or three that would be uncomfortable and disrespectful to step on. She padded out of bed and out of her room, following the chirp. Pause. Pause. Chirp. Pause. Pause.

Joanna crossed the hall and entered her combo office/ guest room in search of electronics. First she checked her mobile, but it was peacefully resting and not emitting any weird sounds. Her laptop was miraculously turned off in her attempt to leave less of an environmental footprint. *Yeah for me!* Joanna thought to herself, pleased she had remembered to turn it off before going to bed. She wandered down the hall, fingertips outstretched as her eyes adjusted to the dark. The chirp was getting louder.

At the end of the hall, where the wall met the ceiling, Joanna spied the little red light where the chirp was coming from. The smoke detector. "Ah...the perpetrator," Joanna murmured.

"Chirp. Pause. Pause. Chirp. Pause. Pause," replied the smoke detector.

Content to find the source, and resigned that sleep was not on the immediate agenda, Joanna contemplated how to reach the damn thing. Joanna was blessed with many things, including an uncanny sense of smell and brilliant green eyes; but at 5 feet 1 inch tall, she was not blessed with height. She turned on a light, rubbed her eyes and blinked away the spots and opened the broom closet to get the step ladder.

Where is it? Had he taken the damn step ladder too? Unbelievable! She thought, irritated. Oh no, here it was, hiding behind the ancient Electrolux her mother had given her when she and Diego had moved into this drab yet pricey apartment.

Joanna wrestled the step ladder into the hall.

Climbed up. Reached high. Still too short; way too short. Undeterred, she tromped back to the closet and located a spindly broom. Back up the ladder, broom in hand she poked at the detector. No luck. She wedged the broom handle against the side of the detector in an attempt to pry it off the wall. Presto! It dislodged and dangled from an old screw, resembling a tiny space ship, "Take me to your ruler," she mumbled, swinging the broom like an insane batter. Astonishingly, she connected hard. It ricochet off the opposite wall, skid along the fake hardwood linoleum and landed somewhere in the kitchen. Joanna dropped the broom and climbed down the ladder. She groped about the kitchen, following the chirp, pause, pause until she found the evil detector; its glide across the floor had been cushioned by a fat and well established dust-bunny. She yanked out the battery; the chirping stopped. Joanna yawned and stretched and sauntered towards her bedroom, first tossing the noisy detector onto the counter and the battery in the trash. She stopped. Wasn't there something she was supposed to do with the battery? Recycle it?

Forget it, she thought, *it's the middle of the damn night. Tomorrow I'll research what to do with old batteries. Right now I'm going back to bed.*

She made mental notes to tell her nephew Leo about her Mays-esque and buy a replacement battery, and then Joanna snuggled down into her bed and closed her eyes; trying to conjure the weird dream, the Fischer house would have been a completely different place with more testosterone around. The dream didn't come. She rolled onto the opposite side of the bed. It was chilly and empty. Joanna burritoed the comforter around herself, perfectly cocooned, and slowly drifted back to a leaden sleep.

Joanna's alarm went off at 7:00am. She blinked at the oppressive radio blaring "Su-su-sudio", astonished. Hadn't she just fallen asleep? It couldn't possibly be time to get up and face the day. She hit the snooze button, rolled over, and promptly fell back asleep. This time the radio screamed "I believe I can fly" and she smacked the off button. The radio reception in the apartment was terrible; so the only radio stations Joanna could get clearly were either in Spanish, which tended to infiltrate her dreams but not actually wake her up, *"Se espera un día soleado, con una temperatura alta en los medios o los altos 60s"*or soft pop which tended towards the softest and cheesiest pop from the previous decades. *Worst radio station EVER,* Joanna thought.

She rolled onto her side and pushed herself into a sitting position, squinting at the light trying to sneak through the cracks in the cheap blinds. She valiantly attempted to get out of bed, the sheets wound around her legs and she struggled awkwardly for their release. Finally free, she started down the hall, yawning and bleary-eyed, promptly tripping over the forgotten broom that slay the smoke alarm and slamming her shoulder into the bathroom door frame. "Just fucking terrific," she mumbled, rubbing her throbbing shoulder, "what a fantastic start to the day." At least her dull job wasn't demanding; just repetitive and mind-numbing and probably better suited for a well-trained monkey. At least there was a minute silver lining: today was Thursday and she had a standing lunch date with her sister, May.

Joanna's title was "Front Desk Coordinator" but she had no idea what that meant, even when confronted with her massive two and a half page job description. She answered phones, greeted guests, filed paperwork. The job screamed "receptionist" but her boss, Helen insisted it was a much more important position than a lowly receptionist; vital to the inter-workings of the firm and therefore worthy of a more weighty title. Helen's title was "Administrative Manager" which to Joanna meant Helen managed paper: "*You, notebook! Get back to work!*" Joanna found it astonishing that Helen, terrified of her own shadow, had worked her way up into a managerial role, overseeing six employees at Miller, Stewart and Sons. Once Helen needed to reprimand Joanna for tardiness and Joanna thought she was going to have a stroke; she was shaking and sweating so profusely. Joanna vowed never to be late again because putting poor Helen through such strain would surely kill her, although, if her goal was to be upwardly mobile at Miller, Stewart and Sons, perhaps this would be a good strategy for getting ahead. Strangely, Helen had a very handsome and rather dashing husband and three very cool grown children.

Once Joanna saw the couple kissing goodbye after a lunch date, and it was the eeriest sight. This anorexic-thin, fluttery-eyed, sweaty bird-like woman reaching up to gawkily kiss this tall, tan, robust, sexy man. Joanna idly wondered about their sex life. It must be painful trying to have sex with that woman, she must be so pokey. Joanna was definitely an advocate of a little cushion for the pushin'.

Joanna suspected that long before the twin towers fell Helen had been excessively alarmist. She had created an elaborate safety procedure manual, not detailing proper lifting techniques and potential hazards, but instead specifying how to meticulously inspect e-mail and properly open post-mail (don gloves, especially for junk mail). "*Be aware of your surroundings and any suspicious-looking persons on the premises*," read the manual. Since Joanna sat at the mammoth mahogany veneered front desk, it was her job to "scrutinize" the guests. Joanna was unsure exactly what she was looking for. The impatient gentleman with the comb-over and the acne scars tapping his well-worn Hush Puppies? Was he "suspicious" or just your average guy waiting to see his divorce attorney? The spindly-thin sad-eyed woman wearing a muumuu? Was she "suspicious" or just unhappy? Delia, who worked in human resources confided to Joanna that Helen had been "spoken to" regarding scaring the shit out of the employees with her doom-laden manifesto. Joanna thought the manual made entertaining reading when the Wi-Fi went down.

"Miller, Stewart and Sons, this is Joanna; how might I

direct your call?" Joanna reached a finger into the potted plant on her desk, the leaves were looking droopy and sure enough, the soil was dry as dust.

"It's me. Can we push our lunch back to 12:30? I desperately need a pedicure." May was predictably dramatic.

"Why does anyone desperately need a pedicure in January? Fine, see you then," Joanna poured some of her bottled water into the plant and made a note to call the overpriced plant service.

Despite the three year age difference, May and Joanna had always been basically inseparable. When May was born, Joanna immediately took her under her wing, a proud three year old mamma to her cute, if whiny, baby sister. Lily was happy to let her do it. Let's face it, motherhood is exhausting. Joanna would feed and diaper wiggling, loud May. She would take her for walks in the stroller and introduce her around the neighborhood. She would dress her in little outfits and bathe her (as an adult, Joanna would marvel at this, that Lily would actually let her bathe her sister, *unsupervised*! Lily denied it.) As the girls got older, Lily would tease that Joanna was the mom and she and May were sisters. Joanna enjoyed playing along until she was about thirteen and decided her mother's behavior was weird and probably abusive. Plus, the comment stung.

May was tall, willowy. Beautiful in a natural; unblemished way. She looked just like Lily, who looked a lot like Dyan Cannon did when she was on Ally McBeal, but with a flower-child wardrobe. May had a huge wavy mane of reddish-gold hair that shimmered like a sunset. Her green eyes sparkled like emeralds against her olive skin. Identical to Lily during her pregnancies, when May was pregnant with Leo she had one of those perfect basketball-shaped bellies, where you didn't even know she was pregnant from the back, showing not an iota of back fat. She also had that lovely pregnancy glow books describe but no one actually has. Her skin was radiant and dewy. May had the kind of beauty that made everyone do a double-take. Men and women would stammer and stare. Once a man wearing his business suit, on his way to work, actually *got off a bus* and chased her down the street just to meet her and beg for her phone number. He didn't get the number. And he was probably late for work.

Despite May's biological good looks, she was forever primping, plucking, shaving or loofa-ing something. Her bathroom was a typhoon of products: gels, creams and balms to beautify every inch of a person. Growing up, May would set up a beauty salon in the backyard and give makeovers to the neighborhood kids (plus a few of their mothers). She'd carefully apply makeup to her customers, lecturing on how this hazel eye-shadow complimented Leah Johnson's green eyes way better than the trendy blue she was wearing; or how just a swipe of rose-toned blush brought out Kate Litman's hidden cheekbones. Joanna provided tasty refreshments for the guests with her state-of-the-art harvest gold Easy Bake Oven. They had quite an enterprising business going.

Joanna, fortunately or unfortunately, more closely

resembled her dad, in both appearance and demeanor. This included his rather pear-shaped figure and penchant for baked goods, but also his calm studious nature. She was shorter, much rounder, often mistaken for the younger sister (a fact Joanna loved to point out as often as possible to her vain sis), and her bathroom routine consisted of Ivory soap and Jergens lotion. Oh, and eye cream. On Joanna's 30th birthday May had presented her with the most obscenely large tub of eye cream Joanna had ever seen, complete with the most obscenely large price tag she had ever seen. "May, I don't own a single item of clothing that costs this much," Joanna told her.

May replied, "It's time to start taking better care of that luminescent skin of yours, Jo, you're gonna get crow's feet soon and look at the little lines you are starting to get in your forehead and..."

"OK, ok! I'll use the damn eye cream!" Joanna's huge green intelligent eyes, her best feature, and one of the few she shared with May and Lily, were framed with long lush lashes. These paired with her pale, smooth skin and dark brown hair inspired an occasional head turning or two of her own. But when your mother looked like Dyan Cannon and your sister looked like May, well, it was easy to get lost in the beauty-queen shuffle. And Joanna preferred to be watching the pageant from the sidelines anyway.

"I'm having the eggplant sandwich," announced Joanna, putting down her menu.

"That's what I'm having. You get the BLT." May

inspected her pedi under the table; her toes had been lacquered a pale peach.

"I don't want the BLT. I want the eggplant."

"We can't both get the same thing. Should we split them?"

"No, May," Joanna sighed "I'm getting eggplant and I'm not splitting today." She smiled at the waitress depositing their drinks, coffee for Joanna and Evian water for May.

This was not a new debate. May always obsessed with ordering. She was concerned she wouldn't like her choice, or someone else's meal would be better, or she was eating too many empty calories. Joanna ordered whatever she felt like eating, much to the chagrin of her mother and her sister, who compulsively discussed the fiber content and other redeeming qualities of everything they put in their mouths. When it came to food, May behaved as if her lineage consisted of huge, repulsively fat woman, rather than the diminutive Lily and their even tinier Bubbie Ruth. Some thought that May and Lily had some type of hereditary eating disorder, which would explain the food obsession, but Joanna knew that they were both just narcissistic.

"Jamie is coming home tonight."

"That's unexpected, isn't it?" asked Joanna, stirring cream into her coffee.

"Yes, I didn't expect him until Friday," May answered, twirling a lock of hair. "In any case, can you pick up Leo for me? I'd like to hit a Pilates class."

"Of course," Joanna agreed.

May and Jamie dated for five years before they were married, but had barely been married a year when they announced they were pregnant. Joanna was ecstatic, and also felt as if she'd been punched in the stomach. Sharing May with Jamie had been tricky enough; thank God her new brother-in-law was an over-achieving workaholic, but a baby? And since when did May want children anyway? Didn't she know what a pregnancy could do to her figure? Apparently nothing as she wore her regular size 6 jeans home from the hospital.

"Well, Jamie wants a big family so, we're having a baby. Nothing will change except I'll be fat for a while and then we'll have a baby to play with. It'll be great!" May leaned back and rubbed her insanely toned and flat belly.

Leo came shrieking into the world after a relatively easy labor of only two hours of pacing at home; two hours of pacing at the hospital; one epidural and thirty minutes of pushing. Once he was cleaned of goop and each person got to ogle him sufficiently, everyone marveled over how he looked just like...Joanna. He was pale with dark, curly hair. Joanna picked up the yelping, whimpering bundle, looked into his baby translucent eyes and found a kindred spirit. Jamie made a special guest appearance for the birth but was back on the road in a flash, and May was barely out of recovery before arranging her post-pregnancy exercise routine with her personal trainer and her post-pregnancy diet with her dietician, so Joanna bathed and rocked and cooed at her mini-me, falling deeper in love by the second.

It wasn't that May didn't love her brand new accessory. She was an adoring and more or less attentive mother, dressing Leo in adorable gowns and hats, oooing and aaahing over each toe-wiggle and sweet sigh. She just didn't take well to the yuck factor. The poop and pee and spit-up were all a little much for meticulous May. Plus, the sleepless nights were horrific on her complexion; which had taken on a bluish pallor more fitting a new corpse than a new mother. And then, there was the boredom. It was stifling. There was only so much feeding, staring, changing, burping and bathing one person could do before she went crazy. She joined a "Mommy and me" yoga class, but that was only an hour out of a very long and monotonous day. She enrolled in a music class but just couldn't stand all the clapping and sing-songy-ness. "Are you sleeping? Are you sleeping? Brother John? Brother John? Morning bells are ringing. Morning bells are ringing. Ding ding dong. Ding ding dong." She couldn't take it. Eventually, it was Joanna who endured the music class, and later endured art and pottery and gymnastics. May hired a Spanish-speaking nanny; Luisa, thinking he may as well learn a second language along with his first", and bought a three hundred dollar breast pump since Joanna insisted on breast milk.

As Leo grew, May enjoyed her son more and more, relishing their early morning cuddles and chats about the sky and seasons and frogs, but as for many first-time mothers, that first baby year was rough as sandpaper. This little person demanding every ounce of her time and energy was overwhelming, and with Jamie gone so much at work, it was hard, and sometimes she was angry and resentful. She loved Leo fiercely and completely, more than she ever expected to love anyone, but sometimes she just felt depleted and done. Did that make her a bad mother? Joanna knew May struggled with this question when Leo was small, despite Joanna's assurances that she was positive every mother felt this way from time to time. Joanna knew that maybe for the first time ever, May felt challenged, really kicked in the ass, and as if she might actually fail at something. And with this particular something, failure was absolutely not an option.

Joanna pulled into the parking lot of Leo's nursery school, waving at mothers and nannies she had come to know in the four years she had been Leo's favorite aunt (poor Aunt Carly, Jamie's sister, was just no fun). Leo's school resembled a miniature college campus; with huge green lawns and high-tech play structures. A teacher buzzed her through the double "*Tighter than Fort Knox*", (said the brochure) security gates. When May first brought Joanna to pick Leo up from Bright Future Day School, "Where every child is a ray of light", Joanna commented, "What, no frisking?" May had given her a look that clearly said, *"Pipe down or I'm going to strangle you."*

"Auntie Jo!" an elated and sweaty Leo bombarded into her from behind, nearly knocking her over, "I ate a cheese for snack and made a elephant picture in art and can we make sagna for dinner and do I sleep over?" Leo smiled up at Joanna happily, a brown smudge (chocolate? mud? better not ask) across his mouth.

"Hey buddy, I'm happy to see you too. Yes we can make lasagna and yes, you can sleep over too and I can't wait to see your elephant picture. Where is it?"

Leo dashed off again to retrieve the picture. Joanna went to his cubby and gathered his sweatshirt, lunch pail and assortment of rocks, sticks and construction paper shreds. Leo returned with the picture, which he rapidly waggled in front of Joanna's face. Joanna couldn't help but be proud that the picture actually looked like an elephant...with a sizeable appendage between his hind legs. Joanna tousled his hair affectionately and said "I like how you made the elephant a boy."

"Yes, his name is Henry. Let's go to the car!" And he was off again like a shot.

Joanna loved having Leo in her apartment. He brought wonderful energy and excitement; he was luminous. He helped Joanna make dinner without complaint. First they made lasagna (Leo liked squishing the ricotta and spinach together), and then a batch of cookies (he was a snickerdoodle boy), and finally he plopped down in front of a Curious George video while the food cooked and Joanna set the table.

In the middle of dinner, Leo said, "My mom is getting a vorce from daddy." Joanna nearly choked on a mouthful of hot pasta. "What?!" She yelped, reaching for her water.

"A VORCE," Leo tended to yell like a deaf old woman

when someone didn't understand him, "Mommy is getting a vorce. That's what she said."

Joanna pondered this. A divorce? May was getting a divorce? And she was discussing this fact with four year old Leo? What the hell was she thinking? And why wasn't she discussing it with thirty-two year old Joanna? Didn't that seem more appropriate?

"When did she tell you this?" Joanna asked casually.

Leo shoveled lasagna into his mouth so quickly Joanna wondered if he was chewing at all. He paused long enough to say "I dunno. Yesterday?" and resumed shoveling.

"Yesterday" was not useful to Joanna, as Leo thought every day, past, present and future were all yesterday, "Slow down, buddy! You don't need to eat so fast! There's plenty! Slow down and just enjoy your dinner."

Leo smiled sheepishly. Joanna understood why Leo was so frantic. He was a child deprived of anything yummy or truly delicious. Sure he got to *sample* the fabulous food of childhood: peanut butter (reduced fat) and jelly (all fruit), chicken fingers (baked), hotdogs ("*well, tofu-dogs but they taste the sam*e" insisted May), ice cream (frozen yogurt, whatever), cookies (applesauce-sweetened) and pizza (low-fat cheese, whole-wheat crust and vegetarian pepperoni). But like Joanna, Leo enjoyed good food along with good company. A picnic for Leo and Joanna involved a crisp baguette and brie with apples. Their morning ritual was lavishly buttered and cinnamon-sugar sprinkled toast with their coffee - Joanna would let Leo have an inch of coffee in warm milk if he PROMISED not to tell May – plus cooking shows and cartoons. An evening stroll to inspect the stars was incomplete without an ice cream cone or in inclement weather, a stop for hot chocolate.

"Leo, do you know what a divorce is?" asked Joanna, keeping her tone neutral.

"No." Leo ate his last bite of lasagna with relish and put down his fork, "Mommy said that enough is enough and if that shellfish prick wants a '*vorce*' then he can have one. Auntie Jo, can I have some more sagna please?"

2

The next morning, Joanna was exhausted. She had tossed and turned, going over the conversation with Leo, and its ramifications, over and over. She dropped Leo off at Bright Future with a big hug and a kiss and immediately reached for her mobile to call May and find out what the hell was going on.

Unable to locate her headset in her bottomless purse, Joanna scrunched the phone precariously against her ear with her shoulder, "Hello, it's May, leave a message," damn, thought Joanna, voicemail.

"May, it's me, everything with Leo is fine. Call me when you can." Joanna tossed the phone onto the passenger seat and braked sharply. The SUV in front of her was not cooperating, slowing at yellow lights, keeping the speed limit and generally thwarting Joanna's feeble attempts to be essentially on time to work and therefore not cause her boss's death. Plus, it was eating up entirely too much gas.

She had been preoccupied with Leo's announcement all night and all morning. Joanna had only ever been envious of May and Jamie's relationship. She had never suspected there was trouble, especially not trouble so severe that she was yelling about a vorce. Especially not trouble Joanna didn't already know about, seeing as she was May's closest confidant.

Joanna knew that Jamie had no ability to wash a dish but liked the house to be spic and span, even as a poor college student he splurged for a housekeeper. She knew he watched the History channel incessantly (a fact Joanna found rather charming, despite the conversations peppered with World War II trivia), that when he drank too much he tended to get overly affectionate with everyone, mothers-in-law included, and if left to his own devices he would wear yellow, a color few can wear successfully, and Jamie was not one of them. Joanna also knew he was an expert lover, not to mention a tennis whiz. For a man with these generous skills, Joanna would have forgiven pretty much anything, except maybe the mother-in-law groping (which Lily, of course, found hilarious and, grossly enough, flattering).

Joanna never could have handled Jamie's constant travel schedule, needy as she was, but to May it was perfect. "Our time together is that much more special; the honeymoon has never quite ended for Jamie and me," she'd say, "and I couldn't stand it if he was always underfoot. You know I need my space." Joanna craved a constant companion, but May liked her independence and REALLY liked the financial freedom Jamie's job afforded them. The Fischers hadn't grown up poor, they were solidly middle-class, but May had always been an upper-crust girl. She turned up her nose at Joanna's hand-me-downs, both clothing and toys. She was embarrassed by their modest California bungalow. She imagined Malibu Barbie dream-houses of epic proportions: she and Ken living happily ever after in a 4,000 square-foot mansion complete with pool, tennis court and movie theatre. There would be hand maidens and foot soldiers and no leftovers. She would have closets of beautiful designer clothes, mountains of shoes and two adorable children who were always tidy, well mannered and nicely groomed. May's life really had turned out a lot like Barbie's.

Joanna was getting annoyed when she still hadn't heard back from May by lunch. She left another message for her: "Hello? Where the hell are you? Call me back please!" and tromped into the lunch room.

Her usual comrades, best friend Delia and side-kick Bruno, were already there, dishing about Earl from accounting. Earl was a very nervous, very sweaty man and today's heckling was focused on his chronically sweaty hands.

Delia offers, "The worst is when he doesn't have a handkerchief so he wipes his sweaty head with his sweaty palms."

"No, no," countered Bruno, "the worst is when he hands you your timesheet and it's damp."

"OK," Delia reluctantly conceded with a shiver, "you're right, you're right. That's absolutely disgusting."

Bruno raised his clasped hands in a victory salute.

"Nice lunch conversation," Joanna said sarcastically,

placing her shopping bag lunch on the counter and removing her container of leftover lasagna.

"Your lunch always looks so much better than mine," sighed Delia, dolefully unpacking a tuna sandwich. Joanna and Delia had quickly bonded during Joanna's first week of work over sharing Joanna's lunch - Delia swears it was a chicken-salad sandwich that clinched it but Joanna recalled meatball – regardless, the friendship had blossomed from there.

Bruno nodded in agreement as he daintily speared some drab lettuce, "It's like there are actual adults cooking meals at your house."

"This may come as a shock, but we are adults, Bruno," replied Joanna as she popped her container into the microwave, "but today you're in luck because I brought you both some lasagna."

"Oh, thank God!" said Bruno, dramatically sweeping his sad salad aside and reaching for the Tupperware container Joanna was extending, "Thank you, Momma Jo!"

"We would starve without you!" Delia popped hers into the other microwave before Bruno could nab it. He responded by sticking his tongue out at her.

"Hardly," Joanna said, smiling. She liked to feed her friends. Unlike ex-boyfriends, Delia and Bruno appreciated her cooking expertise. And Joanna enjoyed how it made them so happy. They were a lot like four year olds.

"Uh-oh, you have your glum face on, Jo, what's up?" asked Delia. She scowled at Bruno's wing-tipped toe tapping impatiently for the microwave "ding".

“Nothing...just a little preoccupied today.” Joanna answered distantly.

Delia dug into her lasagna with gusto and remorsefully encountered a hot spot; she waved her hands frantically in front of her mouth, like a deranged mime, so as not to be scorched by molten cheese.

Joanna picked at her lunch. She felt guilty for being angry with May, but she was confused; she felt betrayed. Joanna knew this was probably a selfish way to feel, given her sister might be getting a divorce. But why hadn’t May talked with her about this oh-so-serious, life-altering turn of events? A DIVORCE! Growing up, Joanna and May were the only kids on their block whose parents were still married by the time the kids had graduated from high school. Lily and Daniel had had some tough patches, like when Daniel decided to shave his beard and looked ten years younger, and then his students began to hit on him. Lily was convinced he was having an affair with a sexy co-ed named Naomi from Michigan who was taking his Comparative Literature course (he wasn’t, but Lily was so irritating during that period of time he for a split-second or two, considered it). There was also the time Lily had bought into a time-share on Maui without consulting Daniel. Woohoo! That was a fight to end all fights. Until of course, the mamma of all fights, the heavyweight battle: the abortion.

Lily had taken time off from nursing school when the kids were small, but when May was three she plopped her in co-op nursery school and set out to finish her degree. With her new busy schedule she had chalked up the exhaustion she was experiencing to, well, exhaustion. Raising two kids, keeping a home and finishing school; plus Daniel's career had taken off and he was finally on a tenure-track, making him less available for day to day help. The morning sickness set off the alarm bells she was pregnant, so she covertly purchased a newly available over-the-counter pregnancy test. After fiddling with the test tube and medicine dropper and re-reading the directions several times, the test was complete and all she needed to do was wait. For two excruciating hours. So while waiting for the results she paced back and forth, then re-potted several plants and baked a zucchini bread and then paced back and forth some more. And then, sure enough, as the package promised, there was the faint little blue line. Not convinced the new technology was accurate, mistakes could be made, no rabbits had died or anything, she made an appointment with her doctor to make absolutely sure.

"Congratulations, Mrs. Fischer!" Doctor Graham warmly confirmed the test's results. "Now, we'll have to proceed cautiously of course..."

Lily was absolutely baffled as to how this had occurred; she was scrupulous about using her diaphragm... wasn't she? Regardless, she was thirty years old and pregnant and another child just did not fit in with Lily's plans. So with Roe v. Wade firmly behind her, she scheduled an abortion and called it a day. And like a cartoon bottle of champagne, Daniel popped his cork.

"HOW DARE YOU," Daniel's modest stature seemed to grow ten feet tall as he thundered at Lily, "not consult me before scheduling this appointment?! We are a PARTNERSHIP, Lily! Partners do not make decisions IN A VACUUM! Who the hell do you think you are, making these decisions for OUR FAMILY?" Daniel trembled in anger.

Daniel's temperament most closely resembled a tranquil stream meandering through a serene forest, so he scared the bejesus out of his family with this explosion of emotion. The abortion incident was the first time Joanna had ever seen her father completely flip out, and there were only two other times since then that she could remember. Both had involved May (big surprise), once when she had defiantly stayed out all night at the tender age of fourteen and the second time when she sneaked Todd Matthews into her bedroom and was caught sleeping, really just sleeping with him, at 3am (Todd was a fierce snorer, more resembling a freight-train than a human being, which blew their cover). Lily, of course, was a different story. Sweet Lily was a sensitive soul who could flip out over a chipped nail and Joanna had actually seen her cry over a glass of spilt milk (Joanna recalled a pot-laced brownie being involved but still, overly dramatic in her book). But Daniel was the voice of reason in their marriage, talking Lily down from whatever ledge she was currently about to jump off.

All of these were tough times for Joanna's parents and consequently even tougher times for the Fischer girls, who tended to sleep in more and stay out later when their parents were arguing. At only six and three, Joanna and May were too young to really understand the abortion fight but in the weeks following, Joanna, May *and* Lily had walked on eggshells around Daniel. But then one day he announced he was done being pissed and they could all carry on with their normal routines. But a divorce? Never in the cards for the Fischers. A divorce was an entirely different animal. A divorce meant custody agreements and court proceedings and "I'm taking the Wedgwood Vera Wang Lace Platinum China; you can have the candy dishes shaped like chipmunks from your Great Aunt Bertha." It meant ending the most important chapter in your adult life, a chapter that began with "until death do you part," included giving birth to another human being and ended with a...a what? Joanna didn't know what had caused May to say the word divorce to Leo, but she knew May was serious about the sanctity of marriage so it must have been some pretty crazy shit.

Delia leaned over and squeezed Joanna's arm, "Joanna, are you ok?" Joanna jumped, startled by the physical contact when she had been lost in her own world. Joanna looked into Delia's petite face, seeing little wrinkles of concern creasing her smooth forehead.

"Yeah, I'm ok, just preoccupied. I think something yucky is going on with May."

"This is the best thing I have ever put into my mouth," Bruno nearly moaned with happiness over his lasagna lunch.

Delia raised her eyebrows at Joanna, "Doubtful," she said smugly.

3

May twisted her slender arm out of the soft grey comforter to hit the "mute" button on her cell. She was reluctant to turn it off in case there was a problem at Leo's school, and she knew it was just Joanna calling, and she couldn't handle Joanna right now. Her mouth was pasty and dry; her head felt like a mouse being squeezed to death by a hungry python, and the sunlight piercing through the cracked blinds was excruciating. It was quite possibly the worst hangover she had every experienced, and that included when Rod Kaplan had continually fed her kamikazes in the hope of coaxing her virginity out of her. His tactics failed, although he did coax a tsunami of vomit out of her and onto his maroon checkered Vans.

That's who I should have married, May thought groggily to herself, Rod Kaplan. Nice Jewish boy. I wonder what happened to Rod Kaplan. After high school he was planning on becoming a fireman like his dad, I wonder if he did that. He would have made a great fireman, adorable guy, tall and strong with that All-American "off to save a kitten up a tree" look to him. Maybe I should look him up. See what old Rod is up to. May giggled and realized she was still a little drunk. This was not good.

It had taken May just about a week to grasp, to really wrap her head around the fact that Jamie had left her. Or was leaving her. That prick was actually leaving her! Or something. "This isn't what I bargained for," he had said, "I just didn't realize, May. I'm so *so* sorry to have done this to you. It was not my intention. I love you and I love Leo, but I think I need to figure out what this thing is. I need to do it for me." Jamie had pounded his chest like a pissed-off baboon, "I need to for ME."

May gaped at Jamie as if he had grown a second head. Did he just tell her he was leaving her...for a man?

"No, May, I'm not leaving you for a man, I'm not gay," Jamie continued, pacing the length of the living room, and dragging his hands through his curly blonde hair, "but maybe I'm bi? I just don't know, but I need to figure this out. This is too important." He flopped into a chair, he was beginning to wheeze. He clutched at his chest as if he could steady his breathing by compressing his lungs.

"Important?" she had parroted, quietly. "This is too important?" Her volume escalated, "Fucking someone else is too important? Man, woman, horse, whatever! Because that's what you are talking about here, Jamie, fucking someone else. Let's not sugar-coat this!" May was shaking.

Jamie wheezed some more, "May, please calm down." Jamie struggled to his feet to put his arms around her shoulders but May shrugged him off.

"No, let me make sure I'm totally understanding what you are saying here. Fucking someone is more important than your wife and your son and this life we have?" May gesticulated wildly, "More important than 11 years? 11 fucking years? Is that what you are telling me?"

Jamie stared at his feet, "I'm so, so sorry, May. I'm not fucking someone else; it was one time, only one. But this isn't just about fucking someone else. It's about my identity." More wheezing. "Please try to understand. I didn't look for this; I didn't ask for this, it just happened. Just one time. I'm so sorry." More wheezing.

"Your identity?" May gaped at him.

Jamie leaned his forehead against the wall, gently banging it, "May, I never, never intended to be unfaithful. I love you. I don't know how this happened. I'm so sorry. Maybe I just need some time to think?"

May couldn't look at her husband. She concentrated on a fly creeping up the lampshade. Maybe if she focused on killing this fly with her laser vision, Jamie would disappear.

But he didn't disappear. Instead he wheezed again and said, "May, we need to talk about Leo."

May's head spun faster than Linda Blair's at a disco, "What about Leo?" she hissed at him.

"May, would you please calm down? We need to talk about what to tell him, how this is going to work, how to make sure I can see him. Whether I should move out while I work this through. There's a lot to discuss..." his voice trailed off as he gasped for breath.

May yanked a drawer open in the bar, rooting around, "God dammit, Jamie, use your fucking inhaler before you keel over!" May threw the thing and it bounced off his chest.

Jamie inhaled deeply and reached behind him for a chair where he sat heavily, panting. "May, I love you, I don't know what happened, maybe I just need some time..."

May really had planned on going to Pilates like she told Joanna at lunch. She had planned on pretending none of this had happened, at least for a few more days. She had planned on going to Pilates and maybe having dinner with a girlfriend, or doing some shopping. Leo needed a few things, new sheets for his big-boy bed, and probably some jeans. But once she returned home she just sat in her living room. Sat and stared, stared out at the lovely view from her living room window, attractively framed by silk shantung curtains. The beautiful living room felt empty and silent; sterile. All she heard was the steady tick-tocking from the antique grandfather clock she had purchased at auction. It was the loneliest, most irritating sound in the world. She couldn't avoid it any longer. She was on her feet and swiftly moving to the liquor cabinet. She plunked two ice cubes into a glass and poured herself two fingers of scotch, just to get the edge off. She downed it and poured two more. May started for the stairs, paused and went back for the bottle. She kicked off her pumps and climbed the stairs slowly. That was yesterday...

May turned onto her side and peeked over the edge of the comforter to see the time. Ugh. 2:15. She had to get herself together so she could pick Leo up by 4:00. May forced herself to sit up; a great wave of dizziness and nausea came over her. She rolled her head, stretching her neck and concentrated on the wallpaper; a pale, icy blue with teeny tiny white polka-dots running through it. Focusing on one spot in the wallpaper, she inched towards the edge of the bed and swung her legs over the side. "You can do this, you're a big girl," she whispered to herself, pushing up onto her feet. Steadying herself on the nightstand, she took a deep breath, ventured a step, and suddenly realized she was going to puke if she didn't move her drunk ass, and fast.

She made it into the bathroom in the nick of time, dropping to her knees and leaning over the toilet as the vomit burst through her clenched teeth, bettering the tsunami that had ruined Rod's shoes. After enduring the wet heaves and the dry heaves, May was empty and the smell was vile. She flushed. Big mistake. The noise was deafening, careening around her whirling head like a fire engine screaming to a 5-alarmer. She held her head and moaned. Shaken, she lay down on the fluffy cream-colored bathmat and pressed her flushed cheek against the cold tile floor. "That's better," she thought, "now I can go get Leo..." her eyes fluttered closed and she passed out cold.

Joanna was back at her desk, trying to figure out how to waste two more hours before she could get the hell out of here and go home. The day was plodding on with agonizing slowness. She was planning on grilling a chicken breast, trying a new dried fig chutney recipe she had picked up and having a glass of pinot, although probably not in that order. She was puzzled when her mobile began to ring from inside her purse; everyone she knew would call at the front desk. One of the very few advantages to being the "not receptionist" was that personal phone calls usually went undetected. She once chatted with May for a record forty-five minutes without anyone noticing. She even sent an e-mail to Helen during the call: *I am just tied to the phone today, Helen; I don't know what is going on!* Her puzzlement elevated to alarm when she saw Jamie's name appear on her mobile. She fumbled with the "talk" button.

"Hello? Jamie?"

"Hi Joanna, I'm sorry to call you during the workday, but have you spoken to May? I just had a call from Leo's school that she hasn't picked him up and I can't seem to locate her."

Joanna's heart-beat quickened and she drew in her breath, something was not right here. "Jamie, I've left her two messages so far today and haven't heard back. I can drive by your house. Do you need me to get Leo?" Joanna was already on her feet and shutting down her computer.

"Can you, Joanna? I'm in Boston, my flight home leaves in about half an hour."

"Boston? Still? I thought you came home last night." Joanna paused in the packing of her purse.

"No, I'm still in Boston," Jamie had a sinking feeling

in his stomach that something was terribly wrong, and he wasn't interested in debating his flight schedule. "When was the last time you spoke to May?"

Joanna was irritated. Jamie should know that Joanna and May spoke daily, usually several times a day. It was not unusual for them to speak first thing in the morning and last thing at night. So, he should be more concerned Joanna had left her TWO MESSAGES May hadn't returned.

"I had lunch with her yesterday. She asked me to pick up Leo and he spent the night with me. Jamie, is everything ok with you two?"

"No, it's not. She didn't tell you?" Jamie was surprised, he assumed Joanna would not only know but would have gone into full throttle May-protection-mode. A loudspeaker interrupted him, "Joanna, they're calling final boarding for my flight. Can you please get Leo and go by the house? I'll call you as soon as I touch down."

Joanna's heart was pounding, she grabbed her purse and practically ran into Helen's office, telling her she had a family emergency and had to leave that instant. Helen responded, her hands fluttering to her throat, with an "Oh my! I hope everything's ok! Go!"

Joanna was too impatient to wait for the elevator, and instead took the stairs two at a time. She screeched out of her parking space, zooming towards Bright Future. She was panicky and tried to calm herself down using the breathing techniques she had learned during May's Lamaze classes. She knew she needed to unruffle herself before she picked up Leo, the kid was frighteningly perceptive. She didn't want to freak him out. In desperation, she phoned, of all people, Lily.

"Joanna," Lily practically purred into the phone, "what a nice surprise. How are you, Honey?"

"Hi Mom, hey, have you spoken to May?" Joanna had no time for niceties; Leo's school was only ten minutes from her office.

"Well yes, of course, I spoke with her...maybe it was Monday? Or Tuesday? Tuesday, it was Tuesday because I saw Fran at the Safeway and she asked how you girls were and I said good, good, fine, but that I didn't get to see you as much as I'd like. And you remember her son Sam? He's the one who had that kissing disease when you were kids? Anyway, he just had a baby..."

Joanna interrupted her mother before she launched into details of the baby's bris and the chopped liver served at the ceremony. She knew it was risky to tell her mother May was...what? Missing in action? But she had no choice, she needed help in what to say to Leo, and for all her faults, Lily was pretty good in these "what do I say?" scenarios as Lily always had something to say, always had something to contribute. So she explained, as nonchalantly as possible that May had perhaps "forgotten" to pick up Leo, you know May, she's probably at a seminar or the gym or something and it just slipped her mind, in any case she was on her way to get him and was a little nervous as to what to tell Leo about his potentially "missing" mommy.

Lily Fischer didn't miss a beat, "What the fuck are you telling me, Joanna Ruth Fischer? Where the hell is May?"

Joanna sighed, "Mom, don't panic. I had lunch with May yesterday. It's just she's not answering her phone at home or her cell and she hasn't picked up Leo so Jamie called me..."

"Jamie called you?" Lily was incredulous and Joanna was instantly annoyed. Of course Jamie had called her, who else would he have called? Should he have called Lily, who lived almost an hour away and was a total drama queen, evidenced by her present behavior?

Joanna was a stoplight away from the school at this point, with traffic surprisingly light for a Friday afternoon, "Christ almighty, Mom, are you going to help me here or not?"

She heard Lily draw in her breath sharply and realized she may have a made a slight tactical error, frankly, a rookie error, but she was starting to freak out, really freak out and as usual, Lily was not seeing the forest through the trees or whatever the saying was. She was sitting in her little Lily-bubble in Lily-land while Joanna was firmly rooted on planet earth. She took a deep, cleansing breath, "Mom, I'm sorry I shouted, but I'm calling for your help and I'm literally fifty feet from picking up Leo and I just don't know what to say to him. I need you," she implored.

Joanna could practically see Lily rearrange herself on her La-Z-Boy recliner as her demeanor softened just a tad. Joanna knew how to flatter her mad-mom and had skillfully done it twofold: not only was her daughter begging for her help but the help was for her only grandson.

"Well," said Lily, "since you're asking for my help," Joanna couldn't help but roll her eyes, "my advice is don't tell him anything. Kids aren't that smart, even my genius grandson. He doesn't need to know."

Joanna jerked into a parking space and leaned her head against the steering wheel with her eyes closed. When oh when would she learn to just call her father?

Promising to call her mother the absolute second she heard from May, she took a deep breath, steadied herself, and got out of the car.

Leo, senses keen as ever, was wary when he saw Joanna approaching. He loved his Auntie more than anything, but he always knew when she was coming and today was a surprise. Also, he knew he was at school later than usual; there were only a handful of kids left; the ones whose parents used the school as childcare so they could work, not like May who used the school as an "enrichment program".

"Hey buddy," said Joanna, running her hand through his soft brown curls. She bent to sit next to him, mindful of how her ass didn't exactly fit into the pint-sized chairs. The teacher caught her eye and made a face which asked "is everything ok?" Joanna shrugged as answer, "I don't know."

"Hi, Auntie Jo. Where's my Mom?" Leo looked up expectantly from the picture he was painting.

"I don't know, buddy, let's go find her," Joanna's tone was forcibly unperturbed.

Leo's clever eyes searched hers, and then his face relaxed, "OK." He got up and began cleaning up the painting supplies and Joanna exhaled quietly, she hadn't realized she was holding her breath.

Once she got Leo into the car, strapped into his car seat, with a box of raisins in his lap Joanna had no idea what to do next. What if there was a really weird scene at May's house? What if May was home and having some sort of torrid affair with the mailman and she was handcuffed to the bed and therefore unable to answer the phone until he finished his route and returned with the key? What if May had a secret, deadly disease which had been in remission but had re-appeared suddenly and she couldn't get off the toilet to get to a phone? What if May was a secret agent and had been called away on a super secret mission involving the President's twin daughters? What if May was a time traveler now being burned at a stake in Salem for her witchy ways? What if May had ran off to Buenos Aires with an Argentinean lover, abandoning this crazy American life? Joanna wanted Leo to have no part of any of these scenarios, but they did seem rather farfetched, and she didn't have a better plan so she decided they should just go and see if May was at home.

Joanna drove into the hills up Fountaingrove Parkway to May's five bedroom, four bathroom "starter home," with pool, tennis court and majestic view. Joanna had gone house-hunting with May, strolling through dozens of model homes as eager agents bombarded them with French bottled water and credit applications. Joanna commented that every floor plan could neatly store everything she owned into the garage (even the one with the puny two-car garage) with plenty of room to spare. A plus in case she ever found herself unemployed and looking for a new home.

Joanna's old Volvo slowly chugged up the winding road, much to the chagrin of the car following behind. She finally pulled off the road, onto a well-wooded cul-de-sac and into a gigantic driveway, right next to May's gold-toned Lexus. Her panicky heartbeat began to slow a little. Leo saw the car too and yelled "There's Mommy's Lex, Auntie Jo! She's home!" He popped another raisin into his mouth and maniacally swung his Stride Rites.

Joanna was nervous as she fumbled with her key to let them in, peeking around the door cautiously and calling out "May?" She noted the house alarm wasn't set. Joanna put her handbag down next to May's on the entryway table and called again, "May?" She had not clued Leo in on the potential need for caution. He whipped past her and was up the stairs in a flash calling "Mommy! Mommy! Where are you Mommy? I'm hoooooooome!!!!!"

May heard her son as if he was yelling through a megaphone, but from underwater and a mile away. It was a ghostly, surreal sound. She opened her eyes, unsure where she was and what she was looking at until she realized it was the bathtub's clawed foot; she was lying on the bathroom floor. "Holy shit!" she said, and quickly got to her feet, using the toilet seat to hoist herself up, realizing too late she was less than steady on her feet, "Whoa, easy does it, girl". She saw the trickle of vomit on the toilet seat and the whole ghastly situation came rushing back to her; Jamie...the drunken night and dreadful morning. She wondered what time it was, what day it was. She reached for the sink so she wouldn't fall over just as she heard Leo burst through the door of her bedroom and march directly into her bathroom.

"Mommy, you are very late!" Leo reprimanded her sternly, "Where were you? You forgot me!" His arms were crossed, his brow was furrowed and he was tapping his toe. If May didn't feel so crappy and guilty she probably would have laughed, he was so grim-faced.

"No, no, Sweetheart," May told her little man, ignoring the queasiness in her stomach to cross the floor to him, pulling his warm, tight body into a hug, "I didn't forget you. Mommy's just not feeling well."

"Apparently," said Joanna, suddenly appearing from the hall. She met May's swollen eyes, red from crying, and her heart ached for her, although she still didn't know the cause of May's grief. May's beautiful luminescent skin was cauliflower white except for the dark, bluish circles around her eyes. May's bedroom, usually an oasis of sophisticated and floral scents, instead smelled like a sour barstool, eau de drunken homeless person with top-notes of barf. To Joanna it seemed May had aged fifteen years since lunch yesterday.

"Come on, Leo, let's get some dinner going and let your mom get herself cleaned up. Race you to the kitchen!"

Leo was off, 0 to 60 per usual. Joanna tentatively approached May, who had moved into the bedroom and was sitting; or sort-of leaning on the edge of the bed. She looked as if she was clinging to a life-boat with all her strength not to slide into the sea and be swallowed up by the waves, "May, are you..."

"No," May interrupted her, holding up her hand to stop her, "I'm not ok," she put her hands over her face, "but can we not talk about it yet? Please?"

"Sure Honey, whatever you need," Joanna put her hand on her shoulder and May erupted into tears. Joanna rocked her and stroked her hair saying "Shhhh, shhh, it's gonna be ok, it's gonna be ok."

May emerged an hour later, freshly washed and smelling like May, wearing melon-colored silk pajamas that fluttered around her slim ankles and a soft, velvety matching robe. Her hair was piled on her head, turban-style, wrapped in a towel. Joanna observed that May still looked like crap, but she sure smelled better, and in fact she was feeling a little better too. May had vigorously scrubbed the toilet, something she probably hadn't done in nearly a decade, and then taken a long, scalding shower. She had scoured herself with lily of the valley bath gel until she smelled and felt familiar again.

"Wow, it smells great in here," said May, lifting the lid off a pot of home-made chicken noodle soup, "I think I'm hungry." May was always amazed by what Joanna could create, especially from a fridge which usually contained just cheese sticks, yogurt, soy milk and ketchup (no high fructose corn syrup).

"I'm starving!" echoed Leo from the living room.

"Where did you find chicken?"

"Freezer, I've stashed a few items in there for emergencies," Joanna admitted.

"You have? When?"

"Uh, I'm always putting stuff in there. How could you not know, don't you ever open your freezer?"

"I thought I did but apparently not."

"It's just about ready. Why don't you go wash your hands, Mister?" Joanna heard the crash of cars parking in a pile-up and Leo scampering into the bathroom to wash up.

"Are you feeling any better?" She looked at May, her eyebrows rose to ask, "Are you ok?"

May nodded. "Thanks for getting Leo."

Joanna nodded. "No problem."

The soup was delicious. May ate two bowls hungrily; she hadn't eaten anything since lunch the day before. She never once asked Joanna how much olive oil was in the soup; Joanna knew she was not herself.

Leo needed some cajoling into his Spider Man PJ's but May promised to read him an extra book after he was tucked in. He chose *Where the Wild Things Are* and by 8 o'clock he had been kissed by both Mommy and Auntie and was firmly ensconced in his bed. Joanna tiptoed out as May sat beside him whispering "The night Max wore his wolf suit and made mischief of one kind and another..."

Joanna cleaned up the kitchen, reviewing the wacky day. Her mobile rang. Jamie began the conversation with "Did you find May? Is she ok?" His panicked words came out in a frightened rush and Joanna felt for him.

"She's ok. I'm here with her now; she's tucking Leo in. She's ok. We haven't even had a chance to speak yet. Where are you?" She sat down heavily at the counter.

"The plane just landed. Do I need to come over?"

Joanna was startled by his question. Did he need to come over? Where else would he go? Didn't he live here?

"Joanna?" Jamie's voice was sharp and strained, bordering on whiny.

"I'm here," Joanna was trying to be patient, but it had been a long, nerve wracking day and she rather felt like whining herself, "But like I said, Jamie, I haven't really spoken to May so I'm not sure how to answer your question. Can someone please tell me what the hell is going on?"

"Shit, I'm sorry, Jo, I just feel like May would want to tell you herself. But the short version is we're separated. We've separated."

"Who are you talking to?" Joanna practically jumped

out of her skin as May came up behind her, stealthy as a cat.

"Jeez, May, you scared the shit out of me! It's Jamie."

May held out her hand, reaching for the phone, and said coldly, "Let me speak to him." Joanna hesitantly handed her the phone.

Joanna strained to decipher the one-sided conversation:

"Hi."

"Yes."

"No."

"I will."

"No, you don't need to."

"I'm fine."

"See you tomorrow then." May pushed the red "off" button and handed the mobile back to Joanna. Then she began to cry and told Joanna the whole sad, ugly story... Jamie had sex, a one night stand with a man. What the fuck was she going to do?

4

Joanna and Delia spent most Saturday mornings doing the same three things: Farmer's market, breakfast, bookstore. The market was really for Joanna's sake. Delia had little interest in fresh produce but she was addicted to the tamale cart, and as she had already been up for hours (Joanna slept late) and had gone for a minimum of a 5 mile run, so by the time she met Joanna, her appetite for tamales was fierce.

They roamed; Joanna meal planning in her head as she happily squeezed and fondled vegetables like little colorful lovers. She poked at melons and sniffed tomatoes. Sampled cheeses and commented on jams. She chatted with the knife-sharpening guy and asked the fishmonger how his mother was, as she'd recently had a stroke. Delia wandered slightly behind Joanna, munching her tamales with glee. Next, they went to breakfast (well, maybe it was brunch for Delia), always at the same little café, usually the same thing. Bacon and eggs, potatoes and toast for Delia and some sort of frittata thing for Joanna. Sometimes they talked, sometimes they read the paper, reading excerpts to each other. Sometimes they stared out the window in companionable silence. It worked for them. Their final activity was the bookstore. Wandering around a bookstore was almost as good as the market for Joanna. She loved the smell, she loved the quiet, she loved the worn sofas and wood shelves. It was like therapy without all the talking and crying and delving into the painful shit that makes up a human being.

This particular Saturday, Bruno joined them for their morning routine, begging "Please, pretty please? I won't disrupt the sisterhood. I'll pick up some extra estrogen to contribute on my way to the market." Generally, Bruno's presence wasn't encouraged. Although they loved Bruno, he didn't quite understand the calming consistency and serenity of their happy habit. For example, he'd inevitably suggest different places for breakfast. Sometimes they would humor him, just to show they could be flexible, usually with disastrous results. Like the pancake place that didn't have any bacon for Delia (who eats breakfast without a bacon-option?) or when he suggested skipping the market altogether (blasphemy!). But since he was so pathetic, they said ok so long as he understood the drill.

"I get it, I get it," he said huffily, "boring market, same old breakfast, dusty bookstore, I'll behave. I promise."

They met Delia, already devouring her morning tamales. She offered a bite to Bruno.

"How on earth can you eat that so early in the morning?" Bruno crinkled his nose and nursed his Starbucks skinny caramel latte.

"You're just jealous, these tamales would go straight to your hips," Delia retorted with delight. She was right. Bruno was prone to chubbiness if he wasn't careful. Delia on the other hand, was Joanna's most athletic friend. She ran an average of ten miles every morning, rain or shine and hit the gym five days a week for Pilates, spinning, yoga, or strength training. Small but crazy strong and bean-pole lean. And what an eater! Delia was one of those rare lucky souls who actually strived to gain weight. She popped the last of the tamale into her mouth. "Yum! Delicious! Joanna, I think you should learn to make these."

Bruno did a pretty good job at the market. Although as Joanna was inspecting a pomelo he did shriek, "What is that thing, a grapefruit on steroids?" This caused Joanna to launch into a lengthy explanation on the various culinary and medicinal uses of the pomelo in Asian cultures.

Delia interrupted her, "This is not especially fascinating and I'm starving, so can we go eat now?"

The trio left the market for breakfast. Bacon and eggs for Delia, artichoke frittata for Joanna and a 3-egg, spinach and mushroom omelet, an order of bacon and sausage, hold the toast and potatoes for Bruno.

"This is what you're eating for breakfast? Are you attempting heart failure?" asked Joanna, incredulous.

"I'm trying the Atkins thing," Bruno replied defensively. Bruno was always trying the newest diet, although despite Delia's comment, Joanna never noticed any fluctuations in his weight.

They wandered into the bookstore, looking over the new releases. Bookstore Guy was there, he waved a little "hello" as they entered and then left them alone. He knew the drill.

Joanna meandered towards the cookbooks with Bruno hot on her trail.

"So, what's with the yummy worker-bee ogling you like the newest Grisham?" Bruno deposited himself comfortably onto a couch with a People magazine.

"Who?" Joanna asked, selecting a Jacques Pépin to thumb through.

"That's Bookstore Guy," interrupted Delia, settling herself on the couch next to Bruno with a David Sedaris, "he's in love with Joanna."

Joanna's head snapped to attention, "What the hell are you two talking about?"

"Your boyfriend," Bruno indicated the bookstore employee with his chin, "he's cute!"

"I have no idea who you are talking about," Joanna searched for who they were discussing, "oh, Bookstore Guy? He is not my boyfriend. And what do you mean he's in love with me? And would you keep your voices down?" Joanna whispered loudly.

Delia laughed and turned to Bruno, "Yeah, he's been trying to get Jo's attention for like, forever. He's always smiling at her and putting books aside he thinks she'd like. She doesn't give him the time of day."

"He's just doing his job." Joanna replied dismissively, flipping through the cookbook absently.

"He never puts books aside for me and I'm here just as much as you," Delia retorted teasingly.

"Delia, are out of your mind?" Joanna said, shaking her head.

Delia grabbed Joanna roughly by the shoulders so she was facing her. It was probably comical to see, Delia was such a teeny thing but so full of verve. "Joanna, you are so fucking dense sometimes," Delia smacked herself in the forehead, "if you weren't wandering around still stuck on that unbelievably stupid asshole and feeling sorry for yourself maybe you would notice when someone interesting was paying attention to you!"

Joanna was stunned silent.

Bruno's mouth hung open, "Holy shit, Delia! Where did that come from?"

Delia exhaled, gathering her composure. She took Joanna's hands in hers, "Jo, you know I love you, Honey, but it's time to GET OVER him and move on!"

The previous fall, Diego left. "I do not like myself when I am with you!" were his dramatic departing words. "I feel like I am a suburban husband. I do not feel like an artist. I am an artist! And that is who I need to go be!"

Within an hour of his ridiculous getaway, May exploded through the front door of the shabby apartment; arms full of vodka and pockets full of M&M'S. She was in a rage "I don't like myself when I'm with you? Are you flippin' kidding me?!" Since Leo's arrival, May was desperately trying not to swear, her words a hodgepodge, "G"-rated assortment of "jeepers" and "yikes".

May had not been fond of Diego in the first place. Really, the only person who had been fond of Diego, besides Joanna, was Diego. "That piece of crap." May added, dropping her load onto the table and her dainty butt into a chair. She teased her locks of red-gold hair into a ponytail.

"He may be a piece of crap," sniffed Joanna "but I love that piece of crap," Joanna blew her nose loudly into a snotty shredded tissue, "and he was my piece of crap."

May sprang to her feet and hugged Joanna, "Oh sweetie, I promise you, there is a man out there who is not a piece of crap, and *he* is your piece of crap." She smoothed Joanna's dark hair out of her bleary, blood-shot eyes.

A fabulous conglomeration of clichés was Diego. Of course, he was an artist; *obviously* vegetarian (except when he just HAD to have a hamburger) and noticeably exotic, or at least foreign. He made women's handbags, wallets, and coin purses out of recycled tires, vegan leather, hemp and feathers. Every weekend, along with dozens of other aspiring artists hawking their wire jewelry, belt-buckles and ceramics, Diego attempted to sell his creations to the students and professors, hippies, yuppies and suburban tourists crowding Telegraph Avenue in Berkeley.

Last Hanukah he gave May a wallet.

"What is it?" asked May innocently. She held the

stiff, square, leopard-patterned pouch gingerly between two fingers.

"It is a wallet," said Diego "for holding your money. See?" He gripped the corner and released the rickety zipper; exposing the sections for holding credit cards, pictures and change.

"How quaint," said May grimly, "thank you."

"May's more a Kate Spade kind of girl," Joanna explained apologetically.

For money, Diego worked for UPS.

The first time Joanna saw Diego she was sitting in front of her favorite coffee shop, nursing a double-espresso and a hangover, courtesy of an over indulgent wine tasting weekend with Delia. It was just his brown uniformed butt sticking out of the brown UPS truck. She couldn't take her eyes off the butt. It was round and firm and perfect, a gorgeous ripe peach. She was inspecting it so intently; it was startling when it began backing out of the truck. Joanna wondered if it was considered sexual harassment to stare at the UPS driver's butt. She imagined being reprimanded, "It is not appropriate," Helen would say, nervous fingers pawing at the buttons on her sensible blouse, "to stare at the bottom of the UPS driver. Please stop."

Finally, the rest of the body followed the perfect butt. Tall, well, tall to Joanna was relative but this guy was at least 5'11". Lean. Coffee-bean skin. Dark hair parted in the middle and smoothed into a thick short ponytail. Dark-chocolate eyes. This was one attractive UPS driver.

Joanna's mouth hung open ("Close your mouth," May would have said if she were there) like an idiot and she lowered her sunglasses brazenly to get a better look. He swung a large cumbersome box effortlessly onto his impossibly broad shoulder and swept an escaping lock of hair behind his ear. Despite the chilly November breeze he wore shorts displaying strong, muscular legs.

As he walked into the coffee shop, Diego looked over said broad shoulder, and smiled a dazzling smile at her.

The following week Joanna was sitting at her desk, supposedly working on a dictation but actually searching for herbal colon cleanses on-line when in he walked, carrying a package and electronic UPS clipboard. "Hello," he said, "I know you."

Joanna was horrified. Had he known she had stared at his ass for a full five minutes and had fantasized about it on a daily basis since? What was he doing here?

Apparently, he was delivering a package.

"You are the coffee shop girl. I am Diego," he extended his hand and she shook it. She still hadn't spoken. "And your name is?"

"I'm Joanna," said Joanna.

"Joanna. So nice to meet you," he handed her the package and the clipboard to sign her name, "see you tomorrow," he again smiled the dazzling smile, "Joanna." The smile exposed a slight gap in his two bottom teeth and a hefty cleft in his chin. He really was perfect.

The next morning Joanna summoned her courage and boldly asked what happened to Joe, Diego's package delivering predecessor. "I do not know for sure," answered Diego "but I heard something about a breakdown. Package overload I guess." And again with the smile.

Their conversation, and flirtation, continued daily. They chatted benignly about the weather. Next they moved on to movies and events in the news. One morning when Diego arrived for his daily delivery, two burly men were hanging a huge oil painting in the waiting room, and like a flower set to turbo-speed, Diego exploded in bloom. After helping the men ensure the painting was straight and low enough ("Most art is hung too high on the wall," he explained) he stood back to admire the painting's "*Lovely texture and perspective.*"

"Are you an artist?" Joanna asked.

Diego smiled, "Yes, I am," he said, almost solemn. He told her all about his handiwork, his affection for fabrics and fasteners. His exuberance in encountering the visual splash of a bright floral or the soft, rich, feel of woven feathers. "I am sorry, this must be quite dull to you," said Diego, a touch of self-conscious smile playing about his beautiful, full lips.

"Oh, no, it's not dull at all!" Joanna answered, mesmerized by his excitement.

Leaning over her desk he searched out her eyes as he told her about an exhibit at the modern art museum he was dying to see, "Perhaps you would like to see it with me?" he asked her, tentative.

Of course she did, having absolutely no interest in art whatsoever, and they had a magical time. The hour's drive to San Francisco was traffic-free, clear and beautiful. The parking Gods blessed them with a relatively inexpensive lot that didn't seem as if you were handing your keys over to a criminal and within a block of the museum. They strolled through the museum, Diego expounding on the use of this material versus that technique in the cluttered collages and confusing paintings, pausing only to answer Joanna's numerous questions. Diego was passionate and interesting and entirely self-absorbed. Joanna was thrilled to be walking with him, and her heart leapt into her throat when he casually took her hand. And when he gently kissed her between a Robert Arneson glazed ceramic and a Gerhard Richter lithograph, she nearly went into cardiac arrest.

The beginning of the relationship, as with many relationships, was pure bliss. Joanna and Diego strolled through vineyards, picnicked at wineries, talked about their lives: growing up, ambitions, and dreams. Joanna made elaborate meals with wine and several courses; they kissed at midnight on New Year's Eve. It was a month down the road and Joanna had already fallen hard when she learned that Diego was not actually foreign. Despite his apparent inability to speak using contractions, causing an odd but entirely fictional accent, Diego was raised in suburban San Mateo, two hours south from where they currently lived, a distinctly un-foreign location. His mother, an IT specialist, and his father, an elementary school principal were also born and raised in San Mateo. They were Mexican, although Diego's knowledge of his grandparents' culture was essentially confined to the family-tree tour of Mexico City his parents took him and his younger brother Alex on when Diego was thirteen. Diego had quickly embraced his newfound ethnicity, at least in his wardrobe, newly resplendent with huaraches and poncho.

One relatively warm night Joanna and Diego lay on a blanket in the park, looking up at the stars. Joanna was tracing the lines in Diego's hand as he pontificated about decoupage when she interrupted him.

"Diego," she began, "don't we seem like rather an odd couple?"

"Why odd?" Diego rolled onto his stomach to look at her with his humungous eyes, blinking his impossibly long lashes.

"Well, you're gorgeous and artsy...I'm short and stubby..."

"Joanna, you are not stubby. I think you are beautiful." Diego reached out and tucked some loose hair behind her ear. "There is something different about you," he paused, "you glow."

Joanna said quizzically, "Excuse me?"

"You glow. You have a brilliant aura about you; you are like a ray of yellow sunshine. Being near you," Diego sat up on the blanket and took her hand, "makes me feel warm and happy and alive," he drew her to him, kissing her deeply.

Practical Joanna, swept up in the magnificent kiss, overlooked the cheesiness of the moment, as well as the impulse to say, (as she would have to anyone else), "You did NOT just tell me that I glow like a ray of flippin' sunshine. Are you kidding me?"

But practical Joanna was nowhere to be found. Soon Joanna proposed May meet Diego, and May was elated. She could not recall the last time she had met a love interest of Joanna's and was thrilled at the prospect. They went out to dinner on a rare evening when her husband, Jamie was available. May wore a necklace which Diego immediately recognized as being designed by a local artist he knew. The two had a lively chat about fused glass and the kooky designer, but despite the promising start, the evening quickly disintegrated. By the end of the excruciating evening of tapas and listening to Diego talk, May's head was throbbing and her disappointment was palpable. Arrogant, irritating and self-centered, Diego was as beautiful as Joanna had described, but he was dull and as transparent as cheap toilet paper. May's older sister was wicked smart and sarcastic, funny and attractive. She deserved someone who worshipped her, who couldn't take his eyes off her. Someone who was well-read and articulate. Someone who could easily hold his own in a conversation about a number of subjects and be interested in someone else's opinion. Someone who was funny and optimistic and kind.

Not someone who had nothing of depth to say about anything. Even his comments on art, although plentiful, were one-dimensional. Having studied design herself, May had hoped that art could be a common ground for the two of them; but when she asked what he thought of the fabulous Ron Arad chair which she knew he had seen at the MOMA because even Joanna, not an art lover by any standard, had commented on how sleek and sexy it was, Diego blinked at her inquiry as if she were a sunspot he was trying to erase. And when she inquired about Prada's new handbag line, his own area of expertise for crying out loud, even then his expression was strangely blank, tabula rasa, and his answer was basic and unsophisticated. And *absolutely not* someone who didn't even bother to *reach* for the bill, even if just for show. And most certainly not someone who would pat her sister's ass *in public*!

"What does Joanna see in that total loser?" May asked Jamie after they dismissed the babysitter.

"Well, he is eye-catching," Jamie replied, pulling May into his arms and nuzzling her neck, "and speaking of eye-catching..." he kissed along her shoulder towards her neck but May pulled away.

"Jamie, I'm serious, this is my sister. I hate that guy! He's vile!" May shuddered, "He gave me the creeps." May climbed the stairs, taking off her shoes and jewelry along the way.

Jamie sighed loudly, "Of course you hated him, you hate everyone." Jamie followed May up the stairs, defeated; all signals were pointing to no nookie tonight.

May whipped around to face him, "I don't hate everyone; did *you* like him?"

"No, I thought he was pompous and boring," Jamie

yawned, "I also *hate* tapas, there is never enough food and I don't like having to share."

"So, what did you think?" Joanna asked eagerly on the phone the next morning.

"About?" May vaguely tried to buy some time; she wanted to tread lightly with this one and needed more time to develop a plan on how exactly to do that. May didn't want to crush Joanna, but she had virtually no ability to censor her reactions. This gave her a reputation of "speaking before thinking" as a child. It was probably lucky May was so wealthy, being married to a man who far exceeded his bosses' expectations of incredible earning potential, because she wasn't good at playing nicely with others, either in the sandbox or in the work world. Like all Fischer women, she was dogmatic and smart as a whip; but her swift tongue tended to get her into trouble.

"Jeez May, you know what about. Diego! What did you think of Diego?" Joanna was irritated by May's nonchalance. If there was one thing you could always count on from May, it was an opinion. And a strong one.

"Oh, Diego...well...he is very attractive as you said..." May was noncommittal.

"And?" Joanna drummed her fingernails against the side of her coffee cup, "You have nothing else to say?" She felt the heat rise on the back of her neck, "Why didn't you like him?"

"Damn it, Joanna, I'm sorry but he's a total ass! He's pompous and condescending and what is with his speech pattern? It is so weird. I didn't get it!" May let it all out in a rush, "I'm sorry Jo but I just didn't like the guy. He seems shifty. And dumb. He seems dumb. He didn't have anything intelligent to say! I'm so sorry!"

Joanna was silent. She was seething. Finally she had found someone truly terrific. Someone fun and interesting and gorgeous and interested in *her* and May was going to shit all over him? May was jealous. May was used to being the center of attention and couldn't handle that Joanna had attracted this great guy. May was selfish.

"Joanna? Are you there?"

Joanna finished her cup of coffee and poured some more before answering frostily, "I'm here."

Regardless of May's less-than enthusiastic reaction, Joanna was in love and those first months were perfect. Joanna quickly agreed to Diego's proposal that they move in together:

"I am here all of the time already. I should just move my stuff in, or maybe we should find a larger place. Do you think so?"

Joanna did think so, and they began to search for a more suitable apartment.

When Joanna was in the 5th grade her mother made her enter a bake off. Lily Fischer was often making her daughters do things. Classes they had no interest in taking (belly-dancing, anyone?); plays they were too young for (*Cat on a Hot Tin Roof* for an eight and eleven year old?); and foods that were frightening, ("They are lychee nuts, not eyeballs, and they are DELICIOUS") all were regular parts of the Fischer girls' lives. Lily was a big believer in experiencing everything, trying everything and eating everything. At least once.

So, true to form, when Lily saw the ad for the bake off in the local newspaper, she did not, like a normal mother might, *ask* her elder daughter if she might want to participate, "What do you think, Honey?" She may have inquired, "Would you like to give it a shot? I think you'd have loads of fun!" No, no, she simply filled out the application, paid the entrance fee and sent it in. A few days later, during dinner, she said, "Oh by the way Joanna, I've entered you in a bake-off. It's a week from Saturday." And Joanna, knowing that arguing was futile, simply said, "Fine."

Another standard element of Fischer life was revolting dinner-table conversation. Lily, a nurse, loved to regale her family with tales of bed-pans gone wrong and bones protruding from unlikely places. Lily also believed in the family eating together nightly; so Joanna and May could not escape anecdotes of weeping abscesses and tarry stools, while eating roast chicken and potatoes. Daniel, Joanna's father, had learned long ago it wasn't worth interrupting her; she would just continue to talk. No one knew if Lily was actually a good cook. The Fischer's, like

Pavlov's famous pets, would sit there stoically shoving their dinner in as fast as they could so as just to be done. The food essentially slid past the taste-buds without registering flavor.

But despite Lily's questionable culinary prowess, even at ten, Joanna could really bake. The bake-off was held at the community center, and each contestant had to make a baked good (Joanna's entry was in cookies) and write a description of said baked good. Joanna baked her famous oatmeal-coconut-chocolate chip cookies. In her description she wrote: "Oatmeal-coconut-chocolate chip cookies: sort of like a macaroon, but not really". When Joanna won the contest she was secretly thrilled but unsurprised. Everyone loved these cookies. Joanna's dad loved them so much he said he wanted to be buried with a batch. Also, the other contestants' offerings were pathetic. Raspberry thumbprints? Give me a break. Better than Toll House? Who are we kidding here? Even at ten, Joanna knew she had it in the bag. She was going to wipe the floor with the other twelve contestants.

The prize was $25 and a blue ribbon. Her mother displayed the ribbon tacked to the kitchen bulletin board; the site of honor in the Fischer household; amongst the expired coupons and yellow-edged recipes for goat's milk carob fudge and seitan-loaf (one of Lily's favorite go-to recipes but known as *Satan loaf* by the rest of the Fischers). The ribbon remains there today, more than twenty years later, curled and stiff with age and kitchen grease.

Looking back, Joanna wondered if this bake-off win was the high point of her life. Had it been the defining moment, her destiny?

She would be a baker. She would wear a white apron speckled with flour; and own a cute little corner bakery with a black and white checked floor. She would bake oatmeal-coconut-chocolate chip cookies all day long and customers would line up around the block for them. She would be happy and fulfilled and her life would have meaning. Lily would insist on sewing curtains for the bakery and telling anyone who would listen: "I made her enter that bake-off! I knew it would be Joanna's defining moment; her destiny! All thanks to me!"

Joanna wondered if she had missed her calling.

5

Diego, Diego, Diego...Joanna's already busy dreams were full of Diego. She couldn't help but play over and over again everything, each tiny tidbit she could recall about their relationship, analyzing her decisions and actions and explanations in an effort to discover where she went wrong, what she did to make this man "not like himself when he was with her." If she could discover the crucial moment that ultimately caused the breakup maybe she could repair the damage, or at least start again. Or learn something. Or something.

One evening they planned to attend the opening of an art show for one of Diego's friends, a flamboyant painter who wore large hats and spoke with a slightly phony sounding British accent, although she actually was British. The evening had begun badly.

"Is *that* what you are wearing tonight?" Diego had asked, critically surveying her outfit.

"Uh, yes," Joanna looked down at her black sweater, jeans and high heeled boots," is there a problem?"

"Well, it is a very important night for Enid, Joanna,

and I thought you might want to dress up a bit more for once," he replied, annoyed.

Joanna was annoyed as well, but pulled in her irritation, "I'll change, it's no problem."

"You do not need to change, it is not *that* important," Diego swung his pleather jacket over his shoulder.

"Well, clearly it *is* important to you so I'll change, it's no big deal," Joanna started for the bedroom.

"No, no, now we will be late, what you are wearing is fine," Diego started for the door.

Joanna stood immobile in the dimly lit hallway, not sure which way to go or what to do. Her mind was curiously blank.

"Joanna!" he snapped, "Let us go!"

The drive to the gallery was silent.

She greeted Enid warmly, praising the beautiful showing. Joanna had attended many art openings with Diego by now, and although she still found the art incredibly boring, she had at least grown to appreciate some of the artists. She found Enid to be one of the few in Diego's large circle who was extremely talented, and she hoped the showing would bring some notoriety and most importantly, profit for the struggling artist. Joanna knew that Diego, although happy for Enid, was also jealous and frustrated. He had struggled so long and had received little if any attention for his own work. She took a deep breath and decided to cut him some slack for being such an ass.

She stood with a glass of wine in one hand and a mushroom canapé in the other, chatting with a small group including Enid and another artist named Saul who made crazy cool sculptures out of wire; huge oddly shaped prehistoric looking creatures. Diego came up beside her.

"Joanna, we are leaving," he said quietly, pulling at her arm.

"Excuse me," Joanna said to her companions, she leaned towards Diego, "What? Why? We've practically just gotten here, did you try these? They're yummy." She popped the end of the canapé into her mouth,

"I am ready to go."

"But Enid hasn't even addressed her guests yet. We should at least stay to hear her, don't you think?" Joanna tried to take his hand but he pulled away, "Diego, what is the problem? I can't seem to make you happy tonight!"

"I do not have a problem. I am not in the mood for these people," Diego was increasingly impatient, pacing and running his fingers through his hair. Joanna noticed he was sweating; his forehead was beginning to shine. "Come on, we are going."

"Honey, why don't you go home and I'll catch a ride with Saul or someone later. I'd like to stay to hear Enid's talk," Joanna instantly knew that Diego, a man jealous by nature was not keen on this idea; he had stopped pacing and stood gaping at her as if she had grown a third eye.

"Saul? You will get a ride with Saul?" he asked, disbelieving, as if she had just suggested she strip naked and perform a cheerleading routine.

"Yes, Saul, he lives in our neighborhood, I'm sure he

wouldn't mind," Joanna tried for nonchalance; she knew Diego was getting angry, but she felt powerless to stop him, he was a runaway train and she was strapped to the tracks by an invisible force field.

"No, I am sure he would not mind at all," Diego was cold, "Fine, Joanna, ask *Saul* to take you home," he turned and left her standing there, vacantly watching his retreating back.

Enid came up behind her, "What's the Prince of Darkness pissed about this time?" she asked Joanna.

"Oh, he's fine," Joanna answered, trying to keep her tone bright and drinking deeply from her lackluster glass of wine, "he's just not so happy with me I suppose." She gave Enid a wan smile.

"He's probably on his period. It's definitely not you, Joanna, it's just Mr. Moody, Mr. Center of Attention," Enid finished off her glass of wine, put it down on a side table with a flourish and clapped her hands, " OK, let's get this show on the road!" she strode back into the gallery, red crushed-velvet hat teetering precariously, wide hips swaying provocatively.

Joanna stayed later than she anticipated. Enid's chat about contemporary painting composition was smart and witty and Joanna was surprised she actually understood most of it. She had moved from a grim discussion on the state of affairs in the Middle East into a lively debate with another group regarding the over-oaking of chardonnay. Before she knew it, it was well-after midnight and Joanna feared she better skedaddle lest her coach turn into a pumpkin.

Saul kept her in hysterics for the brief ride home, doing a brilliant imitation of Tom Hanks, "Do you want me to walk you up?" Saul asked chivalrously, idling in front of Joanna's apartment.

"Oh no, I'll be fine. Thanks for the lift."

"Anytime, me lady!" Saul did a little bow.

Joanna fingered her keys anxiously as she ascended the stairs, unsure what she would find on the other side. A man-eating shark? A psychotic snake? Her loving boyfriend? The last one she doubted.

Diego was sitting on the couch in the dark, drinking wine and smoking, a habit Joanna detested, and one which Diego had agreed to do only outside on the deck. The scene was strangely surreal and would have been almost comical had Diego not been oozing pheromones of fury.

"So, you decided to come home. How was your little ride with Saul?" She heard the sneer in his voice.

"Of course I came home, silly" Joanna answered airily, trying to deflect his dour temper with humor, "I missed you," she sat next to him on the couch, cuddling up, "even if you do smell like a smokehouse," she tilted her head towards him and leaned in for a kiss, but he ignored her. "Diego, come on," she pushed at him playfully, "please don't be mad at me. Can't we just move on here? I really don't understand why you are so upset."

"If you do not understand, I cannot explain it to you," Diego replied, dramatically extricating himself from her arms and leaving the room, trailing ashes and bad vibes.

Joanna sat static. She pulled a cashmere throw, a gift from May, around her shoulders. She'd grown cold.

Diego was fired from his UPS job shortly after he and Joanna broke up.

"It does not matter. I do not have enough time to work on my art with this damn corporate job," he told her on his last day, "I thought you should know."

"What happened?" asked Joanna, concerned and silently kicking herself for being concerned.

"I was sick and tired of them complaining about my hair. As if my hair was keeping me from delivering the packages," he stroked his hair lovingly, as if to soothe its sad feelings over being fired, "Stupid corporate bastards."

"But how will you afford to live without a steady job?" Joanna asked, kicking herself again.

"I have found a new..." Diego faltered.

And then Joanna knew the answer, how stupid could she be?

"...roommate." He finished, evasively.

Joanna told herself she should be relieved to not have to see him every day at work as he delivered packages. Now it would be much easier to move on. It really was a blessing in disguise. Or some such crap.

Joanna was doing her best to be organized and move on. It's just that her best was rather pathetic. She cried with May and Delia. She ate gallons of ice cream and watched *Say Anything* a dozen times. She took a Thai cooking class and a sushi rolling class and a cake decorating class. She hit the gym...once. She went on three blind dates. She re-read *The Bridges of Madison County*. She baked and baked and baked. Joanna didn't want to wallow in the crappy hole she was sitting in, she wanted to be out with the rest of civilization, living above ground, but the sides of the well were so steep and slippery with her feeble tears; she simply didn't have the chutzpah or the upper-body strength to claw her way up and out.

6

When May arrived for her freshman year at the high school, Joanna was a junior. This was the first time since they were little kids the sisters had attended school together and May's appearance made quite an impact on the male population who may have remembered her as a small, red-headed pest. On the first day of school, Joanna was leaning against her locker, chatting with Jason Levine, a clever, studious boy who favored 501s and a brown aviator jacket regardless of the weather. Joanna had nursed a not-so tiny crush on him for years. They were discussing the scary looking new chem teacher when May appeared, striding down the hall towards Joanna, her back straight, fiery hair bouncing. Jason watched her approach, his eyes widening as she walked, and Joanna looked behind her to see what was causing Jason's mouth to gape open so unattractively. *Ah,* she thought, *it's my baby sister!*

"Jo, I can't figure out where my English class is," frustrated and whiny, she held her schedule out to Joanna.

Joanna took the schedule and inspected it closely,

"May, you have Ms. Milton, she's in "C" building, the next one over, I'll walk you," she turned to Jason, rolled her eyes and laughed at his slack expression, "Jason! Wake up!" She snapped her fingers in front of his face, "This is my sister, May. May, this is my goofy friend, Jason."

"Your sister?" Jason said, looking skeptical.

"Yep, from the same womb and everything," said May, "see ya' Jase," she waggled her fingers at him and linked her arm through Joanna's.

"Bye Jason," called Joanna. "See you in Calc." The sisters walked away arm in arm.

May said quietly, "Jo, was that weird?" She was no dummy. She owned a mirror and knew the reflection looking back at her was rather, well, unforgettable.

Joanna grinned up at her baby sister and said, "Nope."

May was not a wall-flower kind of a girl. She had always been loud, brash and exceedingly sought after by the opposite sex, and even her own sex in the case of Linda Walker, captain of the volleyball team, who tried to convince May she must have lesbian tendencies ("Come on, everyone does deep down! Aren't you curious?"). She dated a variety of boys in high school, breaking hearts left and right. She was quickly bored and found most of the boys dull and petty. People were often surprised to find a well exercised brain under May's sheath of red-gold hair.

An avid debater, May heard geeks making fun of her. "Is the pretty girl looking for the mall?" and "Did that cheerleader get lost on her way to tryouts?" She pulverized these nerds on the debate floor, nailing arguments and forming eloquent rebuttals. She was joyful to see their glasses slip down their sweaty, pimply noses as she led her team to victory time and time again with her rapid-fire argumentation. "Take that, pompous dorks," she'd respond triumphantly.

During May's freshman year, her history teacher, Ms. Richards, a ridiculously androgynous woman, complete with mud-colored mullet, sandals with socks and a single, icky, wiry hair growing out of her chin, gave the class an assignment to write an essay about a famous first. The first man to walk on the moon. The first person to receive an artificial heart. The first President assassinated.

They were presenting the papers to the rest of class, and each had to read their opening paragraph. A swaggering Rod Kaplan tediously recounted the first World Series: "The first World Series took place in 1903, an exciting contest between the Pittsburgh Pirates and the Boston Americans, later to become the Boston Red Sox..." The ever glum Samantha Smith enlightened the class on the first woman to serve in the Senate: "Rebecca Latimer Felton served in the US Senate for a mere 24 hours in 1922..."

May rose from her desk smoothing her skirt. She smiled at her captive audience and began to read her opening paragraph about Bess Myerson, the first Jewish Miss America:

"In 1945, Bess Myerson, a 20 year old recent graduate of Hunter College with a degree in music was entered into the Miss New York City contest by her precocious younger sister, Sylvia. After winning this coveted crown, the Jewish beauty decided to pursue the ultimate in beauty competitions: the Miss America title. Despite the blatant anti-Semitism she experienced, including being told to change her name, which headstrong Myerson refused to do, she triumphantly won the title, becoming the first and only Jewish Miss America."

Harvey Kreitler, only a freshman but already varsity running-back passed her a note, "Loved your essay." She smiled at him in response. After class he stopped her in the hall, leaning seductively against a row of lockers, "Yo, Fischer, how about a movie this weekend?" He smiled an expensive smile at her, compliments of recently removed braces.

They went to the movies and began dating. One day they were making out on Harvey's bed. When he got up to pee, May snooped around his cluttered room, inspecting Pop-Warner trophies and league championship medals and ribbons. She picked up a snapshot of the two of them at the freshman dance, Harvey looking magnificent in his tux with May glittering on his arm. Behind the picture, peeking out from behind the tattered mini-blinds, sat a little doll. The doll, clearly a girl from its skirt of leaves, had several strands of auburn hair, *real* hair, as in, from the top of someone's head, attached to its doll-head. Several blue pins were strategically placed on the heart and stomach.

When Harvey returned, May spun around and held out the doll to him, "What the fuck is this? Is this supposed to be me? Is this my hair?"

Harvey admitted that sure enough, the doll was a mini-replica of May, fully equipped with hair from May's head. "But I didn't yank it out or anything, I got it from your hairbrush!" Harvey explained naively, "But it's a compliment, May, it's nothing creepy or nothin'. I just really really wanted to go out with you, you're totally hot and I read this thing about voodoo dolls..."

May dumped him and took the doll with her.

May had experienced heart-break like any other teenage girl, but she was never one to wallow. She had an uncanny ability to turn despair into delight. Dean Richardson broke up with May just two weeks before the prom. Most girls would have crawled into a hole and stayed until homecoming, but not May. She told Dean he was a selfish lay anyway. She would rather stay home and walk her non-existent dog than go to the prom with him. News traveled fast across the quad that Dean had dumped May and even faster that he was a lousy screw and within a day she had several new offers to go to the prom, and Dean's new date had discarded him like yesterday's newspaper. May declined the offers, she was only a junior; there would be other proms. May always knew she was destined for something better than Dean or any of these losers, and the night of prom she visited

Joanna at her dorm where they watched movies, ate nachos and had a dandy time.

James Cohen's reputation on campus quickly reached May her freshman year of college. He was rumored to be brilliant yet down to earth. He was everyone's buddy, a "heck of a nice guy" who threw himself wholeheartedly into everything he did. Even the professors talked of James Cohen as someone to keep an eye on; he was going places.

When she saw Jamie in person, standing under a tree and talking animatedly with a professor-looking type, she knew with an electric jolt: he was the one she had been waiting for. Jamie was intelligent and sexy, with a confidence that rivaled May's. Not an easy feat. He was the only man May had ever pursued.

May monitored his schedule and strategically placed herself in the hall of the Business Administration Building where he was scheduled to walk by between eleven and five after on Monday, Wednesday and Friday. "Hello," she said as he walked by.

"Hi," he answered, eyebrows raised expectantly, head slightly cocked, waiting for this gorgeous vision to continue.

"I want to introduce myself, I'm May Fischer," she extended her hand, eye contact locked in place.

He smiled at her and shook, impressed with her solid, almost masculine grip, "James Cohen. Jamie."

"Good to meet you, Jamie," she smiled at him, a little coy, "could I talk you into a cup of coffee?"

Jamie would later recollect he was utterly taken by her bold move; he knew she was something worth stopping for.

It wasn't love at first sight, necessarily, but it was certainly the possibility of love. That first coffee date, where she drank herbal tea and he drank beer, lasted five hours. Jamie missed economics and May missed art history. So totally engrossed in each other, they didn't notice the morning turn into afternoon, didn't notice the low growl in their stomachs as they missed lunch and didn't notice their heavy bladders until they stood to leave, both running for the bathroom.

May had been dating Kevin at the time. He was also brilliant, also great looking and supremely charismatic. Regardless of Kevin's stellar resume, after that impromptu date, May and Jamie were inseparable, joined at the hip, and May dropped Kevin so fast he was left dazed and confused.

It wasn't long before what May had suspected at the beginning was true. They were embarking upon a majestic love affair. One night, basking in the afterglow, Jamie turned May's face towards him, his eyes searching hers and said, "I love you, May Fischer."

Now, these three words were not new to May, she had heard them dozens of times. Men were always falling in love with her, professing their affection in strange and obsessive ways, including calling off rooftops, renting bi-planes and spelling it out with rocks in the sand. But for the first time, tears sprang to her eyes and she hugged Jamie tightly, their bodies shiny and slick, and she whispered back to him, “And I love you, James Cohen. I love you.”

7

Joanna was more than bruised by Diego's rejection. She was battered black and blue with misery. She didn't know he was unhappy, which made her feel as if maybe she didn't know him at all. "I don't like myself when I'm with you" is what he said. May did her best to convince Joanna it had nothing to do with her, he just needed someone new to feed his astronomical ego, but Joanna couldn't help but blame herself for his sorrow. She was too clingy, too lacking in self-esteem. She smothered him with the cooking and the cleaning and the little gifts and the limitless sex. Of course he couldn't stand her.

Diego was moody and creative and a total night-owl. For the first few months of their relationship, she had tried desperately to keep up with him. Underground clubs, independent film festivals, art exhibits in people's basements, Joanna was totally out of her element. But she purchased a wardrobe (almost entirely black) and could have earned an Oscar for her role of the dutiful, attentive and accommodating girlfriend. After they moved in together, the pace continued. Joanna, exhausted from the late nights, tentatively suggested some changes in their routine. Diego would continue to do what he always did; she certainly didn't want to detain him or cramp his style...but except for the occasional party or exhibit, Joanna would stay home.

Candidly, it was *almost* a win-win for Joanna. She was thrilled to be home with a stew bubbling on the stove, a nice glass of wine, and Netflix. Of course she would rather this be with Diego snuggled on the couch beside her, sharing wisecracks and a decadent homemade dessert (well, Diego didn't like sweets but since this was Joanna's fantasy she liked to pretend he did) and maybe giving her a foot massage; but he preferred to be out and about and she wasn't going to hold him back. She would smile and say "Have fun, Honey!" as he left, stiff pleather jacket slung over his shoulder, like Danny ditching Sandy on the couch to meet Cha Cha to go win a dance contest. But this way Joanna could watch old movies, write in her journal, chat with May on the phone, bake, paint her toenails, and still have the comfort of a warm, beery-smelling body to snuggle up with for a few hours before the alarm woke her up. She thought it was a win-win for Diego too, but apparently, "He didn't like himself when he was with her."

Joanna wasn't always so malleable, and it wasn't as if she had never had a relationship before. Her high-school boyfriend was Ned – she dated him off and on for two years. Ned was sweeter than honey, showering her with attention and gifts and surprises of flowers and picnics and tickets to the theatre. He was soft and doughy and affectionate as a puppy at the pound, absolutely desperate that you TAKE ME HOME AND LOVE ME. That relationship ended, thankfully for Joanna, when Ned left to go to college back East. She told him, "Do what you need to do, date, party, have fun. I don't want to hold you back." She was relieved when he reluctantly agreed, and she was free to date.

Her first college beau was Alan the astronomy major. Astronomy sounded fascinating to Joanna and she was quite excited as a freshman to be able to take a class so outside of her realm of thinking, but it turned out to be quite possibly the MOST boring subject ever. Dating Alan was unfortunately a little too much like sitting through an astronomy lecture, except she did manage to stay awake for most, although not all of their dates. Next there was Michael in the rock band. Michael's major changed with the tides, and Joanna couldn't actually recall his attending any classes. He was a full-throttle partier. Michael was everything freshman year is supposed to be, complete with sex, drugs and rock and roll (very loud and very mediocre rock and roll), only while Joanna was a freshman, Michael was a senior ("Let's hope the third time's the charm," he'd cackle). Michael was a lot of fun, but then Joanna was getting ready for someone more serious. So, in seeking serious she dated Ravi, a gorgeous marketing major. Ravi was in her Classics class and he was so, so, cute to look at, but he was also so, so serious, he bordered on grim, and he wore way too much navy for Joanna's taste, AND he ironed his jeans. That one didn't last long. Junior year she dated Tom the journalism major. Tom was athletic and had the most fabulous blue-black hair, the hair she imagined a vampire would have. He was extremely PC and rode his bike everywhere. Unfortunately, he took himself way too seriously. Joanna realized she needed maybe a wee *less* serious and someone with a sense of humor about themselves, so finally, a few months before graduation she began seeing Mark.

Mark was a breath of fresh air: everyone loved Mark. He was an English major and would be attending U.C. Berkeley for Grad school in the fall. He spent his spare time teaching English to illiterate adults and immigrants, playing chess in the park and eating everything. Mark was funny and magnetic, but down to earth and pleasant to be around. He could strike up a conversation with just about anyone, discussing Gregorian chants with nuns and organic fertilizer options with gardeners. He was completely comfortable in his own skin, happy with who he was. Being with Mark was so easy, they just fit together. Even their friends liked each other. Joanna's parents were thrilled.

They dated for two years. Although from time to time they discussed moving in together, Mark was so involved with his studies it didn't make a lot of sense. They decided to wait and see what happened after he got his Master's, or maybe his PhD. Neither was in a hurry to take the relationship to the next level, they just enjoyed each other's company. They both had a really terrific friend...to have sex with. And Joanna was happy in her life. She was living with a roommate in a quiet suburb and working as a receptionist at an investment banking firm, trying to decide whether her recently acquired BA in Liberal Arts was remotely useful in the real world.

The only sore spot was May. May had already begun to date Jamie, the brilliant MBA student who was also ambitious, attractive, and confident, while not quite pompous. Jamie was really letter-perfect for May and Joanna had never seen her younger sister so gorgeously vibrant, so ecstatically happy and especially so sweetly vulnerable before. Jamie finished his MBA program in record time and had been lured into a lucrative career in the wine business, so he moved to wine country and asked May to come with him. Without blinking twice, May dropped out of college, packed up her dorm room and was off house hunting. They were totally in love, couldn't keep their hands off each other. Joanna was delighted for her sis, and secretly just a tad jealous.

The Fischer parents? Not so ecstatic.

"This is really what you want?" Lily wrung her hands, "For some, some man to take care of you like some fifties housewife? We raised you to stand on your own two feet! What if this doesn't work out? Won't you at least finish your degree?"

Daniel was more sympathetic to May's new love, but just as confused by her decision to drop out of school,

"We raised you to make your own decisions, May, so I trust you know what you are doing here and will reap the benefits or face the consequences of your actions...but you know how we feel about education. We'll wholeheartedly support you, but we just don't wholeheartedly agree with this particular decision."

But the move was a good one for May. Despite her independent nature, she found she loved playing housewife and spent months decorating their new beautiful home. With Jamie's high-paying gig, she could just work part time if she wanted and have plenty of time for lunches and manicures and fashion design classes which she promised her distraught parents she would continue and she did. *Her* only sore spot was Joanna. The sisters were used to seeing each other almost daily and the phone calls were missing that personal touch. They were lonely for each other.

So, Joanna started job hunting. She was getting bored with her job at the investment firm anyway, and the "Front Desk Coordinator" position at a medium-sized law firm sounded like an interesting step up with the "progressive growth" she knew she was supposed to be attaining as a young professional...whatever. Despite the thorough hiring process of a telephone screening, two live interviews and a background check, Joanna was still caught off guard when she was actually offered the position. She told Mark she decided to take the job and they agreed to try the long distance thing. It was really just a little over an hour's drive, but between Joanna's work schedule and Mark's studies, the relationship was primarily on the phone. The couple soon discovered that phone sex wasn't nearly as thrilling as it was made out to be. Joanna missed having someone in her bed at night. Mark missed Joanna's cookies (he gained 10 pounds while they were dating) and the smell of her hair.

But the separation also made the couple realize that although they missed each other, it was easy to sort of... fade away. It wasn't they didn't love each other. Joanna loved Mark, would go to battle for him, slay the dragon and all. But that desire, that yearning, that deep down in your bones I-belong-with-this-man love she was pretty sure existed somewhere...it wasn't there with Mark. So, they decided they would just stay good friends. And they were good friends still.

Joanna's parents were beyond devastated. Daniel, in particular, ADORED Mark and had been fantasizing about their wedding and marriage and grandkids. Joanna thought he might cry when she broke the news. But she knew they had made the right choice. It was her first real adult decision, and she was rather proud of it.

Joanna's parents, like everyone else, didn't like Diego. They could not understand what their sensible and smart elder daughter saw in that egotistical bubble-head.

"Well," Lily said, "I'm sure he's just a transitional boyfriend."

"God let's hope so," Daniel moaned, holding his aching head in his hands after an agonizing dinner, where Diego listened to himself talk for a good forty-five minutes, never noticing the deafening silence around him, "that man lowers the IQ of every room he enters. And he had no concept of social cues! Shouldn't an actor, even a bad one, have a better awareness of his audience?"

"Daniel Fischer! That is not nice!" Lily admonished.

"It may not be nice," added Jamie, "but I'm with Daniel on this one." Jamie and Daniel clinked glasses.

Joanna had been so so lonely when Diego came along. She dated a series of men through her twenties: a butcher named Rick who drank too much beer and hadn't changed his hairstyle since the *Flock of Seagulls* days; an Apple salesman, Paul, who had a slight unexplained limp and aspired to be a race car driver. A financial planner, Andy, who was very nice but so delicate and nervous Joanna was afraid she'd crush him both figuratively and literally. Her dating life had essentially come to a depressing standstill, ending with Simon, a patent attorney who was a great, fun, enthusiastic lay but had almost no discernable personality outside the bedroom. Her hunger for a warm and loving companion was obvious. And then there was Diego's butt. She felt as if one day she was a shabby aging chick with a dull job and a ho-hum life and the next day she was reeking of animal magnetism, a super sexy upwardly mobile superstar. His pursuit of her was so intense, his attention so concentrated she felt as if she was laid out under a warm, probing, joyful microscope. It was heavenly, to feel like the center of someone's world, especially someone as fabulous as Diego. Joanna thrived and grew in the spotlight like an anxious spring flower after a protracted ice-encrusted winter.

And she craved that joy for herself, total and unconditional bliss that came over Diego when he talked about his passion, his art. But maybe deep down, underneath the awe and reverence, Joanna maybe knew May and Jamie and the rest of the world were right about Diego. He was pretty on the outside, but the rest of him, outside of that amazing passion? Maybe not so much...

Joanna chalked up Diego's mood swings to his artist mentality. And sometimes they were charming, just like the rest of him. And then they became maybe not so charming, but tolerable, or at least bearable. That's what you put up with when you're in love, you give and take, you compromise. People are sometimes moody and sometimes selfish and sometimes, well sometimes they are just plain mean. And Diego could be very very mean, in a leisurely, yet deliberate way, where Joanna would find herself frustrated to tears and uncomprehending as to what she did wrong.

"I do not understand why you are so upset," Diego would ask.

Joanna gawked at him through tears she didn't understand herself. Diego could twist her words and thoughts around with the skill of a police interrogator.

"I, I don't know. I guess I'm just sensitive today," she would finally answer, forcing a sad smile.

Mostly vegetarian Diego presented a culinary challenge to carnivorous Joanna but she considered herself up to the task. Subscribing fully to the adage "the way to a man's heart is through his stomach," she was determined to keep Diego's belly full and content.

Lily had been adept at recreating meat-friendly standards into vegetarian edibles. Well, at least they weren't inedible, so Joanna used these as a starting point. She fluffed and firmed her mother's soggy seitan loaf, transforming it into a spicy, mouthwatering Shepherd's pie which Leo polished off unsuspecting and happy and asking for "More shepper's pie please!" Her mom's lentil soup just needed some gentle tweaks to be better than edible, adding a dash of liquid smoke, rosemary and a healthy dose of garlic. And then she branched out with a pile of cookbooks and created meals any self respecting foodie would be happy to eat: three bean chipotle chili, cheese enchiladas with tomatillo sauce, kale, white bean and soy crumble stew, paella with vegetables and tempeh.

One night over an endive salad and pasta with lemon cream, asparagus and peas, Diego sighed heavily and put down his fork.

Joanna noticed he had barely touched his pasta, "Is everything ok?" she asked. "Do you not like the pasta?"

"Yes, it is fine," Diego sighed again, "it is just that... perhaps we could branch out with the meals."

Ouch. Branch out? Joanna was studying vegetarian cuisine like a crazed zealot, making something new on a daily basis. "Branch out? I...I thought I was branching out."

Diego took a bite of his salad and then put his fork down again, "It is not as if I never eat *any* meat, Joanna, I am a man. You know, a hamburger maybe?"

"A hamburger?" Joanna wiped her mouth with her napkin, "Diego, I've been busting my butt perfecting vegetarian dishes for my vegetarian boyfriend and you are asking for a hamburger? Can you not understand why I might be confused?"

Diego's eyes turned in an instant from rich chocolate to chilly fudgecicle, "Well, if a hamburger is too much trouble Joanna, forget I mentioned it," he pushed his chair back and abruptly left the table.

Joanna, flabbergasted, stood up and called after him, "Diego, wait, I'm just puzzled, can't we talk about this? I mean, it's just dinner we're talking about here," Joanna tried to lighten the intense vibe.

Diego grabbed his coat from where he had earlier tossed it onto the couch, "No, Joanna, you are not listening to what I have to say," he left the apartment, slamming the door behind him.

Joanna sat back down, and continued to sit at the table. She drank her wine. She ate her pasta. She went over the incident again and again, dissecting it, peeling it, trying to discover in the layers what she had possibly done wrong this time.

8

Jamie's announcement came totally out of the blue. Jamie was gone a lot, his job demanded a hectic travel schedule, but May trusted him implicitly and never imagined he would step outside their marriage. She knew she was in the minority. Amongst the circle of women she lunched and fundraised with, primarily wives of Jamie's colleagues, all suspected, and some knew for a fact their husbands were unfaithful from time to time. In some cases, they were unfaithful all the time, entertaining women in every port as it were, or mistresses in just one.

Most women in the group religiously relied on a "don't ask, don't tell" approach. As Suzanne Smither noted drily "What I don't know won't hurt me, what I do know might be cause for manslaughter."

"They get lonely, and they're men, they don't know how to curl up with a romance novel and a glass of wine like we do," said Caroline Casper, a tall, skinny woman with fashionable blonde steaks in her probably graying hair. Caroline, the matriarch of the lunch group, was daughter of a renowned surgeon and wife of a notorious ladies man. Her husband, rumor had it, slept with everyone, he was an equal opportunity fucker. Colleagues, babysitters, maids, bartenders. If they were female and not chained down, Steven Casper preyed on them, and as Steven was attractive and wealthy, he was tremendously successful with the ladies. Caroline was not May's favorite in the circle. She was appalled at her blithe attitude regarding her husband's humiliating lifestyle.

And Caroline in turn was almost amused with May and Jamie's "adorable" relationship. After May and Jamie had beaten the pants off everyone else in the bowling fundraiser, Caroline began calling them, with the requisite eye-roll and bemused smirk, "The perfect power couple, aren't they so cute, with the public displays of affection." she'd say, and then down the rest of her drink, motioning the waiter for another, "Better make it a double."

Recently, Amanda Livingston, a pretty girl, newly married to a young hot-shot salesman had come to lunch looking pale and drawn, "Lately it seems as if Brad is always gone just a wee bit longer than before, an extra day here, a flight missed there. There's always some reason, and I want to trust him," she pushed her lettuce leaves around with her fork, "but I don't know if I do..."

"Trust him?" Caroline said, sipping her Bloody Mary, "That seems like a bad idea, but if you want your marriage to last you may need to find yourself a hobby..."

May was disgusted, "Jesus, Caroline, just because you're jaded doesn't mean everyone else should be.

What is this, the fucking fifties?" Caroline shrugged and sipped her thick red beverage, nodding to the waitress for another.

May turned to Amanda, "You need to decide what's important for you and your marriage. Don't listen to these cynical bitches. Ask him what's going on, but be warned, you might be right, and then where will you be? You need to decide what's imperative. If he tells you he's having an affair, do you want to live with that? Knowledge is power, but it can ruin your marriage."

When May first began socializing with these women, she felt like she had gone back in time thirty years. Despite her new suburban address, May had been born and raised by hippies. Women regularly worked and she hadn't met a Republican out of the closet until she had gone to college. So she was stunned at the tolerance of infidelity and confused by it as well. What self-respecting human being would allow themselves to be treated this way? Hadn't these women read a single self-help book insisting they kick these assholes out of their homes and reclaim their lives?

May never suspected she would be in the same boat as these women. Women, to whom, although she liked the bulk of them, she had always felt slightly superior. So, she apparently wasn't so superior after all, although she would never divulge this tasty tidbit to the vultures at the swanky lunch table. She was no dummy.

And what about the fact Jamie had not chosen some young cute girl to diddle around with?

"What about the fact Jamie's encounter was with a man?" asked Elsa, her therapist of many years.

"What about it?"

"Well, I would suspect you would feel something about this."

"No...I don't know why, but that's not what's bothering me about it."

"Honestly?"

"Yes...honestly"

For some bizarre reason, that was the easy part to get over. May didn't believe you could "turn" someone gay, and she knew her husband wasn't gay. She was true in most ways to her hippie roots and believed wholeheartedly that homosexuality was something you were born with, like fat ankles or the ability to spell. She did, however, believe in sexual fluidity, that no man or woman was 100% hetero, or homosexual. She had been attracted to women now and then, someone who stunned her with their brains who happened to be a knockout. But attraction was one thing, emotional attachment was another. Since she knew Jamie wasn't gay, she also knew he couldn't have an emotional attachment to this other man. She thought Jamie was a man, and attached to him was a penis, and his penis was confused. Maybe his penis was stupider than the average penis? Or drunker? Maybe his penis was out cavorting and getting drunk without the rest of him? Specifically leaving his brain behind?

She felt pretty well acquainted with his penis, stupid

or not. And she had experience with a gay penis already, and there was just no similarity between the two.

Anton Barber was hands-down the best all around guy in May's high school. Baseball star, debate team champion, choir soloist. Ivy League bound Anton was an excellent scholar, voted most likely to do anything he wanted to do and most sought after to take off his shirt to expose the most outrageous abs around. Bronzed skin and smoldering eyes, Anton had it all. He and May had palled around together for years: movies, weekends, dances. Whenever they were unattached they gravitated back to each other, no questions asked.

During their junior year they finally slept together, May turned to him and said, "Well, did that help?"

"Oh yeah," Anton grabbed his pack of Camels that had fallen to the floor, shakily tapped one out and nodded thanks to May's extended flame, "It appears I am officially gay."

No, she didn't give a shit if Jamie had fucked a woman, a man or a transvestite bald eagle. But the fact he had gone outside their marriage was more than disappointing, it was heartbreaking. It was unfathomable. It was unforgivable.

Because Jamie, next to Joanna of course, was her absolute best friend. They were two peas in a pod. They were the perfect couple for a reason – they just "got" each other. They were so comfortable around each other, right from the get-go; it was as if they were truly meant to be together, as if they were made for each other. Jamie understood her fears and doubts and what made her tick. She felt valued with him.

And May had never believed in any of that fairy-tale bullshit. She was a pessimist by nature. So when she began dating Jamie it was no time before she realized: Holy shit! This guy is my God-damned Prince Charming! He's the peanut butter to my jelly.

And now that the infidelity was out in the open, May didn't know how to feel and didn't know what to do. Could she be confused? Could she feel rejected? Could she roll herself into a ball and cry until her tears ran dry? Could she eat and drink herself fat and drunk? Could she bludgeon him with a blunt object, shove his dead body into a garbage bag and toss it in the bay? An intriguing scenario...

At the moment, she was making an effort to join the world of humans. Joanna had convinced her she couldn't let her life go to hell in a hand basket, and her therapist Elsa had enthusiastically agreed. So today she had dropped Leo at school, "See you later, Mom," he had said, happily running for the play-structure, "have a good day and don't forget to get me!" She forced her car in the direction of the gym, thinking a yoga class may help to calm her frayed nerves.

May was doing her best to focus, sitting tall in her Lion's pose and breathing in and out. May wasn't familiar with this instructor, a tall, angular man named Ted. Ted's hair was pulled back into a blonde ponytail, exposing multiple hoop earrings and a small serpent tattoo curled at the base of his neck. May couldn't help but think Ted was a silly name for a yoga instructor. Seemed more like an investment banker name. "Hey Ted, want to go play squash this weekend?" "Can't man, I'm off to teach yoga class." It didn't fit. Ted encouraged them to roar, "Let the lion out of its cage and roar!" Students growled and roared around her. May did not roar.

Next, Ted next guided them to stand for *Vrksasana*, Tree pose. "Root your standing foot into the ground," Ted's veined foot nimbly traveled up his leg to the well-defined adductor muscle atop his inner-thigh, "Feel the earth through your supporting foot. Stretch your branches and steady yourself against the breeze."

May didn't feel any breeze, but she did feel as if she was about to fall out of a tree.

9

Dinner with the parents. Oy vey. May drove. She had several cars to choose from and all were so much more comfortable than Joanna's clunker. Today they drove the newest of the fleet; a luminous white Volvo station wagon. May called it "the family car" although Joanna would have called the Honda Minivan the family car. "No, no," said May, "that's the kid car; Leo calls it 'The Big One.'" The car glided along stealthily towards Berkeley. The sisters were quiet on the drive, each psyching themselves up in their own way for the visit. Leo was singing at the top of his lungs.

"B-I-N-G-(clap)! B-I-N-G-(clap)! B-I-N-G-(clap)!" and Bingo was his name-o!"

"Don't forget, we are not mentioning the S-E-P-A-R-A-T-I-O-N," reminded May, casually.

Joanna had been lost in thought so couldn't keep up with the spelling. "The what?"

"The S-E-P-A-R-A-T-I-O-N," May said, spelling more slowly and louder this time, as if Joanna was illiterate and hard of hearing rather than merely spaced out, "I haven't mentioned anything to them as yet."

"Ah, Jeez, May, really?" Joanna slumped against the door, forlorn; she was terrible at secrets. May had learned long ago to not trust Joanna with any information she didn't want leaked. As teenagers, this was often a challenge for the sisters, but as Joanna was May's closest confidante, May needed to learn, sometimes the hard way, what type of secret Joanna could, and could not handle. May sneaking out in the middle of the night to meet a boy? That, Joanna could handle. May taking birth control pills? Borderline, but she could do it. May separating, maybe even divorcing from her possibly newly bisexual husband? Joanna didn't know how she was going to keep that little tidbit under wraps. "OK, then what's our plan?"

Joanna and May loved their parents. But like most people who had parents, they didn't always like them. There was always one parent who was more overbearing and irritating than the other. Usually, this was Lily, although Daniel had his moments. The sisters learned to divide and conquer. If May was feeling particularly vulnerable, then Joanna deflected Lily from her. If it was Joanna who wasn't as psychologically agile that particular visit, May would take her. Daniel was rarely an issue but you had to keep your guard up with him. He was a sly one, wily as a fox. He was deft in acquiring highly confidential information about one sister from the other sister. The good news with Daniel is he only used his formidable powers for good and not evil.

"I don't think we need a plan, Jo, there's just nothing to tell." May was calm. The girls had different strategies for preparing for a Fischer Family visit. May was able to internally compartmentalize all her issues, becoming calm, cool and collected well before the visit. She transcended her emotions with expert precision. Joanna, on the other hand, had to talk herself through it. Today's internal dialogue went like this:

> *So, what are you going to do when Lily looks your outfit up and down as if you stole it from Goodwill moments ago and the tags are still hanging from it?*
>
> *I will smile and say, "Do you like it? It's new!" And then change the subject.*
>
> *So, what are you going to do when Lily asks if you are dating anyone new?*
>
> *I will smile and say, "Not yet but I hope to soon!" And then change the subject.*
>
> *So, what are you going to do when Lily asks when you are getting back together with Mark?*
>
> *I will smile and say, "I don't think his wife would like that, Mom, or his son." And then change the subject.*

"OK, you're right, there's nothing to tell, I can do it," replied Joanna with shaky confidence.

"Of course you can. I know you can, sister!" May put up a hand for Joanna to smack in a high-five, "And don't worry, I brought alcohol."

"Oh thank God."

The car silently glided off the freeway and wove through

the avenues and the girls were quiet as they surveyed the landmarks of their childhood. Their elementary school, remodeled from the crumbling asbestos-laden building where they began their organized learning. Cafés where they had cut classes to drink cappuccinos and gossip. Star Magnolia and cherry blossom trees graced the front lawns in their neighborhood, bare and readying themselves to bud.

"And Bingo was his nammmmmme-ooooooo!" Leo concluded loudly, breaking the stillness.

May and Joanna clapped and whistled vigorously.

Lily and Daniel opened the front door before the car had even come to a complete stop.

"Well hello there! How was the drive? Look at that big boy! Do you need me to carry anything? Look at the new car! So fancy!" Lily, magnificent in her orange caftan was going a mile a minute. She took Leo by the hand, "Give your old Grandmamma a kiss, Sweetie Pie."

Leo planted a sloppy wet one on her cheek, "You're not too old, Grandmamma!" He said, letting go of her and bounding towards his Grandpapa, waiting patiently on the porch for the brood to make their way up to him.

Daniel gave Joanna a hug and a kiss and whispered in her ear, "How are you holding up, Jelly Jo?" Only Daniel could get away with calling Joanna by such a silly nickname.

Joanna whispered back, "Pretty good, Dad. I'm ok."

Daniel held her at arm's length and peered over his bifocals at her, searching her green eyes, "Pretty good?" He smiled, "Are you sleeping at all?"

Joanna kissed him on the cheek, his tanned skin was cool and dry, "Yes, pretty good. Really," she insisted.

"You lie like a dog," Daniel whispered in her ear, giving her a squeeze and ushering her into the house.

They all bustled inside, Leo and Lily talking over each other:

"So how was the drive?'

"We sang Bingo and there was a big truck and it played its horn: BRRRRRR! BRRRRR! Loud!"

"Oh, how nice, Honey."

"And it had a green stripe and a lot of smoke!"

"Oh, well, isn't that interesting?"

Their childhood home had changed little from when Joanna and May were growing up. In the front yard still grew a single huge blue plum tree which monopolized the sun and kept the front room in perpetual darkness. The tree was healthy, green and lush, if messy in the summertime, and the girls had grown up eating handfuls of the fruit, juice dripping down their forearms as well as plum jam in every application: spread on toast, basted on top of chicken, stirred into milk. The living room and adjoining dining room were smallish, simply painted white with dark red trim and dark wood built-in cabinets with rows and rows of books. Black and white portraits of the girls and Leo in various ages and stages lined the walls. The girls' bedrooms were still painted as they had requested as teenagers, Joanna's a pale blue with cream trim and May's wallpapered with tiny little roses. At the time, Lily was disappointed the rooms ended up so...ordinary...she was hoping for black and purple peace signs or multi-colored parallelograms. Joanna's room had since turned into a playroom for Leo and May's served as storage for paraphernalia necessary for Lily's various hobbies.

The old kitchen was still the heart of the home, and now the kitchen bulletin board, still crammed with now even older recipes, Joanna's dusty blue bake-off ribbon, May's debate-team pictures and Leo's numerous art projects threatened to fall off the wall at any moment. Daniel had suggested they relocate the board, or at least replace it with something sturdier but Lily insisted it was fine, fine and would hang there as long as she lived in the house. Even Daniel didn't know how nostalgic Lily was for the bulletin board. At least once a day she took something down and studied it while sipping her tea. A recipe that reminded her of a particular time, May's musical theatre programs or Joanna's 8th grade self-portrait. Leo's crayon art bright against the faded background. She would sip and reflect on her incredible family, and occasionally have a good cry. May and Joanna were taking bets on when it would go, probably taking the cabinet door with it; one decent sized earthquake and that baby was sure to be history. The last über-bohemian remnant from the 70's was the wall of psychedelically-colored glass beads a-la-Greg Brady that hung in place of a door, separating the dining room from the kitchen.

Joanna took the wine from May and started towards the wall of beads which tinkled prettily as she moved through them. She needed a drink, pronto.

"Oh, just a smidge for me, Honey," called Lily.

Joanna moaned, already irritated; it was the same old routine. Lily would pour herself "just a smidge" all night long. Joanna found it interesting that Lily's obsession with food didn't extend to wine.

She expertly pulled the cork and poured herself a wee bit more than a smidge, drank it in one long swallow, and then poured herself some more. This time she smacked her lips, savoring the taste; it was a lovely sauvignon blanc, crisp and grapefruity and clean. There was one thing Joanna and Jamie always bonded over, his carefully chosen and well stocked wine-cellar. She gave him a silent "thank you" for tonight's offering. He might be a cheating bastard but he had excellent taste in vino.

The door leading to the backyard opened, surprising Joanna and causing her to choke on her wine. The surprise turned to happiness when she saw who was walking through the door.

"Nuncle Pete!" Joanna ran and practically jumped into his outstretched arms.

"Hey Jelly Jo!"

Nuncle Pete was Daniel's best friend. Originally, Joanna's parents called him "Not-Uncle Pete" but three year old Joanna scrunched the words together, dubbing him Nuncle Pete, and it stuck. Daniel and Pete lived together as college students and were now lifelong *compadres*. They were best men at each other's weddings (third time was hopefully the charm for Pete, once for Daniel), attended the birth of each other's children (four for Pete, including twin boys, two for Daniel), and grandchildren (three for Pete and one for Daniel), vacationed together (last year Pete and Pearl met Daniel and Lily in Greece) and pretty much saw each other as often as they could, despite their geographical differences. Nuncle Pete's career, or as Daniel maintained, Nuncle Pete's "Selling of his soul to the corporate agenda" took him to New Mexico. So although Nuncle Pete was not a real uncle, he was part of the family.

If Nuncle Pete's buttoned-down bosses only knew what a pothead he truly was! As soon as he set foot in Berkeley it was as if he had never left. His Brook's Brother's suit and tie would seem to dissolve away in a cloud of patchouli and incense as he hit the nearest head shop for a fresh supply of rolling papers. Pete's stylish, graying but not thinning chin-length hair would pull itself into a stubby ponytail. And from the depths of his Louis Vuitton suitcase would emerge every hippie's soulmate and Joanna and May's mortal enemy: Birkenstocks. Hands down the ugliest shoes ever made, revered by hippies everywhere as the footwear of choice.

"I'm half expecting his old VW bus with the bead curtains and bed in the back to drive out of that suitcase," May once remarked.

"What are you doing here? Did we know you were coming?"

"Nothing interesting, boring business," he grabbed a loaf of bread from the counter, ripping off a piece and chewing, "I thought I'd make a surprise visit. It's so good to see you!" He patted her cheek affectionately.

Lily floated into the kitchen, "I see you discovered our little surprise," she encircled Pete's ample waist with her skinny arms. Pete kissed her on the head and excused himself to locate Leo.

Joanna handed her mother a glass of wine with only a smidge, as instructed. "What's for dinner, Mom?" Joanna lifted a lid off of the pot on the stove, although she already recognized the smell of Lily's lackluster lentil soup, a decidedly un-kid-friendly meal, and one that brought up vivid, although not altogether pleasant memories of dinners past, including a memorable stomach-flu episode resulting in Joanna spraying the avocado green walls of the bathroom with avocado green lentil vomit.

Lily drank gratefully and fluttered around the kitchen like a manic butterfly, flitting here and there and accomplishing absolutely nothing, "Oh, lentil soup and salad and bread. Nothing fancy. So, how are you? What's new? Is that a new sweater? It looks great on you! Have you heard from Mark lately?" She finished her wine and smiled over the top of the glass at her daughter.

Joanna blinked at her, uncertain of which question to answer and which to ignore. She chose to ignore the one about Mark. "Nope, it's not a new sweater and I'm well, how are you?" Turning the attention over to her mother was always the best avoidance technique.

"Oh I'm fine, I'm fine. Did I tell you Sam Goldman has a new baby boy?" Lily poured herself another "smidge".

"Yes, you did, so exciting for Sam. And how is Dad's knee these days?" Deflect, deflect, deflect.

Lily tossed her hands in the air as if she were tossing pizza dough, "Oh, who knows, that man won't tell me anything. I ask him, how is it feeling? And he always says 'fine, fine'."

"Well, maybe it *is* fine, Mom."

Lily put her hands on her hips, "Of course it isn't fine, Joanna Ruth, I see that little gimpy-limpy thing he does when he thinks I'm not looking. I wasn't born yesterday, you know!"

Joanna softened, she knew she was too hard on her mom sometimes, a long-held defense mechanism "Sorry, Mom, you're right. I'll try to get some info out of him," she smiled.

Lily began taking silverware out of the drawers, "That would be good, maybe he'll tell you girls. Anyway! What's going on with May these days?" She called over her shoulder, "Is everything ok with her?"

Joanna hid behind a sip of wine, "May? Oh sure she's ok, she's fine." She turned to give the soup an unnecessary stir. She tried to remember the lie she had told Lily as to May's whereabouts that day. Yoga? Shopping? Dead mobile? She had no recollection and felt a trickle of sweat between her shoulder blades.

"Are you sure?" Lily probed, spinning around with a handful of silverware.

"Yes, Mom, everything is fine as far as I know." Yikes, that may have been a tactical error...

Lily jumped on it, quick as a cat on a mouse, "What do you mean 'as far as you know'? You always know everything that's going on with May..." Lily's voice started to climb in pitch.

Joanna put her hands on her mother's shoulders and looked her in the eyes, "Mom, take a deep breath, everything is fine, don't worry," she smiled convincingly, "wouldn't I tell you if something wasn't ok?"

Leo ran into the kitchen, "Auntie Jo, did you see Nuncle Pete?" he asked breathlessly. "Something smells yucky." He wrinkled his nose. Lily's attention immediately switched.

Yes! Thought Joanna, perfect timing, my little perfect nephew, and I didn't even have to pay you.

"What? It smells yucky? Well, that's not very nice to say about your Grandmamma's yummy lentil soup now is it Honey-Bunches? We'll just find you something yummy to eat for dinner ok? What about a hot dog? Do you think your Mama will approve of a hot dog? It's Kosher?" Lily was off and running again and Joanna discreetly left for the living room, beads tinkling, covertly taking the bottle of wine with her.

10

Every other Tuesday, unbeknownst to Lily and Joanna, May and Daniel had a standing lunch date. It wasn't necessarily a secret, and it wasn't as if they would have minded if the rest of the family knew, but neither of them had ever mentioned it. May drove into Berkeley to meet Daniel during his break between classes. She liked to see him during his work day, away from the one-woman show otherwise known as Lily; they had their best talks at these lunches. Today Daniel was pleasantly disheveled, hair needing a trim, wearing an English professor-issue plaid cardigan sweater and the faded 501s he favored. They hugged hello and he smelled familiarly of wool, coffee and....cigarettes?

"Daddy, are you smoking again?"

"This is my 'hello?'" Daniel asked guiltily, ignoring the question.

"Dad, you reek."

Daniel rolled his eyes, "How could I reek from one teeny tiny cigarette?"

"Only one?"

"Only one today, how's that?"

"That's one today too many, but I'll let it go. I'm sure I owe you."

They enjoyed a relaxed, companionable lunch. Daniel drank a beer with his burger and fries and May had a salad and iced tea. May told Daniel about Leo's newest obsession, bugs, the uglier the better, and Daniel told May about a new grad assistant who was driving him crazy and a frightening new hobby of Lily's, archery.

May looked over the top of her iced tea glass, "Are you kidding me? Why archery?"

"I don't know, you know your mother..."

May kept her eyes on her plate and said, "So, I wanted to tell you something. But I want you to not tell Mom, I am *not* ready for her yet. OK?" She looked up at him.

"My lips are sealed, what's up?"

Daniel had grown up with a wimp of a mother and a tyrant of a father. Lou Fischer was a big, burly, forbidding man who was at a complete loss as to what to do with his studious, bookish son. Not that he wanted the boy to be dumb; Lou wanted the boy to be able to get by, he just didn't want him to be smarter than he was, the king of the Fischer fortress with his Queen trembling in the turret and his obedient children making appearances from the cellar to fetch his slippers and beer without complaint. But Daniel was much, much sharper than Lou. He was scary smart. Plus, he was athletic and well-liked. Lou's solution was to try to beat Daniel into the boy he expected him to be. That would teach him to make his father look stupid at the spelling bees and on the football field. Lou didn't experience the pleasure in having strong, confident children, he only saw them as objects to be twisted and fashioned into terrified little wimps. Daniel and his sisters had each run screaming from the house as they turned eighteen, leaving their father behind with barely a backwards glance and their mother waving stoically at the window.

Daniel vowed he would raise his children differently. He wanted strong, self-assured, confident kids, and years of therapy and his big brain helped him understand how to do it. Daniel understood confidentiality and he didn't have any of these pre-conceived notions he needed to tell his wife everything about his kids. May and Joanna trusted him completely, so he knew he had done his job well.

"Jamie and I..." she twirled some lettuce around.

Daniel didn't rush her, but he did put his burger down.

"Well, we've separated," she put her fork down.

"Sweetheart," he leaned forward and covered her hand with his. "Are you ok?"

May nodded, tears quivering in the corners of her eyes. "Yes, no, I'm ok." She took her hand away to root around in her bag for a tissue, instead accepting Daniel's handkerchief into which she daintily blew her nose. "I really am ok. I'm not sure how I'm feeling yet." She paused and shook her hair, composing herself, "He fucked someone else."

Daniel sat back in his chair, mouth hanging open in disbelief.

"I know," May sipped some tea, "I know. I can't believe it either. You know what, this tea is not doing it," she turned around in her chair to flag down the waitress, "excuse me, Miss, may I have a glass of white wine? Dad, do you want another beer? And another beer, please."

May turned back to her dad, "So anyway, that's the scoop in my little world. I wanted to tell you, but can we talk about something else? I don't want to get all emotional..."

"Sure, Sweetheart, whenever you're ready," Daniel twirled a french fry absently in a blob of ketchup, "I'm ready to listen whenever you're ready to talk."

"Thanks, Daddy," May's eyes threatened tears and she drank some tea and choked them back. "So," she rearranged herself and changed the subject, "have you spoken with Joanna?"

"Yes, I just spoke with her this morning as a matter of fact. I think she sounds better, still sad, but maybe there's light at the end of the tunnel. What's your take on her?"

May told him she also thought her big sis was doing better, and asked what he thought about the upcoming Super Tuesday. Daniel was glum about the primary, not optimistic any of the candidates could turn things around. May half listened to her father's trepidation, but found she couldn't concentrate, she was becoming distracted. A man with his back to her, several tables away was droning on and on. May couldn't make out the words to understand what he was droning on and on about but something about him was familiar. The pretty brunette he was with seemed riveted, and May couldn't help but notice she hadn't uttered a single word, not a single syllable in the time she had been listening. The man tossed his hair, and instantly May knew who it was: Diego.

"Dad," she interrupted her father, "Diego is sitting over there."

Daniel turned to look, "He is?"

"I'm going to go say hello to him."

"Be nice, May..." Daniel cautioned.

"Dad, please," May grinned prettily, "I'm always nice," she winked at her dad, wiped the corners of her mouth with her napkin and walked over to Diego's table.

Yup, it's him, she thought, the familiar droning getting louder as she got closer, the brunette was eyeing her warily as she approached, as if she were a Jehovah's Witness peddling the word of God.

She stopped next to his table. She hadn't seen him in months now, but he looked exactly the same: blazing hot and dumb as a post, with those empty eyes of his. "Diego, I thought that was you going on and on about nothing." May smiled sardonically.

"May, what a nice surprise..." Diego began to rise to his feet.

"Oh no, don't get up. And who is this you're with today? I'm May," she extended her hand to the flabbergasted girl.

The girl meekly grasped May's hand in one of those limp girl-shakes May detested, "Vanessa. I'm Diego's girlfriend," she added possessively.

“Well, well. Good for you!” May nodded at the girl, poor brainless thing. She turned her attention back to Diego, “And Diego, what is new with you, besides Vanessa of course,” she smiled at Vanessa.

Diego pushed his hair, a little nervously, May thought, behind his ears, “Not much, not much. Just doing the art thing. I am finally picking up some regulars who like my work so that is good news for me.”

“He’s very talented,” Vanessa interjected, “have you seen his purses? They are, like, so incredible!”

“Yes, yes, I have,” May said, “I do recall you made... stuff...anyway, Diego, interesting to run into you. Treat this one better than you did the last one, won’t you?” She turned back to Vanessa and smiled kindly, “So great to meet you, Vanessa. Take care of yourself, and good luck!” she winked.

She walked away and back to her dad.

“Were you nice?” he wore a small foamy mustache courtesy of the additional beer.

She slipped into her chair, “Nice as pie,” she grinned, reaching for one of her dad’s fries with one hand and her waiting glass of wine with the other.

11

May ran her hand over the silk blouses, the cashmere sweaters. It was time to do a little spring cleaning. She had already gone through Leo's things, the not quite to ankle-length pajamas and the already too tight underwear as they had just finished potty-training. "Yippee! Congrats, big boy!" Joanna had high-fived Leo. "*Thank God*," May said under her breath.

She sneakily boxed up toys she knew he hadn't played with for months, a risky move to be sure, and had even gone through his linen closet, finally packing up the small hooded towels from his toddler days he just didn't fit into any longer, although, she thought, they do make good Superman capes so she tossed a few into his dress-up bin. Now she was moving on to the biggest mission of the clean-up, her own closet. Leo played with his Thomas the Train set on the floor and May promised to take him to the park after she got this project done. She needed to divest herself of some of her stuff; she was certain that would make her feel better, lighter. She swiveled her head on her shoulders, stretched her arms and back and dove courageously into the massive closet. She tossed little worn sweaters and last year's suits onto the bed. Shoes, belts, hats, a blizzard of clothing sailed out of the closet. A black shirt dress flew out, "Where did I get this? Ugh!" May mumbled absently as she tossed it onto the mounting heap.

Leo wandered over to the staggering pile. He pulled down the closest dress and pulled it over his head, laughing as it pooled around his feet. He pulled the pile of clothes onto the floor and dug through until he found a flowered scarf. He tossed it dramatically around his neck and yanked off his tennis shoes to shove his feet into some discarded stilettos. He topped the get-up off with a jaunty sunhat. Not able to walk and barely able to stand, he threw his arms into the air and happily exclaimed "Ta Da!"

May walked out of her gigantic closet (her walk-in closet was bigger than Joanna's bedroom) to see what Leo was up to and doubled over with laughter. Leo looked hilarious, with the cockeyed scarf and dress swimming around the shoes. Leo's tiny boy feet, clad in his favorite bug socks stuffed into the stilettos were really the clincher. May clapped her hands, "You look lovely, my darling! But what you need is jewelry!"

She pulled out her jewelry box and soon Leo was dripping with diamonds and pearls.

Leo strutted in the mirror, "I look fantastic, Mommy!"

"You do, it's true. You are just beautiful."

12

The peppy brunette barista with the eyebrow piercing greeted her with a "Howdy Joanna, here's your medium black!" She slid the cup of coffee across the counter and Joanna handed her a five.

"Thanks," Joanna mumbled. She wondered when she had achieved "regular" status at her favorite coffee joint. She took her change and her cup of coffee, left a generous tip and settled at an outside table, intent on having a quiet lunch time read. She loved hanging with her friends, but some days she just needed some solitude.

Especially days when she hadn't slept a wink the night before. Well, this wasn't exactly accurate, she was sure. Everyone she had ever a shared a bed with told her she was indeed asleep all night long. But Joanna often felt as if she hadn't gotten any rest, as if she had run a marathon or cooked a ten course meal in her sleep. Once she told Mark, "I'm so busy in my sleep that I'm exhausted by morning."

Today she tried to concentrate on her novel, but she was continually distracted by a gaggle of women gathered in a smoky glob in the middle of the courtyard. The women were each gulping huge, slushy, whipped-cream topped coffee concoctions and gobbling over-sized muffins. And so loud! Did they not understand public space? One was particularly grating on Joanna's nerves, wearing pink flowered scrubs and white nurse shoes, sucking on the cigarette as if it was oxygen and cackling "Oh no she didn't!" at the top of her lungs, every minute or so.

Joanna was so preoccupied with this fascinatingly gross display, like a pile-up on the freeway you just can't turn away from, it was rather shocking when the gaggle first quieted as if a switch had turned them off and then parted like the red sea and there appeared Diego, striding directly towards her and smiling that incredibly perfect smile. Joanna hadn't seen him in four months and eight days, not that she was counting. The whole tribe of women looked him up and down as if he were edible. Joanna's catty attitude softened a bit; she couldn't blame them for admiring him so lustily; she had been there. Impulsively, she smoothed her wayward hair and straightened her blouse, cursing herself for going with the comfortable rather than cute outfit she had almost worn. Suddenly she desperately needed to pee.

"Joanna!" he greeted her like a long lost friend, leaned over and kissed her on her cheek, his lips warm and curvaceous, "How lovely it is to see you."

"Diego, hi!" she said, a little too loudly.

He looked, well, splendid. Worn cowboy boots and

trendy bootlegged jeans, plaid well-fitting flannel shirt. Only Diego could pull off the hokey cowboy gear without looking like Woody from *Toy Story*. Joanna glanced down at her own white blouse, navy blazer and slacks, not exactly cutting-edge but not bad, she supposed. Diego's hair was never shinier, his smile never wider, his shoulders never broader and he smelled as intoxicating as ever. Keep it together here, girl, Joanna told herself.

"Soymilk chai?" she asked, indicating the paper cup he was carrying.

"Of course, creature of habit that I am, always soymilk chai." Uninvited, he sat down at her table, "How are you, Joanna?" he leaned across the table towards her and his brow was furrowed, as if he were terribly concerned about her well-being.

"I'm fine. I'm just great. How are you?" Joanna replied, breezily. She felt like her clothes were just a little too tight, as if she were abnormally swollen, like Violet from Charlie and the Chocolate Factory. Maybe I'm turning into a blueberry, she thought. With any luck I'll pop and splatter purple all over him.

He lost the fretful look to collapse backwards in his chair, as if he was just too exhausted to answer such a complicated question, "I am just terrific. So, *so* busy these days," he shook his head as if bewildered the world wouldn't slow down just for him, "my work is going very very well." She had forgotten how he tended to repeat words. It was a little irritating, irritating.

"That's great," she replied.

"And you, Joanna, what is new with you?" he leaned in again, eyes probing hers.

"Uh, well, uh, nothing really new I'd say," Joanna's mind was curiously blank.

Diego drank from his aromatic paper cup, "And how is your family? You know, I ran into May recently, last week? Maybe last week. How is Leo?" Leo? Since when did he give a rat's ass about Leo? Wait, May? Where did he run into May?

"Family is great, really, everyone and everything is just great," Joanna began to gather her belongings, the unread book, her purse and coffee cup; desperate to get away before she said or did something stupid, "My lunch hour's over, I need to get back to work. Nice running into you," she patted him on the shoulder, unsure how else to leave him.

He rose and engulfed her in an awkward hug, Joanna struggled not to drop her hot cup of coffee, "So, so, so good to see you, Joanna. You really are looking well. Give me a call; perhaps we can have a cup of coffee together?"

She forced herself to smile and nod back at him, as if to say, "Sure! Of course! Coffee sounds terrific. I'll absolutely call you!"

Joanna felt a great sadness welling in her chest as she rapidly left, willing herself not to explode in purple blueberry sorrow.

As Joanna rode the elevator back up to her office she remembered it was copy day. One of the more electrifying facets of her thrilling job was copy day, where she, quite obviously, copied and distributed the summary memos, pleadings, discovery documents, and calendars to the partners, associates and occasionally the baby-faced interns. Sometimes the cases were fascinating, so she enjoyed the job, reading greedily about bitter divorces, acrimonious custody battles, and hostile un-neighborly disagreements as the copier did its thing. But more often than not the cases were dry as toast so she would daydream as the gigantic machine copied, collated and bound the mountains of weekly materials, reams of paper she would later shred into an enormous pile bound for the recycling truck.

Today's daydream, not surprisingly, starred the lunchtime encounter with Diego. She mulled over it slowly, reliving the short reunion and scrutinizing it for significance. What did it mean when he said "You really are looking well?" was he telling her he was *surprised* to see her looking so well? Was she supposed to have spiraled into a pit of ugliness after their breakup? Should she have sprouted horns and sallow skin, another chin or unsightly hairs on her upper lip? And what exactly does "looking well" mean? That she looked better than expected? That she looked better than when they were a couple? That she looked better than a monkey's ass? And why on earth had he mentioned Leo and her family and May in particular? Was he trying to show he knew how much they meant to her, and that she meant that much to him? Did he miss her? What did it mean when he said "So, so, so good to see you, Joanna"? Did he want her back? Was he rethinking his drastic and idiotic decision to break up with her? Once he saw her did he realize he was a complete imbecile to have let her go? That the breakup was a stupid, irrational move on his part which he now deeply regretted? And what about that "maybe we can have a cup of coffee together" comment? First of all, he didn't even drink coffee and second, didn't he break up with her? Why on earth...

"Penny for your thoughts, pretty lady," interrupted Bruno, standing in front of her for who knows how long. Joanna hadn't noticed he had entered the copy room, so mesmerized was she with the whir whir whir of the copy machine and her own swirling fantasies.

"Hey Bruno, just, you know, spacing out." Joanna wasn't as embarrassed as she might have been; Bruno knew she had a tendency to...drift on occasion.

"May I cut in here?" he indicated her enormous copy pile, "I've just got a quickie."

"Of course, let it just finish this cycle."

"Gladly," he said, brushing stray paperclips and shreds of paper from the side table and hopping onto it. "So, what are you spacing out about over there? Career fulfillment? Suicide? What?" He inspected his fingernails.

"None of the above," she stretched, "I ran into Diego at lunch," she tried, and failed, to sound casual.

Bruno's eyes widened, "Oh no, how did it go? What happened?"

"Fine, fine, it was fine, I didn't do anything stupid. I don't think I said anything stupid. But Jesus, Bruno, he looked," she paused to shake her head remorsefully, "so, so beautiful. It's still painful. I think I had forgotten how breathtaking he is."

"Breathtakingly evil you mean! I hope you put an evil hex on him."

Joanna laughed. Bruno was so smart, why hadn't she thought of that? A hex would have been the perfect response.

13

May was craving bread. She figured with all the stress she had been under a baguette wouldn't kill her. Carbs were not the enemy here; Jamie was.

She stopped at a little bakery on a side street displaying a simple awning reading "*Sweet*". May bought a small, sandwich sized baguette from the stout woman behind the counter. She hesitated; the cookies were so beautiful, almost too beautiful to eat, and the smell in the bakery was incredible. Should she buy a cookie for Leo? One cookie wouldn't hurt him. A sweet treat for her sweet boy? She was a little worried about Leo, she was certain he sensed something was just not right at home.

The stout woman saw the hesitation, "Can I tempt you with something else, Honey?"

"I'm thinking about maybe a cookie for my son. How about that oatmeal looking one?" May pointed to the healthiest looking cookie in the case.

"Oatmeal-raisin, can't go wrong with that."

She took the bag back to her car and ate the baguette, slowly relishing the crusty exterior and the chewy, tangy middle. Delicious. Quite possibly one of the best baguettes she had ever eaten, or maybe it had just been so long since she had eaten any bread that didn't resemble cardboard or Styrofoam that anything would have tasted good.

She was trying to prevent herself from going home. It was too depressing there. Ironic, May knew, as the house on the hill had been her personal sanctuary for almost a decade. With Jamie's travel schedule, it truly had always been May's house. Even when they bought it, May was the decision maker, well, and Joanna who had accompanied her on the house-hunting trips, but Joanna took more of a consulting role. May had decided what part of the city she wanted to live in. She had researched schools and neighborhoods and crime. She had a size in mind. Huge, but not repulsively so. She chose the colors, both interior and exterior. She chose the extras, pool, tennis court, 3-car garage. She decided which room was for what and what theme would be where. It had May written all over it. Once the house was done, decorated and move-in ready, Jamie saw it for the first time.

"It's perfect!" He exclaimed, agreeing wholeheartedly with all the choices she had made, from the chic living room to the modern cavernous kitchen to the comfy and kid-friendly great room ("For later, when there are kids!" May smiled), Jamie had loved it all. He swept her into his arms and up the majestic staircase, hesitating at the top to ask, "Which way to the bedroom, Baby?"

But now, without him, the house was cold and lonely.

Leo's fabulous little energy rays couldn't fill up the cold empty spots in the corners. And even though Jamie traveled a lot her bed had never felt so drafty, so vacant, so barren. She missed him. She missed him so intensely, she felt like there was a great basketball sized hole in the middle of her chest, the middle of her heart. She imagined this is what an amputee felt like, the phantom pain they described, of their severed limb. Where yesterday there was an arm, today a shirt-sleeve pinned to the shoulder and a deep throbbing ache.

May had already dropped Leo at school, gone to yoga class, picked up the dry-cleaning, dropped the bags of clothes off at the women's shelter, gotten a mani-pedi, and eaten this baguette. She still had hours before she could realistically pick Leo up, and even if she picked him up early, then what would they do? There were only so many hours they could go to the park and play before May had reached her limit. She loved being with just Leo but the other kids on the playground drove her crazy. And she wasn't in the mood for the chatty moms who spent their days carting their kids from one activity to the next. She could take Leo to a movie, but they had already seen *Clifford's Really Big Movie* and unfortunately that was all there was out for the under-5 set.

May reached into the bag and pulled out the oatmeal cookie. It smelled amazing. She broke off a tiny piece and popped it into her mouth. The exterior was crisp and the inside was sweet, spicy and chewy. The raisins were perfectly plump. She took another bite. This time she didn't bother to break off a piece but instead sank her teeth right into the middle of the cookie. Wow, it was so delicious. She sank her teeth in again, and again. And then, catching her quite by surprise, the cookie was gone.

May licked her fingers in order to capture each moist crumb that had fallen and now clung to her yoga pants. Then she grabbed her bag, opened the door and walked back into the bakery.

The little bell rang, announcing her arrival, or maybe her re-arrival and the stout woman looked up from packing a box of cookies. "You're back so soon" she said, grinning.

"Yes, I..." May hesitated, not sure of quite what to say, and didn't know why she felt so guilty. "It seems that I ate the cookie so I wanted to get another one for my son."

The stout woman laughed, "It's been known to happen, although usually the cookie never even makes it out the door," she reached into the case and bagged another oatmeal cookie, "just the one cookie then?"

"Better make it two," she eased herself onto a bar stool, "and, maybe a cappuccino?" May asked tentatively, as if the woman would deny her the cappuccino, saying "What? You're drinking coffee after all that sugar and white flour? Are you insane? Are you trying to kill yourself?"

But instead she said, "You got it," and busied herself making the drink.

May realized too late she had forgotten to ask for nonfat milk, but she didn't care. She sat, people-watching as customers bustled in and out of the warm bakery, contentedly sipping the thick, luxurious coffee, and eating her second oatmeal-raisin cookie, relishing each spicy bite.

Once a week, May volunteered at Bright Future. When the ***Bright Future Volunteer Opportunities!*** notice had been posted at the beginning of the school year, the moms... and one lone dad... clogged the corridor like high school students seeking their grade on a mid-term which would decide their college fate and reciprocally, the rest of their lives. Snarling like rabid pit bulls, they swiftly snatched up highly sought after jobs like *Room Parent*, *Snack Coordinator* and *Art Docent*. May stayed clear of the mob, waiting to see if anything appealing was left. There was only one job left unclaimed, the obviously undesirable *Office Helper*.

So once a week May wrote and typed up memos and reminders, she edited the weekly parent's newsletter and did the office supply order. She sent out requests for new books or art supplies or popsicle sticks or whatever else the teachers needed that particular week. She organized the garden volunteers and the playground volunteers and the library volunteers. It was an oddly satisfying job, especially now when she needed something easy to occupy her time, when she yearned for the simplicity of crossing a completed item off her lengthy to-do list. And blissfully, the job was *outside* of the classroom. There were just too many kids inside. And much worse than the kids, sometimes there were other mothers. Frankly, she had won the lottery with this gig.

Several of these other mothers had expressed sympathy for May: "Darn it!" said stick-up-her-ass Sandy Shafer, wife of a prominent local politician, "You sure got stuck with the icky job!" She shook her head, sympathetically clucking her tongue. Maria Martin wrung her hands together, "Oh, poor May! Maybe next year you'll get a better pick!" Hannah Reynolds, whose son Logan was a buddy of Leo's and probably the only mother May felt like she had anything in common with had said dryly, "Lucky duck."

It wasn't that May was much different than any of these women, this she knew. They volunteered, exercised, lunched and shopped just like she did. And after Leo's birth she tried, she really did. She went to all the classes and trolled the local parks, looking for the Mommy-match she was certain must be out there. But she was stunned to discover...these women were just so boring. It was as if these seemingly normal, once smart and interesting women turned into Stepford Wives in the delivery room. May enjoyed the kid talk as much as anyone. She loved to brag about what Leo was learning, the cute things he said and did. She enjoyed comparing pediatricians and making catty comments about other mothers and voicing her opinion on co-sleeping. She was interested in the disposable versus cloth debate and fascinated by women and the one dad who made their own organic baby food.

But after awhile, May wanted to talk about...something else. Anything else. Something that simply didn't involve children. Maybe politics? Art? Sex? Movies? Fashion? History? Books? There was a whole world out there that didn't just up and disappear because they had children. Sometimes she merely needed a break, some adult conversation about anything but kids.

Plus, the mothers were in two separate camps. First there were the mommies who schlepped their kids here and there and everywhere, volunteering for everything, vigilantly researching convicted sex-offenders in the neighborhood, toxins in the toys and the best French lessons. The other camp fell into two distinct sub-camps, either the über-career types or the ladies that lunched, but both of these groups tended to farm their kids out to a nanny to raise, only to appear when clean, well-fed and adorable. May found herself stuck between these two seemingly diametrically opposed universes.

The director of Bright Future was a kindly 40ish woman named Connie. Connie looked a lot like a giraffe, ambling along with her long legs and neck, a smattering of freckles across her nose, disguising her age. May immediately took notice of her outfit, a rather sharp lemon-colored wrap dress nicely paired with gold-toned sandals, which was more suited to a lunch date than daycare.

"You're looking chic today, Connie." May told her, trying to make pleasant conversation, eager to prolong her day.

Connie halted, mid-amble, "Really? You like it?"

"Yes, it suits you, shows off your legs too."

Connie blushed across her freckled nose, "Thanks, today is my 20th wedding anniversary and I won't have time to go home after work before meeting my husband for dinner."

"20 years! Congratulations! You don't look old enough to be married that long."

Connie blushed an even deeper red, "Well, I totally disagree, but thanks for the compliment!" She ambled away, grinning, a little skip in her step.

"Have fun tonight," May called after her. And then the sorrow hit her hard and fast and she realized if she didn't find some privacy ASAP she was going to cry in front of everyone at the school, and they already looked at her strangely ever since she "forgot" to pick up Leo that day so an emotional outburst was not ideal.

May sprinted into the nearest bathroom, realizing too late it was a "girl's" and not a "women's".

She closed herself into a tiny stall. Feeling like a giant, she folded her long legs in order to crouch onto a tiny toilet, and cried gale-force tears.

May was interrupted by a tiny voice, "Are you sad, lady?"

May sniffed loudly and pushed open the door to see a little girl, Leo's age, with blonde curls, and a wrinkled brow, looking concerned.

May rubbed her swollen red eyes and pulled off a length of toilet paper to blow her nose. She smiled at the little girl through her dripping tears, sniffing, "Yes, I'm a little sad. Thank you for asking. What's your name?"

"Emma. Why are you crying on the potty?"

May laughed, hoisting herself awkwardly off the little seat, "Well, Emma, I had a tough day. But can you keep it a secret?"

"I'm very good at secrets," Emma answered seriously, "and sometimes I cry on the potty too."

"You do? Why do you cry on the potty?"

"When I have an accident, sometimes I cry," Emma answered gravely.

"Well, it's ok to have an accident and it's ok to cry about it." May splashed some water on her face, peering at her puffy appearance in the mirror.

"OK," said Emma.

May started for the door, "Thanks for keeping my secret Emma. Bye."

"Bye," said Emma as she hurriedly entered a miniscule stall, hiking up her purple dress to pee.

14

Although Joanna and May's birthdays were six weeks apart, they pretty much always celebrated them together. That way they could avoid a second Fischer Family get-together in such a short period of time. This year the fun part would be for May and Jamie to pretend everything was hunky dory for the benefit of Leo and Lily. If it were a normal Tuesday night dinner out, it would be easy to explain Jamie's absence, "Oh, he's traveling...you know how busy he is!" but birthdays were a big deal for the Fischer's, often complete with noisemakers and paper hats. So unfortunately, Jamie missing his wife's birthday dinner would raise more than a few eyebrows. May was not looking forward to the task. A root canal would have been preferable, or a hideous case of poison oak. Or crabs.

She was frankly unsure how she was going to get through the dinner at all. As the days passed her emotions felt like a ping pong ball, ricocheting from sadness to depression to red-hot fury and back to sadness. She felt separate from her body, floating overhead, watching herself go through her daily routine, smiling and talking and laughing, but dying inside. And then suddenly she would remember what happened, what that bastard did, and the reality of the situation would slam her back inside her body where she could feel the anger she was avoiding while perched in the clouds, feel it with every inch of her being. And she didn't know which was worse, the anger was fearsome, but the pain was unbearable.

And telling Lily what had happened was not an option. May wasn't sure why, but she wasn't ready to do it. Opening up to Lily meant...*this has happened to my perfect life*...so the only option was to act as if all was status quo. And May was a good actress. She'd held roles in everything from *Fiddler on the Roof* to *Oklahoma!* But this evening would be academy-award winning worthy, if she could pull it off.

Plus, there was that teeny niggling fact she was turning twenty-nine. It wasn't as if May believed in eternal youth or anything, but she was definitely unsettled about her birthday this year. Before this whole fiasco began she had been thinking of broaching the subject of having another baby to Jamie. Not that her age was at all a concern in terms of having a baby, but she knew Jamie had always wanted a big family and they were a few years behind schedule. Plus, she was a big believer in siblings and she knew Leo would be a terrific big brother. He was so patient and kind with other children, she knew he'd be just like Joanna, the best sibling a person could have. But now...who knew what would happen...maybe Leo would end up an only child.

"So what's everyone having?" asked Daniel jovially, covertly tickling Leo behind his ears.

"Spaghetti and meatballs!" announced Leo loudly.

"Leo, remember your inside voice, please," reminded May. And silently she said to herself, *May, you remember your inside voice too.*

"Spaghetti and meatballs, please," Leo whispered, looking to his mother for her approval. She nodded and smiled at him.

"Mmmm, I think its chicken marsala for me," said May, closing her menu and reaching for the bread basket. Lily looked at her quizzically. "What? I'm hungry, I skipped lunch." Lily shrugged as if to say "What? Don't mind me over here making faces, it's what I do."

From all outward appearances the meal was a typical Fischer affair. Lily entertained her family with tales of her archery instructor. A Korean woman, only twenty years old and barely five feet tall, supposedly some sort of archery prodigy destined for Olympic Gold but sidelined with a tragic elbow injury. It was unclear whether Lily was actually learning any archery or just learning about Min-Jung's personal dramas: the heartbreaking loss of her medal, her complicated love life, and unhappiness with her expensive American apartment.

Under the table Jamie's knee accidentally brushed against May's and for a brief moment their eyes met and locked. Jamie smiled apologetically at her but May willed her face to remain stony as she quickly turned away to feign interest in Lily's monologue. *You can do this, May,* she calmed herself.

The food was familiar and tasty and the whole family ate with gusto. Over coffee and chocolate birthday cake provided by Joanna, the Fischer clan sang *Happy Birthday* at full volume.

Leo cheered, "Hurray!" as May and Joanna closed their eyes, wished and blew out their candles.

"Present time!" Lily announced, getting out of her chair to distribute identically wrapped packages to her daughters laps and kisses to their heads. Leo eagerly helped open the packages. Inside they found matching handmade scarves. Teal for May and purple (purple!) for Joanna.

May and Joanna looked at each other instantaneously, their mother was notorious for crappy gifts, and this one was, well, not the crappiest they had ever received.

"Thanks, Mom," they said in chorus.

"Oh, no problem," Lily gushed, "do you like them? I worked very hard on them and I thought the colors were just perfect for you!"

"I can't get enough of teal," said May.

"And I just don't own enough purple," said Joanna.

Lily beamed.

Daniel and Lily had long ago agreed to disagree when it came to presents. Or at least Daniel had agreed to it. Lily was forever annoyed with Daniel's lack of gift giving, calling his use of cash and gift cards as cold and impersonal, two adjectives that certainly didn't describe Daniel by any stretch of the imagination.

"Why should I try to pick out some blouse or jewelry I know they'll just return?" asked Daniel.

Lily would simply roll her eyes at him, "You always get me wonderful gifts, Daniel."

"Yes, Lily, I do, because I live with you and I know what you like. But the girls grow and styles change and I can't keep up with all that, and I want to make sure they like their gift every time."

Because Daniel understood the best gift for his girls, and really any girls, was cold hard cash. That way, Daniel reasoned they could buy themselves whatever the heck they wanted. Even May, whose husband made more money than Daniel by a long shot, loved trying to catch the little folded up cash airplane flying across the table from her daddy each birthday.

"Me next!" Leo was barely able to contain his excitement as he presented his Mommy and Auntie with fabulous macaroni-encrusted picture frames made out of painted tongue depressors. Smiling from the center of each was a slightly blurry picture of an awkwardly smiling Leo.

"This is my favorite present," Joanna got up to kiss her nephew on top of his soft, curly head, "you are a fantastic artist and exceptionally photogenic."

"Mine too, Leo the Lion, I love it!" May leaned over to kiss him on the cheek.

Leo grinned from ear to ear.

Jamie handed a small box to Joanna, "For my favorite sister-in-law."

Joanna smiled at him and opened her package. Inside was a perfect, simple silver bangle bracelet, "Jamie, its darling, thank you, I really love it," she said, slipping it on her wrist and admiring the gift. She got up and hugged him, forgetting she was supposed to be pissed at her brother-in-law. Lily could learn a lot from Jamie, she thought, in the gift giving department. It always amazed her that this man, whom she knew really only through her sister and for a relatively short time in the scheme of things, always got her the perfect thing. While her mother, who had known her for her entire life couldn't get her a decent gift if her life depended on it. Joanna wondered, not for the first or last time, if her mother knew her at all.

"Happy Birthday, May" Jamie said, sliding a box in her direction.

May toyed with the box, turning it over in her hands, as if she was from another planet and had never seen a silver-wrapped package before.

"May," Joanna coaxed, now looking pointedly at her younger sis, saying - keep it together, May - with her eyes, "what did Jamie get you?"

May blinked, took a drink of her wine and said, "Well, let's find out," she slowly opened the package to reveal a stunning necklace made of chunks of butterscotch and honey colored amber. She lifted the necklace from the box and immediately put it around her neck, turning to Jamie to clasp it. "It's gorgeous, Jamie, thank you," she didn't think twice before leaning over and kissing him full on the mouth. She felt the jolt of the kiss deep in her belly and in her knees and she realized like an ice pick in her heart how desperately she missed her husband. And then in the next second she remembered, slamming back to reality she remembered the anger and the pain and she rubbed her temples, feigning a headache, willing herself not to cry.

Driving home from the restaurant, May and Jamie were silent. Luckily, Leo busily peppered them with questions about a variety of topics: The scenery: "Why are fire hydrants red?" and "Why do trees have so many leaves?" Politics: "Why is that man sleeping on that bench?" Fashion: "Why is he wearing that weird hat?" as well as shrewd observations such as: "This road is very bumpy" and "I like apple juice but I don't like orange juice."

Leo's chatter made it much easier for May to pretend everything was fine. Fine, fine, fine.

15

Joanna tossed and turned, unable to sleep as she mulled over Delia's uncharacteristically volatile commentary at the bookstore after their farmer's market outing. Finally she gave up. Throwing back the bedcovers she reached for her robe and stepped into her slippers and padded into the kitchen. She put a kettle of water on, figuring some tea might help her relax and sleep. Waiting for the water to boil she plopped on the couch and turned on the TV, flipping through the stations. She paused at an Infomercial for the Magic Bullet. It promised to "Make your life in the kitchen easier, faster and as effortless as possible." Wow, thought Joanna, if it makes your life in the kitchen so spectacular someone should work on a Magic Bullet for everything else. Yard work? Done! Bills? Paid! Boyfriend troubles? Solved! She continued to flip and paused at a *Friends* rerun. It was the one when Monica is stung by the jellyfish so Chandler pees on her foot, or maybe it was Joey who peed on her foot? Joanna couldn't recall, but she was fairly certain that peeing on a jellyfish sting to ease the pain was a myth. The kettle whistled and she turned off the burner. She reached for her childhood unicorn mug and box of Sleepy Time tea and added the boiling water along with a generous squirt of honey. She watched the rest of the episode, strangely smug she was right in the first place; it *was* Chandler who peed on Monica's foot. She flipped through the channels some more. Bored with television, she turned to the Internet.

Joanna impatiently tapped her foot as the computer slowly revved up; the downside to turning off all the electrical appliances and saving the environment was waiting for them to turn back on again. Probably a small price to pay, Joanna assured herself she was doing a good thing. She had become fairly religious about turning everything off, the coffee pot and the fish tank being the only constant exceptions. There was no way she was giving up the automatic pot, waking up to the smell of fresh brewed coffee made the getting up not quite as horrendous, and the fish would die without their constant pump. Finally she had green lights beckoning her to explore. First stop: effective, non-addicting sleep-aids. "Sleep better with melatonin!" "Sleep better with Cocculus Indicus!" (Joanna couldn't help but chuckle) "Sleep better with classical music!" "Sleep better with yoga!" Joanna marveled at how much crap there was on the Internet, it could suck you in for hours. It really was the modern day drug; hours would pass in a flash with nothing useful to show for it. *Come on, little girl, the first one's free...*All Joanna determined from this mission tonight was the Internet would definitely not qualify as an effective, non-addicting sleep aid.

Joanna surfed from "meditation for a better night's sleep" to "chemical sleep aids" to "Got Depression?" and finally stumbled across Elisabeth Kübler-Ross' five stages of grieving. Well, it wasn't a sleep aid necessarily, but it was interesting. She sipped her tea, it was sweet and warm, and Joanna shuddered in the chilly night, pulling her robe more tightly around her.

The website had varying views about the five stages of grieving, some asserting they were only useful for coping with death, while others argued they could be usefully applied to varying types of loss. Loss of life, loss of friendship, loss of a relationship. Hmmm. Something about these arguments resonated for her, and she began to mull over. It wasn't news to Joanna she was grieving, but what exactly was she grieving for? Was it for Diego? This man with whom she had really nothing in common? Really, what the hell was she doing buying a black wardrobe and staying out to all hours? That wasn't her. And what about sitting at home like a lonely spinster while her boyfriend cavorted around all night doing who knows what...and condoning it? Was she really grieving for her lost relationship? Or was it maybe for the self she lost during this relationship? She was all the Joanna she could be for Diego. The appealing, kind, sexy, fantastic "you'd be lucky to get her" Joanna she knew she was, deep down, that she had been once upon a time. Why was she so dazzled by this man who treated her like a piece of furniture? Delia was right. What happened to confident Joanna? Where were her cajones? And let's face it, she should have known this man wasn't her destiny; he didn't even eat dessert for Christ's sake! Joanna opened a blank document, and began to type:

The 5 stages of getting over Diego:

Stage 1 - Denial – been there, done that! I know this piece of shit left me. No denial here. Check!

Stage 2 – Anger. Really, there is nothing else to be pissed about. Well, maybe there is. I can be pissed this piece of shit left me and made me feel like I was the piece of shit, when it's really him. But I'm over it. At least I think I'm not angry anymore. What is there to be angry about, right? He's the one who is missing out on wonderful me. He's the one who should be angry. Angry and heart-broken he's without me. Done with this one too. Check!

Stage 3 – Bargaining. Hmmm, this is an interesting one. I'm thinking about all those nights of saying "Please oh please let him come back and I'll do something nice for society or the homeless or I'll give blood." Yeah, I'm done with this too. Check! But I really am going to give blood. This week, I am.

Stage 4 - Depression. OK, so here's the Mama of the stages, correct? This is where my sad ass has been wallowing for months now and it's time to be done, done, done! It's time for me to pick myself up, brush myself off and start all over again, isn't that how the saying goes? So, how exactly does one do this? If I could decide to be happy, I would be happy. Apparently it is not this easy. This is why everyone is on Prozac and going to therapy. Do I need to go to therapy? Everybody does it. My mother does it. May does it. Would it kill me? Probably not. Would it cure me? Who knows? Maybe I need to write in my journal? Maybe I need to find my journal...Maybe I need to figure out what I want to be when I grow up and be it? Maybe I need to just be here until I'm done?

Stage 5 – Acceptance. Not there yet.
Joanna paused in her flurry of writing, re-reading what she had written and pondering some more. The cursor flashed at her. She turned back to the website and Elisabeth Kübler-Ross, and then she read something that stopped her dead in her tracks: "Grief is the reflection of the connection that has been lost." Maybe this had nothing to do with Diego, but the connection with another human being she so longed for.

She rapidly typed her whirling thoughts. Maybe this was just all about the fact she didn't want to be alone. She didn't want to be one of those lonely old spinsters with the eleven cats and the housedresses. She was sure that wasn't who she was supposed to be. Maybe what she was looking for was a connection...with herself. *I want a real life,* she wrote, *not a going through the motions life. Not Diego's life or May's life. I want the life I'm supposed to have, the one I know I'm destined to have. And I know I'm not destined to have it alone. I know it in my bones.*

And why was this connection lost in the first place? She stared at the flashing red cursor. Maybe that connection was never really there. That she had so wanted it to be there, willed it to, but it just wasn't. So what was it? The attraction? In a flash she knew. It was almost as if by being with Diego, almost by osmosis; she got to experience a piece of his excitement, *his* unrelenting connection with his own passion. It was something she so wanted for herself.

So next she wrote of all the heartbreak, all the times he disappointed her, all the times he took advantage of her, all the times he made her feel small and insignificant and awkward, and then she took a deep breath and wrote of something else she knew she had to get out. She wrote of the warning signs. The ones she stuffed and choked down. Hard, bitter pills, tricky to swallow, that now lay stuffed amongst the other ugly, festering tidbits she didn't want to see. Those situations that flummoxed her and made her feel cold and empty, those nights where she felt lost and alone despite the warm body in her bed and she wrote and wrote and let it all pour out. Every yucky nugget, every red-flag she had turned a blind eye to and then pressed deep down out of the cold light of day, she brought them all out to stare at, to confront, without any sugar-coated excuses. Joanna wrote furiously.

And then she was done.

She printed the document and read it all out loud. She pondered. And then she turned on her shredder and shredded it, watching her work quickly turn into long curly threads of recycling.

Yawning, Joanna finished her lukewarm tea and turned off the computer and the shredder, (Diego did have some good points and one was to remind her of her hippie upbringing, when she always recycled and turned off lights and composted and only flushed for poop). She walked heavily back to her bedroom. Joanna burritoed herself into her comforter and rolled into the middle of her bed, willing sleep to come.

16

Joanna sat in her sweats on her tiny balcony, feet up on the rickety table. When she and Diego were looking for an apartment they had been attracted to the advertisement reading: "1 and 2 bdrm apts. Clean! Views!" They had laughed hysterically when the advertised "Views!" turned out to consist of the apartment complex parking lot, a foul, shabbily maintained swimming pool, and one lone sickly tree.

The morning was bright and sunny although not especially warm, and Joanna was hoping the cool air would help her wake up. The sky was filled with big fluffy cotton-puffy clouds and so, so blue, the same Crayola Cornflower blue Leo used to color the sky blue. She had a cup of coffee warming her hands, a bagel on the table and her book in her lap, but she wasn't reading. She was waiting for Sundays with Mark.

Joanna and Mark, although not destined for love, were apparently destined to be best friends. They had a standing phone date the first Sunday of every month at 10:00am. It didn't mean they couldn't text or e-mail throughout the month, but this was their designated chat time. They had spoken at the same time each month since their breakup nearly eight years ago.

When Mark's wife, Susan, had gone into labor at 3:00am on a Saturday night, Joanna received an e-mail message in the morning:

I didn't want to wake you! Susan's in labor! I'll call you when he or she arrives! I might miss our Sunday call! Please forgive! I love you!

But Mark didn't miss the phone call. Mason was born at 9:50am, and Mark called her at ten on the nose to give her the news.

Diego had been insanely jealous by the monthly call, as he was insanely jealous of any other men in Joanna's life, including her father, brother-in-law and Bruno, who was as gay as a handbag full of rainbows. The first time Bruno called Joanna at their shared apartment Diego said, "I do not understand why you are friends with all these men."

"Diego, Bruno is not interested in me in any way shape or form, he is gay!"

Diego made a dismissive "tshhh" sound as if to say he'd never in a million years believe a gay man would not obviously want to club Joanna over her head and drag her off into a cave somewhere.

"I do not know why you need to talk with Bruno, you already see him at work and I do not know why you need to talk on this Sunday call. You are not with this Mark anymore, it is over!" he had proclaimed petulantly.

Joanna had sat on his lap, taking his face in her hands and looked into his chocolate eyes, "My dearest Diego, I am with you and you only."

Regardless, he would sulk for the call. Make himself scarce, slamming the door dramatically when her phone jingled. Or, he would make a point of inserting the call into his own conversations. "I would very much like to go to the exhibit with you, but Joanna, she will be waiting by the phone for her boyfriend, I mean ex-boyfriend, to call her today." Or "Hello Mom, yes, we would love to visit Dad in the hospital since he just had knee replacement surgery except Joanna has this phone call with her ex-boyfriend again so we cannot come."

Joanna watched her neighbor, Ken, say goodbye to his weekly one-night stand. This one was pretty cute. She sipped her coffee and fought the urge to wave and call out a hearty "Good morning, neighbor!" She was amazed at the number of one-night stands this guy managed. Didn't he ever get tired? Didn't he ever want to settle down? Ken was a chiropractor. Joanna saw him for a month or so last year when she began waking up with a mysterious pain shooting from her shoulder into her neck and down into her elbow. It was excruciating. Ken quickly alleviated the pain and also insisted she get a new head-set at work to avoid the strain she was apparently putting her poor body under. Diego didn't believe in chiropractors, calling the field "A lot of hocus pocus." All Joanna knew was he fixed the problem without even a mention of drugs, which made her happy.

At exactly 10:00, Joanna's cell phone rang, "Hello?" she answered.

"Hey you," Mark said, a smile in his voice, "What is up?"

Joanna could picture him exactly. He was sitting on his sofa, stroking his cat, Larry. Mason was probably nearby, much to Larry's chagrin. Mark's hair was shorter than when they had dated, and he was a little softer in the middle. Not surprisingly, Mark had married another excellent cook and luckily for their friendship someone Joanna heartily approved of. Susan was a vet and just about the nicest person on the planet, without being so nice that you wanted to punch her in the jaw. She had no problem with the Sunday call; in fact, she was so impressed Mark could continue to be such good friends with an ex it helped to "seal the deal" as it were, for the two of them. Joanna was happy she helped in her own small way.

"Tell me what new tricks Mason is performing."

"Dude! He's got the walking thing down pat and now he's learning to climb up the stairs! It's cool, but scary. And listen to this, he's starting to..." Mark paused for emphasis, "run. He's got this hilarious little hippity-hop run. It's totally awesome." Mark was gleeful, bragging over his son's accomplishments. An eavesdropper would never guess Mark had a PhD in English of all things. When chatting with Joanna he often sounded like an inebriated surfer.

"Holy Cow! Last time I saw him he was barely crawling! Has it really been that long since I've seen him?"

"I know. It's the coolest thing. And it is happening so

fuckin', freakin' fast." Joanna suspected someone had given him a "watch your language!" look. "So JoJo, what's going on in your super boring non-parental world?" Only Mark could get away with calling her JoJo. Well, Mark and her dad.

"Well, lots, actually..." Joanna filled him in on the crazy month since they'd last spoken. She told him about May and her separation from Jamie. She told him about what Jamie had done, how she just couldn't believe it, how she wasn't sure what May was going to do.

She took a breath, and then told him about her conversation with Delia and her new readiness to move on from Diego. She told him she needed to do something just for her, because she felt like she had lost a piece of herself somewhere, although she wasn't sure where, but knew she felt ready to find it again.

"Dude, you hit the nail on the head, JoJo. I'm happy to hear you say that. Sounds like maybe you are on your way back to the land of the living."

"Maybe, fingers crossed." Joanna answered non-committal, but chuckled to herself, "I miss the land of the living."

They chatted about how long it had been since they'd seen each other and they agreed on a date Joanna would come down.

"And bring cookies!" Mark hollered.

Joanna laughed, "Dude, have you just met me? Do I ever come without cookies?"

Usually after Sundays with Mark, Joanna would clean. Just in case her already sloppy housekeeping had fallen behind during the month, she always reserved this time to get the yucky stuff done. Scrubbing the toilet and shower, dusting, vacuuming, cleaning out the fridge, all the blech she never wanted to do she'd make sure to get done after the monthly phone call. But this Sunday she was not unhappily forced to cheat on her dirty house. She instead baked a double batch of oatmeal-coconut-chocolate chip cookies, took a furtive glance over her shoulder at the dust-bunnies doing the Merengue in the corners and hopped into her car to go see Delia. She suspected she owed her an apology, or maybe a "thanks", she wasn't entirely certain which.

Delia lived downtown in a tiny charming Victorian house with her tiny charming husband, Ray and their enormous Weimaraner, Buck. The door was open and Joanna was greeted by Buck wearing an enormous white cone around his neck. Buck had just endured knee surgery and the Elizabethan collar was supposed to keep him from licking his wound. He looked absolutely ridiculous, but Joanna didn't want to hurt his feelings so she said, "I like your new collar, Buck, is your Mom home?"

Delia entered the living room, still wearing her sweaty running paraphernalia, carrying a cup of coffee and munching on what looked to be either a bran muffin or a lump of coal. "Hey Jo, what are you doing here? Buck, would you back up, boy?" Delia nudged Buck out of the way with her hip as he desperately tried to ascertain what the fabulous smell was wafting from the basket Joanna carried.

"Don't worry, Buck, I didn't forget you." Joanna tossed Buck a doggie-cookie which he easily caught, despite the bizarre necklace, and handed the basket of cookies to Delia. "These are for you; sorry I was such a schmuck."

Delia casually tossed her bran muffin onto the piano where it bounced and shed a smattering of dry crumbs and a raisin. She reached into the basket, eyes widening when she discovered what was inside. She pulled a cookie out, inhaled deeply as if it was a rare glass of wine and immediately popped the cookie into her mouth. "Oh my God, they are still warm, YUM! Thank you. How exactly were you a schmuck?" Delia settled herself onto her sofa, tucking her tanned, muscular legs under her in order to work her way more efficiently through the basket. "Sit down, do you want one of these?" she waved a cookie in Joanna's direction, chewing happily.

Leave it to Delia; once she got something off her chest, she was done. No lingering animosity, no long-drawn-out anger, no persistent nagging, she was just done. Delia was in many ways, the antithesis of Diego. Diego could hold a grudge that spanned the millennium. While living together, Diego once *insisted* Joanna give him a haircut. She explained she was extremely nervous about cutting his hair; she had never cut anyone's hair and didn't feel great about using her highly particular boyfriend as a guinea pig for this less-than pressing non-aspiration. Especially as her boyfriend was the vainest creature on the planet, only rivaling May, but possibly edging even her out of the competition. But Diego had insisted she should do this one teensy thing for him, it would be fine, and then he complained for the duration of their relationship about what a lousy job she had done, it was so uneven and called attention to his only slightly less than perfect nose.

Joanna sat on a side chair to avoid sitting on the blanket of dog hair on the sofa, and shook her head no to Delia's question. She stretched, she felt tired but exhilarated from the night and her Sunday with Mark call. "I'm thinking everyone is pretty sick of me feeling sorry for myself. You're right. I need to get on with it and stop acting like a teenager. I hear you. Hey, should we help him?" She gestured to Buck who had dropped part of his cookie and was bumping his head against the wall trying to get at an angle in order to retrieve it.

Delia paused mid-cookie to look over at Buck, "Naw, he'll be ok, and it's entertaining to watch," she took another bite and chewed methodically. "Jo, what did you see in that guy? I mean, he's not even in the same league as you."

Joanna smiled, "Well, I'll take the compliment. Haven't you ever dated an asshole?

"Hasn't everyone?"

Joanna stretched her arms above her head and yawned, the sleepless night was setting in, "I guess Diego was mine," she smiled at Delia's doubtful expression, "it's hard to explain. But I'm working it out.

"You know, Ray has some friends from his cycling club..."

Joanna interrupted, "God no, Delia, I don't need a date. I know I can get a date. At least, I think I can get a date. But first I need to get myself out of this rut. I'm no good for anyone until I do that."

"You're a smart cookie, Jo, I have faith in you." Delia popped the rest of the cookie into her mouth.

Ray appeared in the doorway, wearing a pink t-shirt and sweats. He rubbed a towel over his head, drying his non-existent hair, "You are NOT eating all the cookies my best friend Joanna brought me."

"I am," smiled Delia coyly, clutching the basket to her chest, "every last one."

17

May and Joanna were drinking. They began the evening with a lovely bottle of pinot noir to go with the pork loin Joanna had expertly grilled on May's ultra-modern built-in and never used (except by Joanna) outdoor barbeque. She served the pork with mashed sweet potatoes and sautéed baby artichokes and the pinot was a perfect accompaniment.

Leo loved it when his Auntie Jo came over for dinner. He had one other Aunt, Aunt Carly, but Aunt Carly certainly didn't cook and she barely ate. She was not very much fun in general and Leo knew if she was coming over it was bound to be a boring night. Auntie Jo was practiced at balancing the dinner making with the playing, a skill his mom just did not have, and also his mom's dinners were never fancy unless they came from a restaurant. Plus, the food was always delicious, every last bit of it. Also, there was *always* dessert, and in particular there were always cookies for dessert. Tonight, Joanna had brought not just snickerdoodles (his favorite!) but chocolate chip cookies (his second favorite!) as well. He asked his mom if he could have another cookie and was astounded when she shrugged, winked at him and said, "Sure, what the heck, knock yourself out." Leo looked at his Aunt, who looked just as surprised, but she shrugged and smiled and pushed the cookie plate in his direction. Leo wondered briefly if there was some sort of holiday going on, the birthday bash was last week, but decided to not ask questions in case his mom decided to change her mind. He reached for a third cookie, snickerdoodle or chocolate chip? He wavered and then selected the chocolate chip. Joanna refilled their glasses with the rest of the pinot, and more milk for Leo.

After a very bouncy Leo had been tucked into bed they moved on to a Cab. May, despite her embarrassing blackout, was not usually a big drinker; two glasses were her absolute limit, seeing as her body was a temple and all. So tonight the wine had quickly gone to her head and she was already quite tipsy. Joanna, a sturdier and more practiced drinker, was just starting to feel warm all over.

"The thing is," May was slumped sloppily into an armchair, "I just can't believe he cheated on me. Never in a billion million gazillion years did I think he would cheat on me. Of all of the craziest things..." May trailed off. She ate another cookie, absently licking the crumbs off her fingers.

Joanna sat on the floor, leaning against the cream colored sectional and looking out the huge bay window. The night was clear and she could see millions of tiny stars glittering like sequins in the sky.

"I've never cheated on anyone..." May continued.

"Really?"

"What do you mean, really?" May retorted, irritated. "Is that what you think of me? That I'm the kind of person who would cheat?"

"Jeez, May, don't get your panties in a bunch, of course I don't think you are that kind of person. But you dated, you know, a lot of guys in high school, and you started, you know, having sex rather on the young side. You probably had lots of opportunities is all I'm saying, you were young and beautiful and all that." Joanna swirled her wine and sniffed it appreciatively. "You weren't always so old and wise."

"Ha Ha." May wiggled down off of the chair and onto the floor, "So I'm no longer young and beautiful, is that what you are saying?" May teased.

"Yes, May, that's exactly what I'm saying. You're old as the hills and ugly as a baboon's butt."

"Ouch," May pretended to be hurt. "I slept with my yoga instructor."

"Really?" Joanna was interested, "The one who looks like an investment banker?"

"He doesn't necessarily look like an investment banker. He just has an investment banker name."

"Oh. So why exactly did you sleep with him?"

"I don't know. He was there."

"Was it fun?

"Sort of. He is very bendy. Anyway, I guess I thought it would help somehow. Help me get some perspective on this thing." She sipped her wine thoughtfully.

"Did it? Help...somehow?"

"Maybe. It was a reminder that sex can be just sex, that's for sure," May chewed on her manicured thumbnail. "Does that count as cheating? I'm still married," she paused, "and I feel guilty as hell."

Joanna thought back to the *Friends* episode she had stumbled upon while fighting insomnia; Ross yelling at a furious Rachel: "We were on a break!" She wasn't sure whose side she was on, but Rachel was definitely being unreasonable. "No, I don't think it counts. You're separated."

"I don't know," May stretched her long limbs out onto the floor, looking up at the cathedral ceiling.

"So, why do you think he did it? I mean, we know Jamie, and impulsive is not how anyone would describe him. So what happened? Were you having problems, May?" Joanna turned from the window to look at her delicately featured younger sister.

"No," May said simply, "we weren't" she pulled her long legs up until she was sitting cross-legged, ("criss-cross apple sauce" is what Leo called it), "I have no idea why he did it. And that's what's driving me to drink." She refilled her glass with the nearly empty bottle.

Joanna pushed, "Did you ask him?"

"Of course I asked him, Joanna." May sighed, she was tired. "But I don't think even he knows the answer. He's confused I guess."

"Is an identity-crisis the same thing as a mid-life crisis?" Joanna asked. She was feeling the effects of the second bottle of wine.

"I don't know, maybe, but he could have just bought himself a new car or a motorcycle instead of fucking someone. All I know is I miss him and I want him to come home."

"You know," Joanna began softly, "I had an affair."

"What?! When?" May's eyes bugged out like a cartoon alien.

Joanna sighed, she wasn't proud of herself on this particular topic, although it had happened ages ago, back in her senior year of high school. Joanna's crush on Jason Levine became severe. Jason tended to date smart girls like Joanna, but they were always a little cuter and ALWAYS a lot taller than Joanna was. Nevertheless, she drew little hearts with *Joanna + Jason* inside, which she then blacked out with a Sharpie so no one could see. She fantasized about walking down the aisle in a meringue dress while handsome Jason stood at the chuppah, gazing adoringly in her direction. She named their children, Zoe and Caleb, sensibly born three years apart.

She did everything she could think of to banish him from her thoughts, including a burning sage ritual that Paula, (her best friend from grade-school until college when Paula spiraled into a Quaalude-induced stupor that lasted well into adulthood. Joanna had heard she was clean so was waiting for the phone call of apology for her 9th step) insisted would do the trick, but his cute 501-clad butt kept elbowing, or rather, butting, its way into her head.

One night, after a party (Joanna's parents thought

she was at Paula's, Paula's parents thought she was at Joanna's), there were just a few people left hanging out in Dawn Oberlin's basement. Dawn's parents seemed to be perpetually out of town, and Dawn had followed her elder brothers' stellar example of throwing ragers the moment the parentals left the threshold. She had perfected the party throwing to include advertising and a cleaning service for the aftermath, and Dawn later in life utilized her talents as a highly sought after wedding planner. There were about a dozen kids left by 3:00am, listening to music and making out and polishing off the nearly dry keg. As the music switched to "Need You Tonight," Joanna, taking a cue from Michael Hutchence, "All you got is this moment" drank a swig from her beer, leaned in and planted a wet kiss on Jason's mouth, drinking in his beery breath. Jason reciprocated without hesitation, plunging his tongue in and exploring her molars enthusiastically. He took her by the hand and led her to an upstairs bedroom.

Fifteen fumbling, panting minutes later, the pair lay gasping for breath.

"Why did we wait so long to do that?" Jason asked her playfully, zipping up his jeans and searching for somewhere to ditch the drippy condom.

"Wait a minute," May interrupted, "weren't you dating that Ned guy senior year?"

"Yes May," said Joanna, "I was. Hence the term 'affair.'"

"Wow, Jo, why didn't you tell me?" May asked.

Joanna laughed, "Well, it wasn't one of my finer moments. I was embarrassed I guess. It didn't last long, maybe a couple of weeks, and I finally told him I just couldn't anymore, the guilt was absolutely killing me. Jason and I totally drifted apart, it was never the same between us. Ned never found out...but it wasn't worth it."

The sisters were quiet as they looked at the stars together. Joanna stretched her feet and her hands, little popping noises emanating from her wrists and ankles, when the ground began to shake.

The earthquake was small, just big enough to rattle the pans hanging from the ceiling in the kitchen and scare the shit out of you if you were drunk, and also to knock over a glass precariously perched on the carpet.

"You did not just spill red wine on my cream colored carpet."

"Uh, yes I did," Joanna answered, running to get the salt to pour over the quick-moving stain.

"Oh well," May downed the end of her glass, "it's just carpet."

They listened outside Leo's door in case he woke, surprised or frightened, but he didn't. He just rolled over in his bed, riding the little wave.

18

Every morning when Leo wakes up he immediately looks at his Winnie the Pooh clock. He wasn't allowed to go into mommy and daddy's room until the two hands pointed to the blue tape that meant 7am because otherwise it was just too darn early. As soon as it was time, he'd sprint into his airplane decorated bathroom to pee and then dash into his parent's room and into their bed, snuggling down into the mountain of warm covers, nestling against his mommy's warm, yummy smelling skin. On weekends daddy was usually there too, which was less cozy since it was crowded but more fun since his daddy would tickle him from head to toe and make him squeal like crazy. Mommy days were much lazier. They would lounge around in bed, snuggling and talking and sometimes listening to music until mommy said they had to get up before they grew comforters for arms and a pillow for a belly. They'd get dressed, mommy in her exercise clothes and Leo in whatever Luisa had put out for him the night before and they'd head downstairs for breakfast.

Breakfast came from the freezer in the form of

whole-grain waffles and veggie sausages or from the pantry in sandy packets that turned into creamy oatmeal like magic in the microwave. Leo liked the leisurely mornings before school with his mom. On nice days they would sit outside and eat their breakfast on the deck, talking and laughing. His mommy was excellent at making silly faces and he'd laugh and laugh at how funny she was. If there was time they'd play pirates and he'd make her walk the plank growling, "Aargh!" or they'd be wild animals in the jungle and Leo would roar like the lion he was and mommy would do her "who-who-ha-ha" monkey impression and eat a banana. Then they'd go back upstairs to brush their teeth and then grab his Thomas the Train lunch box and jacket and rush out the door. They had so much fun at home; they always had to hurry to get into the car to get to school so mommy could get to goga, ("Yoga, Sweetie," his mother would purr, "with a 'ya' sound") on time.

Leo loved his mornings with mommy, but lately, he missed his daddy.

19

Joanna approached the door of the blood bank apprehensively, not sure why she was so nervous. People gave blood all the time. In college, when she had a higher sense of civic duty, she had been a regular, faithfully, every eight weeks. She couldn't recall when she had fallen off the donating wagon. She stepped inside and approached the reception desk.

"Hi there, I'm here to give blood," Joanna boldly informed the smiling receptionist.

"Yes, that's what I would think," said the receptionist, her head tipped to the right as if she had a crick in her neck "have you given blood before?"

"Yes, but it's been a few years."

The receptionist continued to smile, head tipped, as she presented Joanna with an IPad. Joanna went through the questions methodically, her health history, sexual history, no new piercings or tattoos in the last year...she handed it back waited to be called.

Forty-five minutes later she was done, reading a People magazine and munching a second graham cracker when she got the thumbs-up she was free to go. She felt good, *yippee for me!* She thought. She rose to her feet, said goodbye to the smiling, still tipped receptionist and was out the door.

Joanna turned the corner towards the parking lot, fumbling in her oversized bag for her car keys, and smacked directly into Bookstore Guy.

He caught her by her shoulders, "Hey there, I know you," he smiled at her, and Joanna noticed his hazel eyes with crinkly corners under his smart-guy glasses.

"Oh hi, sorry for almost knocking you over there," Joanna said.

"That's no problem, I'm pretty sturdy," he smiled some more, "were you just giving blood?" he indicated the band-aid in the crook of her arm.

She nodded, "Yup, I hadn't given in years and felt like I should get started again. Is that where you're going?"

"Yeah, it's an excellent habit I think," he ran his fingers through his hair.

"I think so too," she felt at a loss for conversation and realized her palms were sweating.

"So, what's your type?"

"Huh?"

"Your type, your blood type," he looked at her expectantly, "OK, I was trying to be funny, obviously a bad idea," he shuffled his feet, kicking at a small stone.

"No, it is funny, I'm just a little slow," said Joanna, smiling.

Bookstore Guy smiled again. Joanna couldn't help but notice he had a wonderful smile.

"Hey, I don't think they're going to have a rush on B positive in the next hour, would you like to grab a cup of coffee with me?"

"Oh, I, oh," Joanna fumbled, "today is just not good for me, I'm meeting my mother for lunch," she rolled her eyes, just the thought of the impending lunch was irritating, "But maybe can I take a rain check?" she looked up at him, noticing he was at least six inches taller than she was, a respectable height.

"Sure, ok, a rain-check sounds good," he ran his fingers through his hair again and Joanna noticed fine reddish hairs on the back of his hands.

"Well, I'll probably see you on Saturday at the *Book Nook*, yes?" Joanna began walking backwards towards her car.

"Hey, better be careful walking that way, you could run someone over," he smiled again, "I'll see you Saturday. It's a date...almost."

"Almost," Joanna fumbled to unlock her car door and slid behind the wheel. Bookstore Guy watched her and gave a little wave as she drove past.

Joanna entered the restaurant and quickly spied Lily waving enthusiastically. She made her way over to the table, kissed her mother on the cheek, "Hi, Mom, you look terrific," she told her, sliding into the utilitarian chair.

Lily beamed vainly. She really did look terrific. She was

wrapped in a kaleidoscope of colors and textures. Her hair was piled on her head with silver gray tendrils snaking out of the upsweep to frame her smooth, tanned face.

The waiter, smartly dressed in jeans and white button-down shirt, came to take their drink orders. Lily ordered white wine and Joanna ordered sparkling water.

"Water?" exclaimed Lily.

"Yeah, I'm trying to cut down on the caffeine. Maybe it will help the sleep situation."

"It's just amazing how some things stay with a person! You never have been a good sleeper and I..."

Joanna interrupted her, "I know, Mom. I've never been a good sleeper." She took a deep breath, "So, how are you? What's new? How's the archery going?"

"Oh it's wonderful! Such good exercise, get a load of these arms!" She flexed her muscles, which looked just as skinny as ever to Joanna. "I'm so lucky to have found Min-Jung. She has such a brilliant aura about her. I think she's an old soul, you know?" She sipped her wine, eyes wide.

Joanna nodded on cue. She barely needed to listen to her mother anymore, so practiced she was at nodding and "uh-huh-ing" in the right places. Joanna remembered when she used to hang on her mother's every word, and was unsure of when that had changed. Many of Joanna's happiest girl-hood memories were of times spent with her mother. Tie dying t-shirts in the backyard and managing to tie dye the cat's tail as well. Struggling together through years of agonizing math homework. Teaching

May how to roller-skate, a total riot, as the Princess was really not all that coordinated, not to mention prone to tantrums. Lily teaching both girls to fold origami; deftly folding the colored paper into delicate cranes, baby elephants and intricate ballerinas.

And Joanna used to talk with her mother about all sorts of things. Lily was the first person she told when Ezra Feldman had kissed her at the bottom of the slide on the grade school playground after school. Her first kiss! His lips chapped and a little pinched, his eyes squeezed shut (she knew because she peeked). She had asked her mother if kisses from boys were always so tight, and Lily had assured her there would be all sorts of kisses, soft and yielding, strong and firm, and some she would feel deep in her belly or even all the way to her toes! Joanna remembered nodding sagely, drinking in this new womanly wisdom her mother was sharing with her.

But Lily had also been the source of some of Joanna's most traumatic childhood memories as well. She remembered being thirteen on a hot, hot July day. Joanna and her best friend, Paula Gilbert were sucking on Popsicles and gossiping about boys. At the moment, Paula was in love with Kevin Lott, a spindly kid with huge feet yet to catch up with the rest of his body, while Joanna was harboring a slight crush on Eric James, a quiet boy with a slight lisp and dimples. Paula was convinced Kevin was also in love with her, as evidenced by his inability to look her in the eye even when directly confronted with a question like, "Hi Kevin, how are you today?" Joanna concurred it was clear Kevin was surely in love. Lily appeared from the house wearing a tiny macramé bikini, enormous sunglasses and espadrilles. She stretched out on a lawn chair to sun herself. Lily was considered a cool mom so the Fischer household tended to be a popular haunt. The girl's friends were used to Lily hanging out with them and welcomed her contributions to the conversation. She immediately remarked how cute Paula's new haircut was, "It's so becoming on you!" And Paula was sufficiently flattered, flipping her bangs and smiling wide-eyed at Lily, "Thanks!"

Grape Popsicle dripped and splattered on the pavement. Joanna and Paula moved from boys to a discussion regarding their new bras, both having recently graduated to B cups. Joanna commented the thicker straps were cutting uncomfortably into her shoulders, little did she know at the time, but that was because those B cups lasted about a week before Joanna needed a C cup. Paula was particularly boastful of her new size, making snide comments regarding other girls they knew who barely needed to wear a bra as yet, like Melissa Dowd who remained flat as a board and Angela Milton who looked essentially like an 8 year old boy. Little did Paula know that Karma is a bitch, and a B cup was as big as her breasts were ever going to get. Lily lowered her glasses, peering over the top and interrupted them, "Remember girls, your boobs should always stick out further than your tummies!" She then flipped herself over like a human pancake to sun her back.

Joanna stopped sucking, mid-slurp. There was no question Lily was referring to her, seeing as Paula was stick thin. Joanna let the rest of her Popsicle slide slowly down the stick and melt onto the pavement, leaving a sticky purple puddle, thinking: *my mother just called me fat*. There would be many other times Lily would make some backhanded comment about her weight, remarks that stung and cut her to the core. Paula pretended to ignore the comment altogether, and changed the subject back to boys.

Joanna knew it was natural for relationships with parents to ebb and flow. That they would disconnect and reconnect countless times, depending on who they were or what they were doing at that particular time in their lives. And time could be so tremulous, so transitory. But as she looked into her mother's familiar green eyes, those same eyes that belonged to May and Leo and Joanna, she wondered when their relationship would flow again. She'd thought they would be back together again by now, but there was always something missing, a lost connection, an awkwardness and an exasperation Joanna couldn't quite put her finger on the reason for, but was as real and prevalent as the proverbial elephant in the room.

The waiter returned for their lunch orders, a salad for Lily and a grilled chicken and arugula sandwich for Joanna.

"So Honey, tell me how you are," Lily reached out and patted Joanna's hand affectionately. "I feel like I haven't really talked with you lately."

Joanna was wary, "Uh, we talk all the time, Mom."

"No, no, I mean really talk. So how's work?"

"Work is fine. Nothing really new or interesting to report there." She drank some of her sparkling water, wishing it was coffee. She tried to ignore the caffeine deprivation headache creeping around her temples.

"And are you dating anyone new?"

"Mom, don't you think I would tell you if I was dating someone? I mean, don't you think that might be a pretty significant change to report?"

"Well, I don't know, Honey, you seem so secretive lately. I don't know if you would tell me or not."

Joanna didn't respond as the waiter delivered their lunch. "Thank you," she said.

"Enjoy!" He answered.

"I'm not being secretive, Mom."

"Well, I just think it's time you get over that Diego and get on with it. You are a smart and beautiful young woman and I hate to see you moping around."

Joanna took a bite of her sandwich to avoid answering hastily. What she wanted to say to her mother was, "Moping around? You want to see moping around? Can't I deal with my life in my own way?" She chewed her bite of sandwich slowly and swallowed, giving herself time to formulate a non-snappy response, "I'm not moping around, Mom. I'm actually doing very well, perhaps I've even turned a corner," she smiled and lied. But this time, it was just a little lie. She really was feeling better somehow. Lighter. Definitely less mopey. More positive. More awake. "Today I gave blood."

"Well, that's terrific, Honey, although I'm not clear how that connects to getting over Diego but I'm all for it," she reached forward again to pat Joanna's hand, "you know I just want you to be happy, Sweetheart." Lily's brow was furrowed with concern.

Maybe she needed to cut her mother a break. She was just trying to help, to be interested, to be a mother. Joanna decided to let her. "Thanks, Mom. I really am better, and I'm working on happy." She wiped her mouth with her napkin, "So, really, tell me more about this archery business, how on earth did you discover archery in the first place?"

"Oh! Well, it's just a fascinating sport..." and Lily launched into the history of archery, as explained by Min-Jung, and Joanna did her best to actually listen.

20

May and Jamie agreed it was premature to tell Leo anything as yet except daddy was working more than usual to explain his absence from the home front. They didn't want to unnecessarily alarm him, since they hadn't made any decisions as to what would happen next, so decided the best thing to do was carry on per usual. It wasn't difficult, as even when Jamie wasn't traveling he often didn't arrive home from his office until Leo had already eaten his dinner and was getting ready for bed.

So Jamie continued to arrive just before bedtime. They would talk about guy stuff like baseball and bugs and then Jamie would tuck his son into bed and kiss him and snuggle him, perhaps read him a story or two, and then instead of coming downstairs to spend time with May he would come downstairs and leave the house for the small, cramped apartment he had rented downtown.

May would remain in the kitchen, drinking wine and picking at the remains of Leo's discarded dinner. Pretending Jamie wasn't there at all and it was just she and Leo now. Jamie had fallen off the deck of a cruise ship in a bizarre accident and now she was a widow, sad and alone. And Leo was a bastard. Poor kid.

At first it really wasn't so hard to imagine. Catastrophic things happened all the time. People die. People get swept away in floods and crushed under falling pianos. People are carjacked. People get hit in the head with baseball bats and lose their memories and don't recognize their families. People are gored by bulls. People fall through thin ice. People disappear off the face of the planet without a trace.

But more likely, May would pretend it was just a typical day or at least what used to be a typical day for the Cohen's. Jamie would tuck Leo in and would come downstairs shortly. Maybe he would have changed into sweats and a t-shirt or maybe pajamas, the blue and white striped ones were May's favorites. If it was warm, he may be shirtless. Maybe he'd have taken a shower so he'd be damp and clean, jaw smooth from shaving and smelling of sandalwood soap and aftershave. He'd sneak quietly up behind her, surreptitiously slide his strong arm around her waist and pull her to him. Pushing aside her cascade of hair, she'd feel his quick hot breath at the nape of her neck, anticipating his warm mouth. Finally he'd go in, kissing and sucking gently and then aggressively along her hairline. He'd pull her close until he was pressed up against the length of her backside, mouth circling her neck, hands deftly moving under her sweater and unzipping her jeans and sliding his strong hands inside. He would turn her around by her hips, pulling her against him and kissing her urgently, his hands everywhere: in her hair and running down her body, over her breasts and stomach, pulling at her clothing and finally lifting her onto the kitchen counter...

Jamie cleared his throat, "Then I guess I'll be going, May."

She was jolted out of her reverie, seeing her husband standing in front of her, today looking particularly dazzling.

"Is everything ok?"

She nodded, took an unintentional step towards him, propelled briefly by lust. She hesitated.

"Everything ok with Leo?" Jamie ran his hands through his hair. His nervous signal.

"Oh yeah, he's fine," she smiled feebly, feeling awkward and uncomfortably moist between her legs.

"OK, I'll be going then. I'll see you tomorrow." He practically ran out the door.

May sighed, took another tater tot off of Leo's plate and chewed.

21

Diego and Joanna lived together for over a year before Diego made his infamous exodus. The summer prior to the breakup, Diego's brother Alex was married.

Diego shared little in common with his younger brother, as Alex symbolized everything Diego considered evil. Alex worked in a corporate job as a middle manager at a bank; he played on a softball team and was involved as an alumnus of his college fraternity. He spent weekends hanging out with his buddies, watching and participating in a variety of sports. In order to fulfill his sense of community responsibility as a successful Latino male, he volunteered as a mentor to a fatherless kid named Esteban at the Boys and Girls Club. Alex was maybe not quite as attractive as Diego with his stocky build and his hair in a very short, bordering on military short buzz-cut, but he was plenty handsome, with the same coffee-bean skin and dark-chocolate eyes as his older brother. His fiancée, Annie, was a local weather reporter with the most unfortunate laugh, quite resembling a cat in heat. Nevertheless, she garnered the highest ratings due to her flirtatious smile, unnatural and blindingly blonde hair and enormous boobs a la Pam Anderson.

One of Diego's many artsy talents was his beautiful, sent straight from God singing voice, and Alex asked if he would do them the honor of singing at his wedding. Annie had her heart set, not surprisingly, on the John Denver classic, "Annie's song." Diego agreed to sing, it was the least he could do for his younger brother and his beautiful bride to be and he began to practice incessantly, strumming his guitar along as Joanna sang in her crackly, always slightly sharp voice to familiarize him with the lyrics:

"You fill up my senses, like a light in the forest,
Like the mountains at springtime, like a walk in the rain,
Like a storm in the desert, like a sleepy blue ocean,
You fill up my senses, come fill me again!"

Although, maybe not so surprisingly, the practice didn't go quite as smoothly as planned. For one, Diego hadn't picked up his guitar in years, in fact, Joanna didn't even know he played at all (and he really didn't play more than a few cords), so he was extremely rusty. But the much larger issue at hand was Diego could not for the life of him remember the lyrics to the song. So the practice went more like this:

"You fill up my senses, like a storm in the desert, shit!
You fill up my senses like a light in the, shit!
You fill up my senses, like a light in the forest,
Like a storm in the desert, shit!"

Joanna did everything she could do to help. She made him flashcards, she drew pictures, and she played a demented game of charades, acting out the images. She sang the song to him over and over again until the neighbors were probably holding their heads in pain. Nothing seemed to help and as they got closer and closer to the date Diego's mood became darker and darker until he was a total wreck in full-throttle panic mode. And as Joanna easily remembered the simple lyrics and found herself inadvertently humming them, she merely added to Diego's dour temper.

The wedding day arrived. Alex and Annie were being married at a multi-steepled church in the South Bay, the same church Diego and Alex had reluctantly attended while growing up, and ironically, the same church Annie had reluctantly attended while growing up. "Isn't that a riot?" Annie had exclaimed when telling Joanna of the coincidence, her smile exposing a row of perfectly straight, blinding white teeth.

Sunlight streamed through the stained glass windows on a picture perfect June day. Diego wasn't scheduled to sing until the end of the ceremony, right before the vows, so in the meantime he had locked himself into the car to practice. He banished Joanna, saying she was driving him crazy and he needed to be alone.

At a loss of what to do with herself, seeing as the ceremony was not set to begin for another forty minutes, Joanna decided to sit in the church with the slow trickle of early arrival guests. On her way over she spotted Alex pacing and so veered in his direction to say congrats on his happy day. He greeted her with a warm hug, told her how beautiful she looked and then leaned over to whisper in her ear, "Where the hell is my God-damned brother?"

Joanna hesitated; she didn't want to alarm Alex, especially seeing as it was his wedding day, probably the most important day of his life thus far, so she smiled soothingly and assured him Diego was back in the car, continuing to work on the song as he wanted to make absolutely sure it was perfect. She kept her tone airy. Alex searched her eyes, suspicious, "Really, Alex, he's just going over it one more time. Don't worry and just relax and enjoy your special day," Joanna kissed him on the cheek and headed towards the church.

She sat and made small talk with Diego's aunt and uncle and cousins inside the church. She never felt particularly comfortable in churches, was never sure if it was ok to put your feet up on the prayer kneeler or not. Of course Diego's relatives asked where Diego was and Joanna did her best to smile and tell them he just had his own case of wedding-day jitters due to his big performance. The wedding was due to begin at 4pm so when 3:45 approached and still no Diego she excused herself and left the church to check on him. She walked quickly to the parking lot but couldn't recall where they had parked the car. She could have sworn they were in the second row on the left but where she expected to see her old Volvo sat a fat, enormous, pearl-white Escalade. The lot was crowded now with the two hundred guests who were expected to attend the wedding. She called Diego's mobile, but he didn't pick up. She checked her watch; it was 3:54, so she half jogged back to the church to her seat, praying Diego was waiting in the wings somewhere. She would of crossed herself if she thought it would help, but she wasn't sure how.

The wedding began with eight bridesmaids gliding down the aisle in their pink strapless dresses. The flower girls were adorable, yanking at their matching fancy dresses, and the ring-bearer dragged his feet, appearing sufficiently bored with his job. Annie was gorgeous in her ankle-length sheath of shimmery white, complete with plunging back and enormous veil; the wedding guests sufficiently held in their collective breath when she appeared on her father's arm and murmured to each other how beautiful she looked. A few began dabbing at their eyes so as not to smudge their water-proof mascara. Everyone simultaneously sat on the Priest's command and Joanna clutched her tiny, practically useless but quite fashionable (said May) blue purse in her lap and said another silent prayer Diego would appear on schedule. The Priest read some miscellaneous bible passages. Annie's sister read a poem about trust and love and Alex's best friend read something she couldn't quite follow that sounded vaguely sports-related. Alex and Annie gazed into each other's eyes and clasped hands. And then the Priest said, "And now I'd like to introduce the groom's brother, Diego, who will sing Annie's song."

The wedding guests looked expectantly towards the back of the church. Joanna watched Diego's mother in the row ahead of hers lean towards Diego's father and whisper something in his ear. Joanna held her breath, certain Diego would come bounding into the church, huge smile dazzling, and charm the pants off of everyone. That's not exactly what happened.

The good news was Diego did appear at the back of the church. The bad news was he was clearly drunk. And we're not talking a little, just enough to take the edge off tipsy; Diego was totally and completely hammered. Joanna had no idea how he could have gotten so drunk so quickly, but, over-achiever that he was, he had accomplished the task with expert precision.

His eyes bright and glassy, Diego weaved almost comically towards the front of the church, clutching his guitar by its neck. Something had spilled onto the front of his jacket causing a dark stain, and his pant leg was bunched up around his knee. He tripped up the stairs to the altar, landing in a heap at his fuming brother and stunned soon-to-be sister-in-law's feet, looked up at Alex and said, "Hey bro."

Before Alex could respond, Diego was on his feet and began to strum the guitar, and unbelievably sang the song with absolute perfection:

"You fill up my senses, like a light in the forest,
Like the mountains at springtime, like a walk in the rain,
Like a storm in the desert, like a sleepy blue ocean,
You fill up my senses, come fill me again!"

His voice reverberated beautifully through the church, soaring towards the vaulted ceiling. He closed his eyes as he sang and his audience was riveted. It was gorgeous, it was touching, and he left not a dry eye in the house. And then he finished the song, opened his eyes, swayed slightly on his feet, and vomited into the choir box.

22

Trying to schedule something with Lily, something as simple as dinner, or a play date with Leo, was like trying to schedule a presidential hopeful for tea during the California primary. Lily had an ability to complicate the simplest of affairs. Case in point:

"Hi Mom, what time are you coming up on Saturday to take Leo to the zoo?"

"Oh hi, Honey, yes, Saturday, we're on."

"Yes, but *what time* are you coming up?"

And here the drama begins...

"Well let's see, I've got tai chi at eight, and then I need to do a quick shopping and get my hair done. And I promised Daniel I'd clean out the hall closet, did I tell you that a whole shelf collapsed? Your dad says I overloaded it, but isn't that what a shelf is for, to put things on? Anyway, that shouldn't take too long, and then I'll be up to see Leo!"

"So...like two in the afternoon?"

"Oh no, Honey, I'll be there by ten. Or eleven, I'll be there by eleven."

"OK, Mom, just to be clear, you are going to tai chi, shop, get your hair cut and clean out the hall closet and still be able to leave your house by ten am in order to be here, at my house by eleven, is that correct?"

"Well, maybe I can move my hair appointment, and I'll work on the closet tomorrow instead..."

May clenched the phone, willing herself not to scream at her mother. "Mom, do you want to call me back on this?"

"No, no, Honey, I'll be there at ten, ten thirty at the absolute latest. I can't wait to have some Leo and me time! Oh! I need to stop by the toy store to get him that Thomas engine he wanted, what's his name? Spencer? Toby?"

"Rusty, Mom, he wants Rusty," May said. They had discussed this particular train a minimum of six times.

"Right, Rusty! I'm going to go pick that up right now." May heard her mother scratching a note to herself, most likely on a Post-it note. Lily considered Post-it notes to be one of the best inventions of the 20th century, better than super-glue, instant coffee and the jet engine combined. At any given time, Lily could be counted on to have at least 3 blocks of different colored Post-it notes inside her purse, not including the probably dozens of loose notes scratched with reminders and lists. Lily's Post-it obsession was one of many topics of hilarity to her daughters, especially seeing as she didn't actually post the Post-its anywhere, she just stuffed them into her purse where they stuck to tissues, gum and loose change.

"OK, Mom, I'll see you at ten am on Saturday, Rusty in hand," May attempted to neatly terminate the conversation.

"Yes, I'll be there no later than eleven. See you then!"

When the appointed day arrived, May and Joanna had coats on, purses in hand, ready to walk out the door for lunch, a movie, maybe some retail therapy. May ventured her mother would arrive at eleven twenty, so twenty minutes late, and bring the wrong train. Joanna said no way, thirty minutes late minimum, agreed regarding the wrong train but would make it up by bringing additional track or accessories. The five dollar wagers were never paid but the sisters kept track of the wins as if they were tossing heaps of chips on the table.

Twenty minutes passed and May watched, glum, as Joanna did a victory lap around the kitchen. When forty-five minutes passed and still no Lily, Joanna tried her cell but was derailed by voicemail. Next, she called Daniel.

"She left over an hour ago, but still...she got a late start," Daniel told her, unruffled, "so let's not panic for a few more minutes, ok? Call me back in half an hour or when she arrives, whichever happens first, ok Sweetie?"

"Mommy, when's Grandmamma Lily coming?" Leo, gecko-like, climbed up May's long leg and wrapped himself around her waist.

"She'll be here soon, Pumpkin, how about we pull out some Tinkertoys in the meantime, ok?" May busied herself getting Leo set up with his Tinkertoys as Joanna began to pace.

Thirty minutes later, no Lily. May called Daniel back: "Hi dad, nope, no sign of her," she tried to keep her tone breezy for Leo's sake, but her heart was fluttering. An hour and fifteen minutes late was very late, even for Lily.

"Did you try her cell again?"

"Yes, but I keep getting her voicemail..."

"I really am not worried, Sweetie, she's probably stuck in traffic somewhere, don't worry, she's a big girl."

"What did he say?" asked Joanna.

"To chill."

"I'm getting a little f-r-e-a-k-e-d out," Joanna spelled.

"I know me too."

Joanna turned back to her perch by the window, "Wait! She's here!"

May ran over to the window and the sisters watched, disbelieving, as their mother calmly extricated herself from the car, gigantic shopping bag in tow. They watched as she stretched her back and leaned back into the car to retrieve a huge straw hat which she then put onto her head. Slowly venturing up the walk, she stopped and fingered the leaf of a rosebush and then leaned to pluck a weed the gardener had missed. When she put the shopping bag down to inspect a bug or a crack in the cement or something, May yanked the door open and yelled down to her, "Mom, what the hell are you doing? You had us worried!"

Lily looked up at her, alarmed, "What? Worried? Why? Am I late?" She looked at her watch, "it's only 11:20!"

"Mom, it's not 11:20, it's 12:20! You are over an hour late!"

"It is? I am? Oh, I see, you're right, it is12:20. Well I had no idea; I thought I was so early so I stopped at the outlet mall on the way up. Why didn't you call me?"

"We did call you, Mom," said Joanna, joining May with hands on hips, "repeatedly."

"Well, I didn't hear the phone even once," she reached into her purse and pulled out the phone, "oh look, I have a message, is it you?" Lily held the phone out to May, as if she could telepathically decipher who had left her a message by looking at the phone.

May took the phone and inspected it, "Mom," she said grimly, "it's on silent," she held it up for her mother to see and Joanna slapped her hand to her forehead in utter annoyance.

"It is? Well no wonder I couldn't hear it. Anyway, here I am, and I have a present for you!" she tousled Leo's hair and pulled a train from the enormous shopping bag, "Look Honey, its Thomas' friend, Toby!"

23

Joanna was excited to see Leo. They hadn't spent much time just the two of them in recent weeks and she missed their private time so she jumped at the chance when May asked her to pick him up. It was too cold for a park visit so she was planning on taking him to the library. After the library she was thinking sushi for dinner.

She drove up to Bright Future, pulling her Volvo next to a new Tesla. She looked into the window of the new car, wondering if it was the one with the bat wings. Busy snooping, she didn't see the car's owner approaching and looking none too pleased Joanna was peering into her windows.

The woman, firmly gripping the hand of a plump pink-faced boy sadly dressed in corduroy, cleared her throat and Joanna jumped, startled.

"Oh! I'm so sorry, is this your car? I'm totally in your way!" Joanna stepped back to give the woman space.

"Yes, excuse me" She opened the non-bat winged door and strapped her glum, silent child into his car seat.

Joanna noticed the tell-tale signs of tears streaking his dull pink face.

"Sorry again! Joanna obtusely ignored the woman's cranky non-verbal cues as she got into the car and sped away.

Jeez, thought Joanna, watching her flee. Her mobile rang.

It was May, "Are you there yet? I just got a call from the school..."

Joanna interrupted her "Yeah, I'm in the parking lot. I just tried to make conversation with the rudest woman. She is driving one of those new Teslas? Do you know which one I mean? She was not interested in talking to me at all."

"Black hair, scrawny, perpetual scowl?"

"That's the one, what *is* her problem?"

"Well, today her problem is that my kid bit her kid..."

After she buzzed her in, Leo's teacher motioned for Joanna to join her in the office.

"Hi, Alice. May just called me. It sounds like Leo had a tough day, huh?"

Leo's teacher Alice was young, maybe twenty-five, with a purplish birthmark spiraling around her right cheekbone and into her hairline. She wore her strawberry blonde hair in a pageboy which helped cover the mark. Joanna liked Alice; she had an excellent sense of humor. When Leo was new at the school he asked Alice about her face and she told him she drank so much grape juice as a child her skin started to turn purple! "Now, I stick with water or milk," she added, winking at him. Leo had stared, open-mouthed, not sure what to make of her.

"He did have a tough day," Alice motioned for Joanna to sit down, "he's been not quite himself lately. He's getting upset easily and his stubborn streak is really apparent. I hate to ask, but is everything ok at home?"

Joanna hesitated.

Alice continued, "I don't want to pry. It just seems he's been exhibiting some unusual behavior. At least unusual for Leo."

"Like...biting other children?" Joanna tried to add some comedy to the not-so-funny situation.

"Honestly, I'm so not concerned about the bite. Between you, me, and the wall? Andy had it coming. But Leo's not a biter and he just seems a little, I don't know, not himself, off. Can you let May know I mentioned it?"

"Of course," said Joanna, relieved. She wasn't sure exactly what she should reveal about Leo's home life right now.

Joanna sat next to Leo on one of the tiny chairs. Leo was sitting by himself, looking at a picture book.

"Hey, sweet boy."

"Hi, Auntie Jo."

Joanna put her arm around her nephew's bony, warm shoulders, "Want to go to the library with me today?"

Leo nodded.

"How about now? Should we go now?"

"OK." He didn't budge.

"What's up, Leo?"

"I bit Andy." His eyes welled up with tears.

"I heard, Sweetie," she gave him a squeeze, "do you want to tell me what happened?"

Leo rubbed his eyes with his little fists, his face a little scowl, "He said I was a poop-head and I bit him."

"Ah, I see," Joanna remarked, "it's not very nice to call someone a poop-head, is it?"

"No."

"And it's also not nice to bite people, right?"

"Right," he looked at his red sneakers, "I know. Member Collin bit me on my back that time and it hurt a lot." The tears trickled down, creating little muddy rivers down his cheeks.

"I do remember. And I know you're sorry you bit Andy." She rubbed his back, bowled over at the empathetic abilities of this small ingenious person, "Is there anything else you want to tell me?"

"Can I have a tissue, please?"

Joanna laughed, "Of course you may have a tissue," she dug around in her purse until she came up with a ragged, possibly unused tissue.

He rubbed his nose with the tissue, "Can we go to the liberry now?"

"Sure we can to the lib*rary* now, let's go."

They gathered his usual paraphernalia, this time including acorns and some unidentified fuzz from his cubby and Joanna signed him out, waving to Alice as they left.

The children's librarian gave her a withering look when her mobile rang. "I'm sorry." she mouthed, as the crinkly woman pointed to the large "No cellular phones" sign.

"May, we're in the library," she whispered, "I'll call you back."

With two Dr. Suesses and a Shel Silverstein under her arm they exited the library with Leo skipping happily beside her, the trauma of the day forgotten behind him.

"Leo, let's park here and call your Mom back, ok?" she indicated a bench.

May picked up on the first ring, "So what's the story, did he really bite him? Was there blood? Are we talking a lawsuit here?"

"Chill May, yes and no and no. All is fine; I'll give you the details later. Don't you have some deal you need to get to?"

May groaned, "Don't remind me. I'm dreading it."

"I know. I'm sorry, call me after, ok?"

May absently gazed around the huge conference room. It seemed inappropriately large for one divorcing couple and two eager lawyers. It seemed something smaller would have been sufficient, but maybe the big room came with the bigger price tag of the lawyer's services. Or maybe smaller was too intimate for such yucky business. The walls were muted beige, accented with a darker brown trim and several large potted plants. There was a large bay window with a less than spectacular view, and a large cabinet on the far wall, May assumed it contained a screen for presentations. May looked at her watch. She was early. Her lawyer's assistant had called to say he was running a bit late, he was very sorry, and if she preferred to reschedule that was fine. May hadn't preferred to reschedule, she wanted to be done with this. She didn't know what she would be moving on to, but she was determined to get started. She would not let this man break her.

May was the one who had insisted they begin discussing the logistics of a potential divorce.

"Doesn't that seem premature, May?" Jamie had said tentatively, "I mean, can't we just do this separation thing for a little while before we move towards such a huge step?"

But May had replied, "No. I don't want to be dicked around while you figure out who you want to dick around with."

They had already discussed the mundane stuff, and Jamie, to his credit, was doing his best to give her everything. And May, to her credit, was doing her best to take everything. Today they were moving on to the horrible stuff; on today's agenda they were discussing Leo.

Jamie smiled stiffly as he entered the room, escorted by the irritatingly perky receptionist. He sat across from her at the shiny, enormous conference room table. May noted he was wearing the gray suit she had picked out for him on their trip to Milan. The journey had been dubbed "The last hurrah before the then-unnamed baby's arrival and the shit really hits the fan." They had an incredible time, a wonderful second honeymoon. May remembered the vacation wistfully; now it seemed like a million years ago.

Jamie also wore the cobalt shirt she had given him for his birthday last year and finally the rather avant garde tie she had picked up in a boutique in San Francisco (although, could a tie be avant garde? She didn't know. This would have been a question for that nincompoop Diego to extrapolate on, she supposed.). She bet she had purchased his shoes as well, although she wouldn't stoop to look under the table at them, and she had certainly purchased his socks and underwear, items he hadn't purchased for himself in at least a decade.

"Where's your lawyer?" May asked.

"Late," Jamie smiled stiffly.

"Mine too."

The silence stretched between them. Jamie tapped his fingers nervously, instantly putting May's hackles up. Why was he so fucking anxious? This was all his idea.

Finally he spoke again, "It's great to see you, May."

May narrowed her eyes suspiciously at her husband. It was not so great to see Jamie. Upon closer inspection, he looked like shit. His dapper clothes were rumpled, as if he'd just removed them from a suitcase or had slept on a park bench in them. He had dark circles under his eyes, and his hair was disheveled and a little greasy looking. May, doing her best to keep her icy composure, fissured just a tad. "It's good to see you too, Jamie."

A look of relief crossed Jamie's face and his eyes were suddenly swimming with tears. Abruptly he was on his feet and moving quickly around the mammoth table towards her, "I'm so glad to hear you say that, Honey," he slipped into the huge leather chair next to her.

May instinctually leaned away from him, this man who had broken her heart, this man who had betrayed her, something no other mortal had ever done.

The tears in his eyes glistened, threatening to escape. He reached for her hand and she let him take it. His voice was merely a whisper, "May, I've made a terrible, terrible mistake." His head was bowed, and when he looked up at her, she saw the tears had overflowed.

It wasn't as if he had never been curious. Like any red-blooded American male Jamie had checked out his share of Internet porn and occasionally meandered into a little guy-on-guy action. He didn't find it repulsive, but it wasn't a particular turn on either. It was just something interesting to watch.

But Austin was a different story. There was something intriguing about this man. Austin had this thing about him. This energy. This charisma. Jamie was drawn to him, as guys are drawn to guys. And it was cool, because it was just guys drinking beer with other guys. They hung out a lot, traveled the same routes. Jamie wasn't sure when the "hanging out" had crossed the line into actual flirting. He still wasn't sure if the line had ever really been crossed to flirting. As far as he knew, he had never flirted with a man before and he wasn't sure if he had ever flirted with Austin. And had Austin flirted with him? He didn't know. The whole weird scenario was a just a blur at this point.

Jamie and May hadn't been going through a particularly rough patch, sexually speaking. Although her usually healthy sex drive had never completely rebounded after having Leo, she and Jamie always found time to connect. It wasn't as if he was finding himself frustrated and unfulfilled on a regular basis, just an occasional one. But he was lonely when travelling, and when Austin made advances, well, it was as if he had emerged from a forty year drought. His curiosity, and shots too numerous to count, got the better of him. Jamie, like May, had an excellent bullshit detector. There had been tons of women throwing themselves at him throughout his life. He easily saw through them all in his search for his equal and true partner in May. But apparently, this was Austin's shtick. He liked the rush, the challenge, of sleeping with straight men. That way he had a constant cycle of virgins, or at least, "sort-of" virgins. It was a turn on, it was fun, it was his sport of choice. And Jamie was the perfect specimen. Terrific looking, confident, smart. To Austin, he was the perfect mark, a good chase.

Maybe Jamie wasn't a teenager any more, but clearly he wasn't immune to the advances of this particularly slick operate. When Jamie next bumped into Austin at a sales event, he felt none of the lust he had before. He sat next to him at the bar and ordered a beer, trying to summon the courage to ask him what the fuck happened between them, when Austin piped up.

"Look Jamie, you're adorable. You're adorable to women, and you're adorable to men. And you were drunk, so I thought I should take it upon myself to take advantage of that. Lots of straight men dabble, you know."

"I don't know any straight men who dabble. I've never dabbled."

Austin snorted, "Plenty dabble! But my guess is that your dabbling days are over. Look what a wreck you are! You're a straight man who loves your wife, Jamie. Worse things have happened."

Jamie haltingly relayed the pathetic story to May. He couldn't meet her gaze. He's ashamed, May realized, an emotion she had never seen in her husband before.

Jamie had enlisted the aid of a therapist. The therapist helped him come to the same conclusion that Austin had, that the one night stand was exactly that, a one night stand, no different from any other. It meant nothing in the long run, it was a huge, idiotic mistake, and he was pleading his case to May, and his argument was temporary insanity.

Now it was May tossing and turning the night away.

Her head was reeling. Can you love someone and hate the choices they made? Of course you can. What about the spouse of an alcoholic, or the child of an alcoholic. They love that fucker, but hate their behavior. But are they stuck? Well, the kid is stuck. What is that kid supposed to do? Scream and yell and get themselves grounded? But the spouse might not be stuck, they can leave. But where's that line? And how many chances should someone get after they blow it? One slip up and they're out on their ass? What about the kid who cheats on his spelling test? Does he get kicked out of school on the first offense?

This was a pretty huge infraction. How could she ever trust he wouldn't do it again? He had never done it before, but maybe he had, maybe he had been unfaithful and she just didn't know. No, no way. Although Jamie's announcement had been a total shocker, deep down in the pit of her stomach, May knew something had happened. She hadn't figured it out yet, and hadn't even thought there was a problem to figure out, but once she really began to ponder the declaration, she realized she knew, she knew.

But, but, but thought May, *but we're different! We really are that perfect couple! We really are immune from all this crap that other couples endure! We don't fight about money, or Leo's bedtime or not having enough sex. We treat each other with respect and dignity, and believe in a partnership. This doesn't happen to couples like us...right? Right?*

May put her hands over her ears, trying to shut out the screaming in them so she could forget it all and simply sleep.

24

"Miller, Stewart and Sons, this is Joanna; how might I direct your call?"

"It's Delia. Can you get out of work?"

Joanna lowered her voice, "Delia? What are you talking about? Aren't you here at work?" she glanced at her computer clock, it was nearly ten.

"Fake a stomach-ache or something. Come on, we're playing hooky."

"We are?"

"Yup, meet me on the corner in five," Delia hung up.

Joanna smoothed her skirt, formulated her plan, and walked over to Helen's office. She knocked lightly on the open door until Helen looked up.

"Helen?" Joanna began tentatively, "May I speak with you just a brief moment?"

Helen was very much like Lily, and taking Lily into your confidence was the best way to get, well, whatever you wanted. Later curfew, the last cookie, whatever. Joanna suspected the same would work on Helen.

"Of course, Joanna, please come in." Helen removed her glasses and gestured to the chair.

Joanna closed the door behind her and sat down and looked at her hands twisting in her lap.

"I know I've been missing a lot of work lately, and I'm sorry about that. But if it's not too much trouble and ok with you," she paused for effect, "I need to leave early again today. Like, I need to leave right now."

"Are you all right, Joanna?" Helen's bird-like features were screwed up with concern, making her appear even pointier than usual.

"Yes, yes. I'm fine. I mean no, no, not really. I'm just having a rough time these days. Boyfriend blues or ex-boyfriend blues is more like it. You know how that is," she gave Helen a wan smile, "I just can't seem to shake it; I think it's making me physically ill. I'm so nauseous today I can't see straight. I think I just need to, you know, take care of myself right now and take the day off to try to feel better. Would that be ok?" Joanna looked up from under her eyelashes as innocently as she could.

"Well, Joanna. You have been missing some time, but it is so important to take care of your mental health, I wish more people would do it! In fact," Helen looked left and right as if they were in jeopardy of being overheard in the middle of a crowded room rather than her empty office, "last month when I took that 'vacation' time?" she made little quotation marks with her fingers, "I was actually on a...retreat of sorts," she sat back in her chair, grinning like the Cheshire cat and letting her revelation sink in.

"Really? A retreat? What type of retreat?"

Helen grinned, "Well, it's rather private," she looked around again, "but I know I can trust you."

Joanna stifled a laugh; she couldn't think of why Helen had any reason to trust her, she obviously didn't know about her little problem with secrets. "Only if you're comfortable..." Joanna began.

"Oh, I'm just bursting to tell someone. It was just fascinating! I discovered it on the Internet?" She said "Internet" like a question, like, are you familiar with that crazy brand-new concept of the "*Internet*?"

And then Helen launched into how while she was trolling around the "Internet?" she was looking for, she claimed, some relaxation ideas, as she was just so stressed out lately, what with her son's wedding and the crazy workload. In any case she stumbled upon a website called not so cryptically, meditatethebigO.com.

"Meditate-the-big-O?" asked Joanna, cautiously.

"I know, I know, it sounds a little out there," Helen giggled like a schoolgirl, "but trust me, it's the most fantastic thing I've ever experienced." Helen pretended to swipe some imaginary sweat off her brow. "Talk about relaxation!"

"So the gist," Helen told Joanna, gesticulating animatedly, "of meditate-the-big-O is to learn how to silence the internal chatter in your head so you can truly focus on what causes the O in the first place," she leaned forward in her chair, elbows on her desk, "but not necessarily while doing anything sexual, but really anytime, anywhere, everywhere!" Apparently the founder of the movement claimed orgasm is a state of mind, and the more you can "live there" the better your chances will be at achieving one as often, and as easily as possible. The website was full of testimonials of frigid women finally getting that big O.

One testimony, Helen explained, was particularly compelling, causing her unable to resist forking over $99.99 on the 2 DVD set, (including *Meditate the big O*, *Meditate the big O for couples* and the bonus, act now to receive your free copy of *Meditate the big O while driving or at work or in a crowd*, your choice!) sent not-so-secretively in a brown-paper wrapper. Arlene was a plain, sad housewife in her 50's married for 34 years to a cold, aloof office-supply salesman. Despite being a self-described "avid masturbator," Arlene was unable to achieve the big O, or any size o for that matter while actually participating in sex with her distant bore of a husband. Now that their three kids were out of the house, Arlene was petrified of spending the rest of her life cooped up with this man unable to find her clitoris with stadium lights and a well-highlighted map. And then, while taking a "Getting to know technology " class at the local community center, she came upon the MeditatethebigO.com website, immediately whipped out her credit card and in stepped this miraculous 2 DVD set (Arlene chose *Meditate the big O while driving* as her bonus DVD and found dozens of reasons to run extra errands. *Forgot the tomatoes? I'll just run to the store! Dry cleaners? No need to stop after work, Honey, I'll be happy to run out and pick it up. New snow tires? Leave that to me!*) Within weeks, salesman Frank called in sick for work and he and Arlene holed up in their modest brownstone, experiencing their own summer of love.

"Not that Jerry and I were experiencing any sort of drought, but even old married couples like us could use a little help in that department from time to time if you know what I mean," Helen said, "anyway, they do these fabulous workshops for individuals and couples, they are just wild! MeditatethebigO has really turned my whole world around." She sat back in her chair and glided from side to side, twirling a lock of graying hair and looking out the window rather wistfully.

Joanna was more than a little weirded out by Helen's admission. She didn't exactly know how to respond so she said, "Wow, Helen, that's so interesting. Thanks for sharing with me."

Helen stopped her sideways glide to smile conspiratorially, hands fluttering to her throat, "You go get some rest and let me know if you're interested in talking about this some more, or if you'd like to borrow one of my DVDs!" Helen winked at her, and Joanna had to close her eyes for a moment and say a quick silent prayer she wouldn't burst out laughing until she was firmly ensconced in Delia's car, "This really might be the thing you need to help get you out of your breakup funk!"

Joanna stood, "Thanks for everything, Helen; I'll see you on Monday."

"See you on Monday," Helen replied, smiling and turning back to her computer where her frolicking kitten screensaver had taken over, pouncing back and forth between a toy mouse and a roll of yarn.

Joanna packed up her purse and as she hurried down the stairs she thought to herself, *is it sexual harassment if your boss divulges she is into orgasmic meditation?*

"What took you so long? Is everything ok?" asked Delia, "You look like the cat that just swallowed the canary."

Joanna slid into the backseat as the passenger seat was already occupied by Bruno. "My boss...told me something crazy, I'm just digesting. So, where are we going?"

"Well what a silly question, my dearest Joanna, where else would we go at ten-thirty in the morning on a beautiful spring day like today?" she started the car, "We're going wine tasting!"

"Yippee!" exclaimed Bruno, clapping his hands like a child anticipating a birthday cake high.

"Ah, of course!" Joanna smacked her hand against her forehead, "What else would we be doing on a Friday when we're supposed to be working, but drink copious amounts of wine? I'm totally in." She fastened her seatbelt and secured her hair in a ponytail, anticipating the windy ride, "Somehow, I think ole' Helen would approve of this excellent plan. Let's motor. "

Delia, who was always the designated driver, cautiously pulled her car into the light mid-morning traffic. Delia loved to drive, it gave her a rush and she had hands-down the coolest car. Although the competition with Joanna's Volvo was not so steep, Bruno did drive a snazzy silver Audi. But Delia's car was truly a classic, a blue 1968 Chevy Impala convertible which had belonged to her father-in-law. He was the original owner and took better care of the car than he ever did his wife and sons. Upon his death his other two sons were royally pissed that he left the car to "My favorite daughter-in-law, Delia." The other daughters-in-law were equally pissed. Delia and Ray were absolutely delighted. Another reason Delia was always the DD was because she was a complete lightweight. A lot of swirls, just a few sips, lots of spitting. Although she could eat like a horse Delia knew her tiny athletic body could only handle limited alcohol. Plus, "its way more fun to watch the two of you get plastered." Joanna and Bruno, excellent sports that they were, were always up for the challenge.

Delia sped north up the 101, exiting at Dry Creek Road and curving towards the magnificent vines of the Alexander Valley. It really was a perfect wine-tasting day. The sun was shining brightly but the spring air was deceivingly crisp. The grapevines had recently sprouted beautiful shoots of green, rose-bushes lined the vineyards and wild dill grew along the edges of the roads.

The trio had a marvelous day. They meandered lazily, not in any particular hurry. They swirled and drank and spat leisurely. They tried to outdo each other to see who could come up with the most asinine descriptions of the wines: "This pinot tastes like starfruit with hints of cinnamon and elbow grease." "This cab reminds me of being punched in the jaw on a warm summer's day in Rome." "This chardonnay is reminiscent of apple blossom shower gel and duck-liver pâté."

Delia had thoughtfully brought a picnic lunch and they sat hunched together on a blanket, watching ducks in a gray pond fight over scraps of bread some picnicker had left on the shore. They sipped more wine and hungrily ate smoked turkey sandwiches and fruit. Bruno lay on his back and interpreted the cloud formations. "OK, over there I see a deer wearing a cowboy hat and over there it looks like a pirate ship and see over there where those geese are flying? If you look closely at that one, see right there?" he pointed wildly at the sky, "You can see the Statue of Liberty." Joanna and Delia just grinned and nodded at him, like you would an elderly relative or a small child learning to talk.

Delia dropped Joanna off at her car and gave her a hug. "Hey, did I say thanks for the cookies?"

"WHAT??" Bruno screeched, "Why did Delia get cookies and not me?"

25

Delia, Ray, Bruno and Trudy were already laughing and drinking when Joanna and May arrived. *Appellation* was their regular stomping ground, and the wine bar's owners, a young hip couple waved hello from behind the bar and Joanna half-expected a "Norm!" as a welcome.

"So what are we drinking?" Joanna asked by way of a hello, leaning over Delia to give Ray and Trudy kisses.

"Trudy brought a few bottles," answered Bruno.

"Yippee!"

Joanna was surprised and pleased to see Trudy, Bruno's hilarious roommate. Trudy was a winemaker, a boisterous bean-pole of a woman, red-headed with not an iota of her open delicate face not covered by freckles. Joanna loved it when Trudy accompanied Bruno so they could talk food and wine. She jovially scooted Bruno aside with her ample hip so they could chat uninterrupted. Joanna also knew this would take some coaxing. Trudy, like many winemakers Joanna met since her move to the North Bay, complained the romance of wine-making was gone, replaced by the day to day drudgery of budgets, investors and celebrity that too often accompanied the role. Frankly, it was rare for Trudy to be seen drinking wine. "Beer is my alcohol of choice," was her mantra.

May said her hellos to Joanna's gang and took a big sip of Trudy's luscious offering, a delicious zin exploding with juicy raspberries. She asked Delia about a new spin instructor she had noticed at their gym. Delia, a hard-core athlete, was always in the know of the best trail to run, the best shoe to wear for what activity and the best moisture-wicking attire. Her finger was firmly on the pulse of the county's best instructors and gyms. Rising daily at 4:30 to run, Delia would then hit the gym for spin class or yoga or strength training. May admired her tenacity, not to mention her seemingly endless energy. Before Leo came along May would have considered herself at least medium-core, now...not so much. Cancelling on her personal trainer and that little cookie habit she was developing was not helping the situation either.

"She's an animal. Totally kicking my ass," Delia snapped a bread stick in two, eating one half and using the other to poke at Ray.

"So I should probably stay away?" Occasionally, May was as obtuse as Joanna.

"No, no, I mean she's terrific, you should come! Hey, what do you think of Ted's yoga class?"

Joanna turned to May semi-mockingly, a small amused smile playing in the corners of her mouth.

May smirked at Joanna, "I like it, he's...challenging."

“He’s cute too,” said Delia, munching the other half of the bread stick.

“I hadn’t really noticed,” said May, coy, ignoring Joanna.

May looked around the wine bar. One thing about having a spouse in the wine business, invariably there would be someone she knew, some colleague of Jamie’s, especially at an out of the way space catering to the well-tooled wine crowd. She was relieved to spot no one familiar.

Quickly feeling warm from the wine, May shrugged out of her leather jacket. She shook out her mane of hair, her gaze settling on a lesbian couple sitting at the bar. One of the women was tall and slim with an almost elf-like face and pointy, well-pronounced cheekbones. She wore a stylish blonde spiky haircut, white button-up shirt and black and white pin-striped trousers. “Very nice ensemble,” thought May. Her friend was short and round, with a huge mane of fluffy and flying blonde hair, presumably to bury a rather unsightly large nose and extra chins. She wore a floaty dress with layers of alternating green and blue. May thought them an odd pair, the tall woman was so angular and striking and her date so soft and schlumpy.

She wondered about being with a woman. Would it really be so incredibly different as being with a man? Sure, the equipment was different, but would the experience really be so bizarre? She wondered what went through Jamie’s mind as this man, this Austin, leaned in the first time for a kiss. Was it, "Oh shit, I'm about to cheat on my wife!" Was it "Oh shit, I'm about to cheat on my wife... with a man?" Was it "Oh shit..." at all?

The tall woman rubbed the shorter woman's back affectionately then leaned down to kiss her, a sweet, slow, tongue-filled kiss. Did a woman's tongue taste different than a man's? Was the kiss softer? Harder? Wetter? Would she feel it deep in her knees, spreading heat and longing into her groin as when she was kissing Jamie or another man? Although she hadn't felt much when kissing Ted. It was comparable to the practice-kissing she used to do on her Baby Alive doll.

The group laughed, apparently Ray had said something funny and May smiled, a little self-conscious that she had wafted away from the group's conversation. Joanna leaned in to pour wine into May's empty glass and speak discretely into her ear, "Everything ok there, baby girl?"

May nodded and drank from her newly refilled glass, "I'm looking at this cute couple at the bar," she indicated the snuggling pair, "they are very sweet."

Joanna scanned the bar, looking for the couple May indicated. "May, that's Lisa and Alison. They live down the hall from me, I think you met them at the Cinco de Mayo party Diego and I threw last year. I'm going to go say 'hi,'" Joanna rose, "do you want to come?"

"Oh no, I'm content to sit here and ogle from a distance."

Lisa, the tall woman, smiled happily to see Joanna

and kissed her full on the mouth. Alison gave her one of those awkward "on the side" hugs. They turned as Joanna pointed to May and the three waved. May waved back.

Bruno beckoned May to move closer since Joanna had vacated the space. May scooted in and plucked a bread stick from the glass centerpiece in the middle of the table. Bruno put his arm around her and gave her a little squeeze, "Hey there, May May, long time no see."

They chatted about the world. Bruno complained about his new boss, an apparent micro-manager who was severely cramping his style. May wondered how much Joanna had told Bruno and Delia about her current sticky situation. Knowing Joanna as she did, probably everything.

Her eyes wandered to Delia and Ray. They had been high school sweethearts, bonding over track meets and fun-runs and long-distance races. They married young and had just celebrated their fifteenth wedding anniversary with an enormous drunken bash. May watched as Ray leaned over and tweaked Delia on the nose, she laughed and kissed him as a response. May smiled. They were so happy. Maybe the happiest couple she had ever seen, although, once upon a time, she was sure people would have said the same thing about her and Jamie. Once upon the time, they *were* the happiest couple, and frankly, once upon a time wasn't so long ago. It was crazy what could change in just a few short months...a whole life could change.

"I see you have a case of the Joannas today," Bruno told her.

"The Joannas?"

"You know, how Joanna will just disappear for awhile into her own little world? She always comes back at least."

May laughed, "Yes, I know how she does that, did I just disappear on you?"

"It's ok, I'm used to it. Anyway, since you're back, Roger said to give you a hug and kiss and to tell you he misses you madly."

May smiled, she adored Roger, Bruno's on-again off-again, but mostly on-again boyfriend of probably a decade by now. Roger was May's dermatologist, and due to her fair skin and some suspiciously funky-looking moles she needed to remove a few years back, she saw him regularly. He was a stark contrast to Bruno, and she suspected their differences helped complement the relationship, while adding much needed drama. Roger was extremely calm, very gentle. His bedside manner was impeccable. Unruffled, he stoically endured Bruno's brazen style.

"How is Roger? Is he coming tonight?" She sought eye contact from the waitress, she needed a more substantial snack than the meager breadstick was offering.

"Roger's great, working a lot, you know him, career-oriented and all. The practice is going well and that's good news. He should be here at some point," his eyes flickered to the door.

"I'm thrilled the practice is going well, so risky to start your own business these days." May was well aware of Roger's reluctance to leave his partners, but was glad he had. His new office was much more modern with sleek furniture and contemporary art (the old place was straight out of the 80's, complete with burgundy-colored couches and a Nagel) and it was fun to see Roger's name on the door: *Dr. Roger Burlap, MD*. "I'm referring everyone I know his way."

"I'm sure he appreciates the business." Bruno drank some more wine, "We're talking about..." he looked around furtively, Joanna was deep in conversation with the lesbians and the rest of their table was occupied, "moving in together," he whispered, then slapped his cheeks in an excellent impression of the Home Alone kid, "can you believe it?"

"Wow, after all these years?" the waitress gave her the "I'm on my way over," nod.

"Yeah, we're madly in love and all that. And we're getting old, at least Roger is," Bruno winked, "so we decided it was time to take the leap," he yawned, stretching his arms over his head.

"Well good for you, such exciting news. So what's Trudy going to do without you?"

"Oh jeez, she's been trying to get rid of me for years; she'll probably throw a parade! Anyway, it'll be good for her to stand on her own two feet," he feigned a sniffle, "they grow up so fast, don't they?" He smiled impishly and took a long drink of wine, "So speaking of growing up, how's your cute kid and hot hubby these days? Leo must be what, ten? Eleven? Twenty-four?"

May narrowed her eyes, again wondering what exactly Bruno knew. Maybe not as much as she had originally suspected after all, she didn't think he would ask so obtusely otherwise. Before she could formulate a witty response the waitress arrived with an appetizer menu which May seized eagerly, telling Bruno, "I skipped lunch and I'm starving!" She ordered half a dozen appetizers for the table, and launched into a Joanna-esque rant about Leo's latest escapades.

26

A week and a half before Mark's wedding, he completely freaked out. He called Joanna at 2am, blubbering something about his lost youth. Joanna said she'd come get him despite the late hour on a work night, the forty-five minute drive to the bar he frequented, and the fact she knew there would be consequences.

When she arrived at the bar, now closed, she could hear Mark singing through the closed door. It was Prince, although she couldn't put her finger on the name of the song, which in itself was very odd as Mark was into old-school rock and roll. He believed the sun rose and set on Mick Jagger.

She peered in the tiny window and knocked. The bartender cleaning up for the night let her in, saying, "Your boy here is blitzed and the singing is intolerable." Joanna noticed his arms were heavily inked with sea-life: crabs, lobsters, sea-stars, and fish. She wondered idly if he was a Pisces.

"Thanks for taking care of him. Does he have a tab I need to pay?" Joanna asked.

"Joanna!" Mark noticed her and stumbled off of his

bar stool, embracing her in a full-body, vise grip of a hug. "You came!" he kissed her sloppily like a Saint Bernard finally let out of the house after a long day while his owners toiled at work, "You came!"

"Of course I came, Sweetheart," Joanna patted him and hugged him back and then wiggled out of his grasp in order to breathe.

The bartender laughed, "Naw, we know him so I'm not worried about the dough. I feel bad he got so drunk; he must have been drinking before he got here. Anyway, I think his honey is out of town..."

Joanna knew Susan was having a Bachelorette weekend in Carmel. "Thanks for taking care of him," she said and ushered Mark as quickly as she could out of the bar and into her car.

"Please, please don't puke in my car, Mark," she told him as she leaned over him to buckle his seatbelt.

He grinned at her dreamily, his eyes blurry with tears, and touched her cheek, "I love you, Joanna."

She touched his cheek back, "I know sweet cheeks, I love you too, now let's get you home and to bed," she gently closed his door and quickly moved around the car, slid behind the wheel and started the engine.

"No," Mark leaned over and put his hand over hers on the steering wheel, "No, I LOVE you, Joanna. I really do. You always take care of me." This was not Joanna's first experience with a drunk Mark so she understood every word, despite the fact it sounded like: "Dough, dough, I LUV you, Anna. I weally do. You alays take care uf me..."

She smiled at him, wrinkling her nose at his alcohol-laden breath. "I know you love me, Mark, I love you too."

Mark resumed the singing on the drive home, and Joanna identified the song as "I Would Die 4 U." Suddenly, as if he turned off the drunk switch, Mark stopped singing and said, perfectly sober, "JoJo, what if I'm making a huge mistake marrying Susan? What if you and I are supposed to be together?"

Joanna pulled the car in front of Mark and Susan's house and patted him on his knee, searching in the dark for the whites of his eyes, "Mark, that's the liquor talking. I love you and I know you love me, but we are not destined for each other. Susan is the woman you are supposed to be with, to love and have children with, and I am the woman who will continue to be your best bud, fattening you up with cookies." She brushed his hair out of his face, "You're taking a huge, exciting step, of course you are nervous, but I promise you it will be worth it."

She led him inside and pulled off his shoes, tucked him into bed (leaving a big bowl beside the bed, just in case). As she was tip-toeing out he called, "JoJo?"

"What Mark?"

"Diego isn't the man you are supposed to be with," he said, and then he rolled over and began to snore.

Joanna stood motionless in the dark for a few minutes before she let herself out, locking the door using the spare key hidden in the cactus on the porch and began the long drive home.

Diego didn't speak to her for three days.

27

Joanna incorporated the knocking into her dream. She was dancing with Madonna on a beach, somewhere tropical with swaying palm trees and tiki torches and Polynesian dancers. Madonna was radiant as ever, curls bobbing and abs exceptionally tight. The sand was rough and warm on the soles of Joanna's bare feet. They were having a wonderful time, laughing and boogying as if no one was watching. The knocking was perfectly in synch to the music. "Like a virgin, knock, knock, hey! Touched for the very first time, knock, knock, knock. Like a vi-ir-ir-gin, knock, knock."

"Joanna! Joanna! Are you in there?" Joanna's eyes popped open; suddenly wide awake she sprang out of bed and tripped over her slippers. Madonna was gone. She'd know that voice anywhere. It was Diego.

She stood in her dark bedroom motionless, questions galloping like un-tethered race horses. *What the hell should I do? Should I answer the door? What is he doing here?*

"Joanna!" Joanna jumped. "Are you awake? Answer the door!"

Joanna grabbed her robe and raced into the hall and then paced back and forth like a 50's dad in the waiting room, eager to meet his newest asset. *What do I do? What the hell do I do?*

"Joanna, it is freezing out here! Please answer the door."

Joanna went to the front door. She looked through the peek-hole. Sure enough, it was Diego. *What the hell should I do?* She unsuccessfully smoothed her tattered pony-tail.

"Joanna. I can hear you in there. Please answer the door," he implored.

"Shit!" Joanna muttered crazily. She tightened the belt on her robe and unlocked the door. Taking a deep breath, she opened it a few inches.

"Joanna," Diego smiled that beautiful smile at her, exposing the adorable gap, "Hello. How are you? It is so cold out here. May I come in?"

For a moment, Joanna hesitated. *Of course he couldn't come in! What the hell was he doing here, at God-knows what hour? Hadn't he done enough?*

"Please, I just want to talk with you," he leaned his tall, masculine trunk against the door-frame, "please?"

Against all better judgment, Joanna stepped aside and opened the door.

Diego smiled and closed the door behind him. He looked amazing and smelled even better.

"It is so good to see you, Joanna. You look just great."

Joanna furrowed her brow. *She looked great? At*

1:00am, when she was shaken out of bed she looked great? In her ratty Morrissey tee-shirt and ancient sweats she looked great? "Diego, what are you doing here? It's like one in the morning," she asked him, her voice hoarse with sleep.

But she knew the answer. Joanna was a lot of things, but she didn't just fall off the turnip truck. Men only showed up in the middle of the night for two reasons, to tell you someone was dead or to get laid. And seeing that Diego would be a lot less smiley and chipper if he were reporting a death, she guessed it was the latter. Suddenly, she became extremely aware of her teeth. Her whole mouth felt pasty and slimy and generally unclean. She covered her mouth with her hand.

This was not the first time Diego had stopped by "unexpectedly" since the breakup. The first time he had made a late night visit, they had been barely broken up a month and Joanna had still been bloody from the original battle. The wounds were so fresh they hadn't begun to scab over and she was vulnerable as a newborn learning to cry it out. He was a magnificent apparition at her door and she accepted his fumbling, inebriated kiss hungrily, as if she were starving. She clung to him tightly. He was back! He missed her! He loved her! They were barely inside the apartment and hardly made it to the bedroom before he had entered her with a contented moan. They barely spoke during the twenty minute visit that essentially consisted of torn clothing, a lot of groaning and an anti-climatic shudder, at least anti-climatic for Joanna. It was over before it had begun.

Afterwards, as she watched Diego rapidly zip up his stylish blue jeans, tuck in his shirt and lick his fingers to control down a wayward strand of hair, Joanna was embarrassed and ashamed. And when Diego leaned over to kiss her goodbye, she turned her head.

"Oh baby, do not be angry with me," he took her face in his hands and made her look at him, "please?"

"I'm not angry," Joanna lied and succumbed to a slow smile, he was so hard to resist! But as quickly as the apparition had appeared, it was gone, leaving only damp sheets to wash. Joanna wept bitterly when he left, kicking herself for her stupidity and shame, her heart squashed and ruined on the floor yet again.

"I am so sorry to come here unannounced," he paused, "But I miss you. Ever since I ran into you I can not stop thinking about you. I just needed to see you." Diego moved towards her and Joanna realized he was going to try to kiss her or hug her or attempt some sort of physical contact and that absolutely could not happen. She stepped backwards, directly into her ficus plant. It toppled with a crash as Joanna and Diego watched, helpless to intercede.

Joanna struggled to right her plant, straightening the smashed leaves and gathering the spilled soil into her hands.

Diego ignored the mess and walked into the apartment; he sat down on the scruffy thrift-store couch, all the while smoothing down his collar and running his hands through his hair, giving it a gentle fluff.

Joanna looked after him with disbelief, "Diego," she began, tentative, "What are you doing? I haven't invited you to stay and sit." She felt her color rise, "It's the middle of the night! I don't understand what you are really doing here. You need to go."

"Go?" He looked genuinely bewildered.

In his befuddled gaze, Joanna saw something she had never seen before. She saw this selfish and self-centered boy, this deer-in-the-headlights child. Not a man. She puffed up her chest, and like a lion stalking an antelope, Joanna felt how powerful she was. She felt muscle all the way into her toes, and she felt something she hadn't in years. She felt in control, "Yes!" She threw her hands into the air, "Go! Do you not remember that you left me, Diego? That you told me that you didn't like yourself when you were with me? The single worst thing anyone has ever said to me? Does any of this ring a bell?" Joanna's skin felt electric and cold.

"But Joanna, can we not just sit and talk? Can two friends not just sit and talk?"

"Friends? Are we friends now, Diego? When exactly did we become friends? And do 'friends'," Joanna made quotation marks with her hands, "usually stop by in the middle of the night to chat? Of course they don't."

Diego rose to his feet, "Well, if you do not want me to stay..."

"No, no, Diego, we are not playing that game." Joanna shook her finger at him like she was scolding a child, "You are the one who left. Don't try to turn this around to something I did. Because do you know what, Diego? I didn't do anything but love you. And I was very good at that. And you walked out on my love," she paused, breathless, "and now, Diego, now you don't deserve my love."

"Joanna, please let me explain," Diego was begging, "I miss you!"

"Explain? What is there to explain? That you are confused as to why I won't sleep with you? The perfect and fabulous Diego? There's nothing to explain except I'm just not interested. I'm done. I have set my sites higher than you." She tightened the belt on her robe again and looked up into his eyes. This time she didn't see limpid pools of chocolate. This time she saw a big, wet mud puddle. This time, she didn't melt.

Diego, probably the worst actor ever, could not meet her eyes and instead looked at his feet. "I should not have come here tonight," he said quietly pathetic.

Joanna could practically see the script:

Diego, crestfallen, exits the building.

Joanna, triumphant, slams the door behind him screaming, "And I don't like myself when I'm with you, either!"

But instead Joanna crossed the room to open the door and said, "We had a good run, Diego, but it's over now. Goodbye."

Diego, tongue-tied for once, left.

And then she closed the door behind him. She climbed back into her bed, languidly stretched like a contented cat and yawned a terrifically loud lion-yawn. And then Joanna burritoed herself into her comforter and soon fell into a hard, satisfying sleep.

The next morning Joanna woke up before her alarm. She stared at it, mystified. She could not remember a single day in her entire life that she had woken up without some sort of aid. Alarm clock, bullhorn, bucket of water, something. She got up to shower, singing to herself. She strode into work wearing her high-heeled boots, lipstick, and an attitude adjustment, displayed attractively, she thought. She walked with poise and verve. She smiled at her coworkers and winked at Helen, who jumped a little, as if Joanna had stuck out her tongue or something equally rude. Tossing her purse onto her desk, Joanna shrugged off her coat and hung it on the coat rack. She felt invigorated, on top of the world. Whistling quietly, she spun her chair around and sat down, missing the seat just enough so she slid off the side and landed solidly on the ground, on her ass.

"Shit," she said, and threw back her head and laughed. She knew it was going to be a good day.

28

Jamie told her he was ready to do whatever it took to win her back. For starters, he asked her to go to couple's therapy with him, and May couldn't exactly refuse. After she had hurled herself out of her drunken stupor, it was Elsa's number she had reached for. She believed therapy was a healthy way to keep oneself in check, so she was silently pleased Jamie had gone this route, one he had scoffed at on more than one aggravating occasion. Pilates for the outside and therapy for the inside.

But sitting on the couch with her bi-for-a-night husband, facing the moon-faced therapist who was not her familiar Elsa, May felt uncomfortable and nervous. She fingered her platinum, Princess-cut diamond engagement ring, twisting and turning it around her finger.

"So," the therapist, Linda began, "May. I've been working with Jamie for about a month now, and we both thought it was important for you to come in and hear what he has to say, and maybe talk a little about it. Is that ok with you?"

Well, obviously it's ok with me since here I am, thought May, but out loud she said, "Yes."

Linda leaned forward, tucking her rather cute suede flats under her chair, "Good. Very good. And it's important for you to know," May detected a slight Midwestern drawl, "Jamie has been working very hard on getting to the root of this situation. Now it will be up to the two of you to work together to decide what happens next in this relationship."

May nodded, bracing herself for what she was about to hear.

"Jamie, what do you want to say to May?" Linda folded her hands in her lap.

Jamie cleared his throat. "May, First I want to tell you I'm sorry. I'm so so sorry that I did this to you. To us. To Leo. You have known me a long time, since we were kids practically, and you know me better than anyone..."

May interrupted, "I thought I did know you, Jamie."

"You do! You do know me, and that's why I know, or at least I hope I know, that deep down you can find it in your heart to forgive me. Forgive me for being so blind and so stupid and such a fucking schmuck." Jamie used a monogrammed handkerchief to mop some sweat that had sprung onto his forehead.

"What else, Jamie," prodded Linda, "did you want to say to May?"

Jamie turned back to May, "May, I love you. I know I've hurt you terribly, and I'll do whatever you need me to. If you want to divorce me, I'll understand. But I hope you don't, May. I hope you want to see if we can get over this horrible ordeal and try to patch it up. I love you, and I don't want to let you go. I want to work on whatever we need or whatever *I* need to work on. I won't let you down again."

May blinked at this man who was her husband. He was a little chubbier than when they had started dating all those years ago, his softly curled hair was turning a gentle gray around his ears and flecks of silver speckled his short goatee. His eyes looked sunken and tired and when had those crow's feet cropped up in the corners?

"Jamie, you told me you might be bisexual; that this was about your identity and not just about sex..."

"May, that's the absolute truth; I hadn't desired anyone else since you and I got together! And that's the truth! Not in a dozen years have I taken more than a glance at anyone else. So maybe my ego wouldn't let me believe it could just be plain, ordinary, run-of-the-mill... horniness."

"Jamie, are you telling me you put our marriage in jeopardy because of a confused dick? For one night of strange?" May asked him, incredulous, "Because frankly, that is so fucking pathetic!"

Jamie sighed and slumped a little on the couch, "Pathetic is the word for it. I thought I was above my penis making decisions for me. Apparently I was wrong. I was stupid and wrong," he turned to her again, "May, I'm not trying to make excuses for my actions. They were my actions and I'm taking responsibility for them. I'm just asking you, I'm begging you, to believe me.

I've never stopped loving you, not for a second. I just fucked up." His eyes searched hers, and for the first time in a long time they connected, locked together and she really saw those eyes she was so familiar with, "I made such a stupid, idiotic mistake. May, I miss you and I love you and I want to come home. Please can I come home?"

May pulled her gaze away as confusing thoughts whirled through her head, she couldn't see straight. She didn't know what to say. She opened her mouth and nothing came out.

She thought back to the session she had just yesterday with Elsa:

"I want to get back to the fact that this affair was with a man," Elsa prodded.

"Why do you want to get back to that?" May was impatient.

"I just want to make sure we're not missing anything here. So not only did your husband sleep with someone else, but the someone else was a man..."

May interrupted her, "I know it's weird, but I don't really understand why that's what you are focusing on. I feel like this is about the betrayal, the infidelity. Why should his sex make a difference to me? He cheated, that's what I care about."

Elsa leaned forward slightly, her elbows on her knees, "The reason I keep coming back to it is that a man is something you could never possibly be." She paused, "I wonder if you may feel 'how can I possibly compete with a man?'"

May paused and thought about it. How could she compete with a man? But really, how could she compete with anyone? She couldn't make herself younger or shorter; she couldn't change the essence of who she was, her opinions and passions. There were so many things she couldn't be, and frankly wouldn't be for Jamie.

"I don't need to compete with anyone. This is not a competition to me. The only person who I'm going to be is me. He can take it or leave it."

Elsa had studied her intently and then finally said, "Ok, May. I see your point."

Linda cleared her throat and interrupted her reverie, and May remembered she was in a totally different therapy session, "May, Jamie has just said a lot of emotionally-charged things to you. Maybe you need to ruminate on what he's told you before we can really discuss and dissect it. How does that sound to you?"

"OK." May said, grateful for the reprieve. She didn't know yet what she wanted, her mind was reeling.

Linda leaned forward and patted her on the knee, "You've done a very brave thing, coming here today. This is not easy stuff," she smiled, exposing her laugh lines.

May stood with her husband outside Linda's office, discreetly located amidst accountants and lawyers.

"So, what do we do now?" May asked him.

"What do you want to do?" Jamie put on his leather coat.

"I want coffee. Can we go get a cup of coffee? Together, I mean? Can we do that?"

"Coffee? Of course we can," he smiled, "let's go."

May met Daniel for lunch, their regular spot.

After they ordered, Daniel told her Lily had made a trip to the emergency room. She needed stitches in her finger due to an archery accident.

"How does one require stitches from playing archery?"

"This is your mother we're talking about here, May. You should be surprised the injury is so minor."

"Excellent point. Should I call her?"

"No, she's mortified; don't tell her I told you, she'll kill me. Anyway, what's up with you?"

May told him about the therapy session and about coffee afterwards.

"What do you think you're going to do, May?" Daniel asked.

"I don't know yet. I keep going back and forth. I'm so confused! I never thought I was the kind of woman who would take a man back who cheated. But Dad, I believe him when he says it was a mistake. I believe him and I love him. Am I an idiot? Am I being stupid?"

"May, the last thing anyone would ever call you is stupid. What does your gut tell you?" Daniel said.

"I've been with him for eleven years, Dad. Eleven years and we've barely even fought. We've had this wonderful life I've probably taken advantage of," she looked out the window at the streams of students hurrying to grab lunch between classes, "I've trusted him all these years, Dad. Do I throw all of that away because he's human? My gut says he fucked up and he knows he fucked up," May pulled her mane into a ponytail and then let it go, letting the sunset swirl back around her shoulders, "but what if I'm kidding myself?"

"I can't tell you what to do here. I can tell you to be careful and I can tell you I'll support whatever decision you make," he paused to thank the waitress dropping their orders on the table, "May, have I ever told you about Irene?"

May frowned; she seemed to recall something about an Irene, a snide comment from her mother perhaps? "I don't know, Dad, seems familiar..."

Daniel cut his burger in half and took a big bite. He chewed thoughtfully and took a swig of beer. "Well, maybe this is a good time to tell you."

So Daniel launched into his tale. Along with a sea of others from the East Coast, he left his parent's house for UC Berkeley in the 60s. They moved for freedom, for change, for college. It was a fascinating time to live and go to school in Berkeley, right in the middle of everything.

"Dad," May interrupted, "Please, I'm well aware of the wonderment of the 60s..."

Daniel waggled his hand to shush her, he was getting to it.

He met Irene at a co-op health food store. He was looking for something, *anything* edible amid the weird, foreign looking vegetables and unsavory looking meat-free options. "You've got to remember May; I had never even seen an avocado before I came to California!"

May nodded, she knew, she knew.

So Irene, who was working in the deli, made him a sandwich. Evidently this was the best sandwich Daniel had eaten to date. It had falafel, it had avocado, it had sprouts, it had tomatoes and cucumbers, and it had tahini. The whole delicious mess was tucked inside warm pita bread that crackled when he bit into it. Daniel described the sandwich as if he had eaten it moments ago and was licking the remaining crumbs from his fingers, rather than thirty-five years ago.

"Got it, someone named Irene made you a really great sandwich."

Daniel drank another long drink of his beer, "Patience, May!" he admonished.

So enamored by the sandwich, Daniel began frequenting the shop daily between his morning classes and his afternoon job. Irene always had the sandwich ready for him when he arrived. And one day, he found a note rolled into his napkin. It said, "I'd like to see you eat this sandwich naked."

"Dad!" May nearly spit out her wine. "Eyew!"

"What? I was a cute guy back then. What's wrong with someone wanting to see me naked?"

"Dad, way too much information..."

So Daniel invited Irene to "have a sandwich together" the next day. The one night stand grew into an absurdly fantastic relationship. Irene was the quintessential flower child, complete with the appropriately tie-dyed wardrobe, hair flowing to her butt and lack of bra. She lived in a large ramshackle house where people came and went, worked and paid as they could. An enthusiastic gardener, she grew vegetables and flowers and pot. Irene introduced Daniel to a whole new world of dashikis, anti-war demonstrations and drugs. She made vegetarian stir-fries with vegetables Daniel had never seen before. She baked carrot-walnut bread they ate and sold at peace rallies. Daniel tried his first tab of acid with Irene, on the garage roof of the ramshackle house, and she held his hand and talked him down as he hallucinated skeletons and snakes dancing in the sky. She was the first person he had ever told about his violent father, and his troubled upbringing. Irene was an excellent listener, folding Daniel into her arms so he wouldn't be embarrassed by his tears.

Daniel was intrigued by her lifestyle and awestruck by her total freedom and he soon fell in love with this offbeat beauty. They were together through Daniel's whole undergraduate schooling, and into graduate school.

"Wait, I thought you were with Mom during grad school," interrupted May.

"I proposed to Irene during grad school."

May's eyes nearly popped out of her head, "Holy shit, Dad! Are you kidding me?"

"Uh, nope," Daniel drank some more of his beer and

he sighed heavily. "Irene and I were engaged. We were planning our wedding. My nonconformist lover became strangely traditional during the planning ...in any case, I proposed, met her parents, the whole nine yards. And then, one day, Lily was hired at the co-op."

May inhaled sharply, "And you dropped Irene like a hot potato?"

"And I dropped Irene like a hot potato."

May was stunned; she didn't know what to say, she simply stared, open-mouthed at her father, her lunch forgotten.

"I met Lily, and it was all over. I fell, head over heels for her. We went to dinner one night and talked until dawn. She was everything I had been looking for, that I didn't even know I was looking for. She was the one. Lily and I married within months and Joanna came along the year following," he sighed sadly, shaking his head, "I broke Irene's heart. Marrying your mother was the best decision I ever made. But I wish this divine, brilliant woman hadn't been a casualty."

May was quiet, letting her dad's confession sink in. Daniel, her beloved dad, this pillar of a man who she loved and respected maybe more than any other human being, had cheated. Finally she said, "Dad, I don't even know what to say. That is so intense."

He nodded, "Yeah, intense is a good word for it."

"Do you hear from her, do you know what she's doing?"

"I did, I kept tabs on her. Berkeley's a small town and

I knew the circles she ran in. Last I heard she was married with kids," he paused and wrinkled his forehead, "hell, she probably has Grandkids by now!" he shook his head, "She's living in the City, as far as I know," he exhaled and reached to take May's French-manicured hand, "May, I'm not a bad person, but I made a choice that affected another human being in a profound and heart wrenching way. A human being I truly loved," He looked into her eyes, "Jamie isn't a bad person either; I don't believe that for a minute, but he too made a choice, and he made a bad one. The good news is Jamie is right. People make mistakes, and if you decide to take him back you better believe he will spend the rest of his life making up for this mistake. I'll be sure of that."

"I love him, Dad, I've always loved him. He's my Ken."

"I know, Barbie," he smiled, "and you need to do what's right for you, and I think you already know what that is."

29

Bookstore Guy's name was David and he was very nice, and since Delia had clued him in Joanna was single and finally ready to mingle he pursued her unabashedly. Delia reminded Joanna a date didn't mean she had to marry him. But she needed to get out there and meet new people and this was the way to do it. And he was very nice. And rather cute, what with his hazel eyes and brown curly hair and glasses. And he had good taste in books. So that was a pretty promising trifecta.

Every Saturday David stepped up his game. The first week he brought Joanna a single perfect dahlia. He handed it to her with a flourish as she was leaving the bookstore with a grin. She couldn't help but smile back. The following week he presented her with an autographed copy of Rose Levy Beranbaum's "The Cake Bible". *Very well played*, Joanna thought.

The following Saturday, he wrote her a song:

"Oh Joanna!" (Sung to the tune of "Oh Susanna!")
Oh Joanna!

Please have a date with me!
We'll walk, we'll talk, we'll sit and gawk
Underneath a tree.
Oh Joanna!
Please oh please say yes
I'll take you out to dinner and
I won't spill on your dress
Oh Joanna!
Please have a date with me!
We can go to a museum and
On Tuesdays they are free

Both Delia and Bruno agreed the song should have been the clincher and took to humming it around the office each time they passed her desk, but Joanna wasn't quite there yet. She was enjoying being pursued, it was good for her decrepit ego. And it was fun to see what was next up his sleeve...

The next week, David was conspicuously absent from the Bookstore.

Joanna inquired of his absence to the prominently pierced and tattooed replacement, who vaguely told her David was sick that day, or maybe someone else was sick and he was taking care of them, or something. Joanna was surprised to realize she felt...disappointed she wouldn't see him.

Delia teased, "Oh, you are so sad he's not here! How sweet is that? Or are you just missing his super-cool gifts?"

Joanna rolled her eyes at Delia. She was trying not

to stare at the teenager's enormous tongue ring, which Joanna found to be the ugliest and least practical of the facial piercings. Why on earth would anyone find this attractive? Not only was she slurring, sounding slightly drunk, but she kept playing with it, impulsively biting it between her lips. She asked the young woman, "If I leave him a note, will you make sure he gets it?"

Joanna wasn't 100% convinced the grunt of a reply she received was a "yes" but she pulled a scrap of paper from her bag and wrote:

Hi David,
Missed you today. Hope you are up and about shortly.
Fondly, Joanna.

The following Saturday, Joanna was surprised to find she felt both relieved and happy to see David when she walked through the door of the Bookstore. "Hi," she said, "you're back."

"I am. Thanks for your sweet note," he smiled. Joanna couldn't help but notice how the corners of his lip curled up rather adorably and how the smile lit up his face.

"Are you feeling better?"

"It actually wasn't me who was sick, it was my nephew. But thanks for asking. And I have something for you," he extended a small, fragrant pastry bag to her and she peered inside.

This week's gift was an absolute show stopper. It was

hands-down the best *pain au chocolat* she had ever eaten. It was still slightly warm with inconceivably crisp yet tender buttery layers and intensely bitter chocolate. It was heaven in a pastry. Joanna immediately agreed to go out with him. Anyone who knew the whereabouts to score such excellent baked goods was worthy of a date. But before she would go anywhere with him, she insisted on knowing where he bought the ethereal pastry.

The bakery was tiny, with a faded blue awning reading simply: *Sweet*. The little bakery stood practically unnoticed on a side street, tucked between a florist and a tchotchke shop, one of those places you never understand how they stay in business selling the occasional bobblehead or bubble-gum flavored condoms. She swung open the door and a bell tinkled to announce her arrival. The smells of yeast, coffee and chocolate smacked her full in the face. The shop was meticulously clean. Along the length of the small room there were three bar stools and an antique-looking espresso machine. Large empty baskets were lined up along the back counter, apparently to hold bread which had sadly already been sold. The modest pastry case was also nearly empty but Joanna spied a *pain au chocolat*, what looked to be an almond croissant and a gorgeous Florentine cookie.

A woman's voice called from the back, "Hi there! Sorry! I'll be right with you!" From the back of the bakery toddled a 50ish woman almost as wide as she was tall. Her hair was pulled into a loose bun with gray hairs wildly straying and she wore an ample, open smile on her plump, pink face. "Although there's really nothing left, it's a pretty sorry looking situation in here. You just take it all. It's time to close up anyway."

Joanna looked at her watch, it was 10:15. That seemed a little premature in the closure department.

"Oh I know, I know," the woman continued, bagging up the three pastries, "it's a weird time to close. But there's no reason to stay open if there's nothing to sell!" She handed the bag over the counter to Joanna's outstretched hands. Joanna's mouth was practically watering.

"You make the best *pain au chocolat* I've ever tasted," Joanna told her, "the texture is just perfect." Joanna handed a $20 dollar bill over the counter.

"Oh no charge, Honey. It's the end of the day so it's on me. Besides, you are saving me from eating them myself so I should probably pay you!" She patted her square middle, and gave a resonant, generous laugh.

It seemed like the beginning of the day to Joanna, but she didn't want to argue. Instead she reached into her bag to pull out the almond croissant. She pulled the edge away to peer inside and then took a bite. The buttery pastry crackled, the almonds on the outside were sweet and toasty, a lovely contrast to the rich and creamy center of the croissant. She rolled her eyes in ecstasy, "Oh my God, this is delicious. May I ask...is this almond paste or marzipan?"

The woman blinked at her, "Well, funny you should ask, Honey, it's both. I find the marzipan to be a little sweet and the almond paste a little too thick so I whip the two together. I think the combo works great, don't you think?"

"I do think. This is spectacular."

The bell tinkled again and a man ran inside, absolutely frantic.

"Oh no! Am I too late?" He practically wailed, "Marjorie, tell me I'm not too late." He was rather pathetic.

"I'm sorry, Dan, its Sunday! I didn't expect you. I didn't put anything aside for you."

Joanna watched the exchange, rapt, as she ate each crackling, tender morsel of the croissant.

"I know," he slumped into a bar stool, defeated, "I was just having a crummy morning so I thought..." his voice trailed off.

"Let me see if there's anything in the back I may have missed, I'll check." Marjorie was off, waddling in her clogs, her ample bottom swaying under her peasant skirt. Dan turned to Joanna.

"What did you get?" he asked her wistfully, swiveling back and forth on the stool.

She told him.

"Oh! Those Florentines!" Dan spun the stool around and looked up as if the Florentines were dropped straight from heaven, and he was hoping one would miraculously land on the counter in front of him, "This stuff is better than crack. I'm totally addicted. The almond-tea cakes are my favorites. Have you had them?"

Joanna shook her head "No" as Marjorie came back

around the corner empty handed; Dan's face rose and then fell.

"You know what, I'd be happy to share, I don't need to be greedy." Joanna said, "Which would you like, the Florentine or the *pain au chocolat*?"

"Really? You'd do that?" His eyes widened and his face lit up.

"Well, sure, you are obviously desperate, which would you like?"

Dan hesitated, this was clearly an enormous decision, "May I have...the Florentine? No! The *pain au chocolat?* No, no, the Florentine. The Florentine." He scrunched up his face, and hunched up his shoulders, as if to shield against the possibility of her saying no.

"Is that your final answer?" she asked.

"Yes, yes, absolutely the Florentine."

"Well, I don't know..." she joked.

Again, his face fell.

Joanna marveled at how much power she wielded! "Kidding, just kidding, here you go, it's yours, enjoy." She handed him the cookie.

Dan looked the cookie over as if appraising the color on a fine wine. Satisfied, he leaned in and took a whiff. Finally, he took a big bite. He chewed slowly, savoring the nuts and caramel and chocolate. "Now that," he paused, "is perfection in a cookie." Turning his attention to Joanna he asked, "What's your name, little lady?" A rather funny thing to say, as Dan was maybe ten years Joanna's junior.

"Joanna."

"Well, Joanna, you just made my day. You are an angel from heaven." He clasped her hands sincerely, "Thank you!" He gave her a little bow and then turned to Marjorie, "Marjorie, see you tomorrow."

Joanna and Marjorie erupted with laughter as they watched him bound out the door like an excited toddler, cookie in hand. His gait was very similar to Leo's. Tears sprang up in the corner of Marjorie's eyes which she wiped with the corner of her apron.

"Come tomorrow, Honey, I'll save you a Florentine." She paused, then cocked her head to the side, "Or how about if you come into the back right now and I'll show you how to bake them."

Joanna's hand stopped mid-way to bringing the *pain au chocolat* to her mouth, "Are you serious?"

"Sure, sure, come on back. I need to get started for tomorrow and it's not often someone even knows the difference between marzipan and almond paste so I suspect you know your way around a kitchen." She smiled warmly and held the white swinging door, separating the front of the shop from the kitchen, open for Joanna.

Joanna put the pain au chocolat back in the pastry bag and without hesitation, walked through the open door.

Joanna spent the rest of the glorious day in Marjorie's pocket-sized kitchen. Marjorie taught her how to feel the croissant dough with the heels of her hands to determine whether it needed more flour or water, how to knead it into a smooth, elastic ball and what it should look like when properly proofed. Next they grated frozen butter into delicate little strands and layered the butter with the dough, pressing them together just so, to produce the flaky, delicate layers of tomorrow's croissants. She learned to shape the slim Florentine's so they formed a perfect, golden brown disc, ready to be dipped in chocolate; and how to temper the chocolate just so it crackled, but didn't shatter as you bit into the cookie. "Nothing worse than chocolate on your white shirt while you're indulging in a cookie on your lunch break!" Marjorie laughed.

Joanna learned to expertly whip egg whites, creating frothy meringue for the almond tea cakes, folding it gently into powder-fine ground nuts so as not to deflate its fluffy texture. They made a half dozen types of cookie dough and cupcake batter and several flavors of icing. Marjorie's knowledge was cosmic, and she was happy to share it, and Joanna was an enthusiastic and gracious beneficiary. Several exhausting and exhilarating hours later, Marjorie announced they were done for the day.

"Thank you, Marjorie; this was exactly what I needed." Joanna removed her flour-spattered apron. "You have no idea."

"Well, I know a thing or two about baking therapy, I suppose. It's the only type of therapy that's ever worked for me."

30

Joanna called May on Sunday morning.

"Hi, what are you doing?"

May looked guiltily down at the coffee and croissant, as if Joanna had super-sonic vision and could see what she was eating through the phone. "Uh, having some breakfast. Leo is out with Jamie."

"Excellent! Then you're free to go on a walk with me."

"A what?"

"A walk. Some fresh air, nice conversation. A walk! I'm sure you are familiar."

May grinned to herself, "Yes, Jo I'm familiar with the concept of a walk. Are you aware that a walk constitutes exercise? My understanding was you didn't subscribe to fanatical religions."

"Ha ha. Come on, May, I'm feeling like exercise would be good for me. Are you in or are you leaving me to my own devices?"

May sighed heavily; she of course, had already exercised early that morning. It had been a particularly brutal session with her personal trainer. Ivan had literally kicked her softer, wider ass. But it was Joanna so she said, "OK, I'm in."

They met at the trailhead, May in state-of-the-art walking shoes and a practical expensive windbreaker, Joanna in ancient Nikes and a sweatshirt.

"Joanna, are you sure those are safe?" she indicated the dilapidated-looking shoes with a skeptical look down her nose, "They look like they were run over by a bus." May stretched out her tight calf muscles.

"Well, I found them wedged in the back of my broom closet. But they work, it's not like I've worn them for vigorous exercise. They're just a wee bit smushed. They'll do the job. Let's go!" Joanna bounded up the hill in an unexpected burst of energy.

May finished her stretch and needed to jog a bit to keep up with her, "What are you on today?"

"I don't know, I just feel good today. Happy. Alive!"

Twenty minutes in and Joanna's pace had slowed considerably. The sun was beating down on them and the sisters stripped off their outer layers and tied them around their waists.

"So," Joanna was slightly panting, "guess who stopped by the other night."

"Hmmm. Stopped by. I'm a little scared to guess..."

"Diego. And it was more like the middle of the night..."

"What the fudge? Who the heck does he think he is?" May was sputtering, and then she stopped walking, "Oh God, Joanna, please don't tell me you..."

"No no no, of course I didn't sleep with him! I'm not that stupid." May resumed the walk, quiet.

"Really May, I swear I didn't. I know I did once but that was a long time ago..." Joanna shook her head, banishing the memory, "Remember, we had just broken up and I still thought maybe by some miracle we would get back together. Now, I wouldn't get back together with that catastrophe if you paid me."

"Thank God," May said, "So, what did happen?"

Joanna smiled, "Absolutely nothing."

"Nothing?" May was still skeptical.

"Nothing, nada, zilch. Oh, except I kicked him out on his gorgeous but sorry ass."

"You did not!"

"I did so!" Joanna gulped some air; the incline lined with wild blackberry bushes was shortening her breath, "I didn't succumb to his wily ways, I told him to leave, I was done with him and it was over. You would have been so proud."

May stopped walking, "Jo, you are the bomb! Good for you!"

Joanna took advantage to sit heavily on a bench, reaching over for a dark berry and popping it into her mouth. "I'm pretty proud of myself. But honestly, it wasn't that hard. I know I deserve better than Diego. I'm done with him." She picked another berry and stood up, "Really. It's over. I feel good about it."

They curved around the blue lake, slowing to watch a heron circle and then dive for a fish. Geese flapped as they passed.

"I actually ran into Diego the other day," said May.

"You did?" Joanna's breathing had slowed from the

brief rest, but she hoped the end was in sight, this exercise business was exhausting.

"Yeah, I was having lunch in Berkeley and there he was. He was there with a new girlfriend. Vanessa. Pretty girl. Terrible handshake. One of those limp-wristed things. I hate those."

Joanna was less interested in the handshake than the girl, "A new girlfriend, huh."

"Yup."

Joanna was quiet and May wondered if she had made an error in judgment. Maybe Joanna was not quite ready to hear about Diego's thriving love life, although she certainly shouldn't be surprised. People like Diego needed women around them. They needed someone to constantly feed and care for and attend to their massive egos, and that took a woman with a lot of time, a lot of patience, and not a lot of brains. Although, May rationalized, that probably wasn't fair. Her sister was awfully brainy; she'd just been temporarily insane during this relationship. Evidently, temporary insanity was the defense du jour.

"Well," said Joanna, planting her foot up on a bench to tie her shoelace, "I hope you warned her," she looked over her shoulder at May and smiled.

31

"Miller, Stewart and Sons, this is Joanna; how might I direct your call?"

"Hi Sweetie, it's Mom, how are you?" Lily began.

Joanna involuntarily winced at the sound of her mother's voice and then instantly felt guilty. She relaxed her tone, reminding herself that her mother was just trying to mother, "Hi Mom, I'm fine, how are you?"

"Oh fine, fine. I was just calling to say hello, see what's new, see how you are."

So here was yet something else grating about her mother. She didn't seem to understand Joanna had a regular 9-5 job which required her to actually work during normal, regular work hours. Now, to her credit, as a nurse Lily had worked a variety of odd hours, including a brief stint on the graveyard shift, and as a professor, Daniel taught the occasional evening class and was therefore home during the day, and then May, well, May hadn't had a regular full-time job ever. But Joanna, since college, had worked in the standard business world along with the bulk of society, and she found it endlessly irritating that it never occurred to Lily that she couldn't just "sit and catch up" on the phone during the work day. Now, honestly, Joanna had no problem sitting on the phone with anyone else, chatting about anything to pass the time from sports to weather to a celebrity's latest hi-jinx, but with her mother it just irked her to no end.

"Nothing really new to report, Mom."

Lily got right to the point: "So what's going on with May and all the bread?"

"Huh? The bread? What are you talking about?"

"Joanna, don't play dumb with me. May is not acting like herself; she's eating all this bread, *and* she's looking a little thick. Something is going on! So, tell me..." she paused, probably for dramatic effect, "Is Leo getting a sibling?" Lily could hardly contain her excitement.

Joanna involuntarily let out a laugh, "A sibling? No Mom, absolutely not, May is not pregnant." *Although she did admit to herself that her mother was correct, she wasn't thick necessarily, but definitely...fuller.*

"Well, something is going on with her." Lily was clearly disappointed. Although Lily never imagined herself to be such a traditionalist, she yearned for more grandchildren. She was surprised to see how happily she fit the stereotypical spoiler of a Grandmama. But she also wanted May to experience the greatest joy there was, having a daughter. And she especially wanted this for Joanna, her strong and competent eldest who so deserved happiness...

"Mom? Are you still there? It seemed like you were about to say something else."

Lily cleared her throat, remembering they were discussing May, "I've never seen her so blasé about her waistline! Frankly, I've never seen her waistline expand at all, besides when she was pregnant with Leo and even then it was practically imperceptible. I can't believe you haven't noticed!"

"Well, Mom, there are many more important things in life than the narrowness of one's waist, you know."

"Oh, I didn't mean anything about *your* waistline, Dear, we all know you are much more evolved than we are."

"I'm sorry, was that supposed to be sarcastic?" Joanna asked, irritated.

"No, no, Dear, it's just that you don't care about these things and it's so enlightening, so carefree. I admire you for it, really I do!" Lily backpedaled.

Joanna sighed and continued to work as Lily continued to yak. Joanna was an expert at the non-conversation with Lily, having perfected the art over many years.

Blessedly, another line buzzed in, "Mom, I have to go, my other line is ringing, bye!" she hung up quickly before Lily had a chance to protest.

"Miller, Stewart and Sons, this is Joanna; how might I direct your call?"

"It's me."

"Oh my God, May, I just hung up on Mom, and guess what she just asked me..."

32

May sat at the counter at *Sweet*, savoring her cappuccino and oatmeal cookie. She had begun to switch it up a little, steadily working her way through Marjorie's delectable bakery case: The heavenly cookies and flaky croissants, the muffins bursting with fruit and nuts, the sweet cupcakes and crisp, chewy baguettes; all were delicious, although she tended to return to the oatmeal cookie. It had a satisfying chew she adored, and she had convinced herself that it was practically health food, not to mention helping to keep her regular.

May enjoyed the hustle and bustle of the tiny bakery, the regulars whose orders Marjorie had bagged long before they reached the counter. She had become a regular herself mid to late morning when the bakery was usually close to closing, which could be anytime between nine and noon, depending. Once she had arrived to tragically see the doors locked and the: "Sorry! Sold out!" sign displayed. She asked Marjorie about increasing her production in order to increase business, not to mention prevent the mournful late arrivals salivating at the door.

Marjorie had laughed like a hyena, slapping her plump thighs, "Now why on earth would I do that? I work a short day and make a good living, its absolute perfection!" May never saw anyone else working in the front of the bakery, unless you counted Marjorie's husband, Hal, who would jump behind the counter to refill his coffee cup or grab another muffin before being swatted by his territorial wife. There was also a daughter Marjorie had mentioned who helped out on weekends, although May had never seen her. Occasionally she glimpsed a few passing shadows in the back, one of which looked remarkably like Joanna, so much so she had done a double-take mid-bite.

May scooped the last bit of cappuccino froth up with the end of her cookie and popped it into her mouth, savoring the last bite and talking herself out of ordering another. Instead she asked, "Marjorie, may I ask you a hypothetical question?"

Marjorie was brushing crumbs out of the empty case, "You can ask me anything, whether I answer or not is a different story entirely."

May chuckled. "What would you do if Hal cheated on you?"

Marjorie removed her head from inside the case to look at May with an unadulterated view, "This is your hypothetical question, now is it?"

"Purely hypothetical."

"Well, I'd beat the living hell out of him is what I'd do," Marjorie went back to cleaning up the case.

May sighed, "Yeah, that's what I figured you'd say,"

She hopped down from her barstool and pushed her cappuccino cup across the counter, "see you tomorrow, Marjorie." Marjorie waved a goodbye.

Joanna was spending as much time as she could at *Sweet*. Each day that Joanna returned, Marjorie began the day with: "How about if I pay you today?" And each day Joanna replied with "Nope, not today but thanks for the offer." Joanna was getting an education one just couldn't put a price tag on, and she adored every minute of it. She even relished the aching back, sore legs and especially the burning arms which she was convinced would result in a totally cut physique. Each night she sipped a glass of wine and read her book while happily soaking in an Epsom salt bath to help soothe the satisfying pain.

She began going in before dawn, well before her work day at Miller, Stewart and Son's began to help Marjorie bake the breads and pastries that had been waiting overnight. Since she was so chummy with Helen these days she boldly asked if she could change her work hours, and Helen amazingly agreed to the change, although some of Joanna's co-workers were vocally irritated they were stuck on phone duty in her absence. So now on Tuesdays and Thursdays she stayed at the bakery until nine in the morning and stayed into the evening at her real job to make up the time. She went to the bakery on weekends and worked in the back while Marjorie and her daughter, Emily tended to the crush of customers. Joanna preferred the quiet chaos of the kitchen to the pandemonium of the shop, finding it enormously satisfying to whip up a buttercream to frost a quick dozen cupcakes or pull the last baguettes from the oven while enveloped in flour and butter. She worked with Anita and Esteban, the Spanish-speaking brother and sister team who had been working for Margie since the week *Sweet* had opened. Despite the language barrier, they quickly familiarized Joanna with the ins and outs of the bakery and they soon worked together like a well-oiled machine.

The morning she met Hal, Marjorie's husband, Joanna was juggling a tray of almond croissants and a basket of carrot muffins when she inadvertently bumped a pan. Unsure if hot water had sloshed into her slowly melting chocolate, she peered anxiously into the double-boiler, searching for the tell-tale graininess of seized chocolate. She knew it wasn't the end of the world if the chocolate seized, she could use it for something else later but she had intended to dip the last batch of Florentines before the end of the morning rush. She suspected she was going to need to trash the batch and start again when a booming voice came from the back door scaring the crap out of her: "Hey Marje, you back here, Sweet Cheeks? Oh hey, you're not Marje, you must be Joanna! I'm Hal!" the barrel-chested man put out a hand to shake and then realized Joanna's were occupied, "How about you unload those on me, I'll bring 'em to the front so you can work on yer chocolate situation there," he indicated the gloppy, grainy chocolate mess.

"Shit! I mean, darn it!"

"Hell, don't worry about my delicate ears, Sweetheart, you've met Marjorie right?" he winked and whisked the baked goods into the front of the shop while Joanna tossed the bowl in the sink to start again.

The kitchen finally restored to calm, with Florentine's properly dipped and cooling, Joanna went to the front of the shop to have a more proper introduction to Hal.

He was drinking a cup of coffee and eating a *pain au chocolat*, "Well, there she is," he smiled warmly at her.

"So, I see you met Hal," said Marjorie.

"Yes, sorry I was so rude, things got a little hairy back there," Joanna extended her hand towards him and then realized the smear of chocolate across the back of it, "Jeez, I'm a mess today!" she wiped it on her apron and tried again.

Hal was big in every way, his smile was enormous and his laugh hearty and abundant. Joanna never considered Marjorie would be the quiet one in the relationship until she got to know Hal. He was telling a story, and although Joanna missed the beginning, she was laughing along with everyone by the end. He was so engaging, a natural story-teller with a deep, melodious voice and a terrific sense of comic timing. His eyes twinkled like Santa Claus.

As Joanna surveyed the pair, she understood how Marjorie had fallen in love with him, his gregariousness was easily contagious. And they had an easy, companionable way about them, the way couples of many years had. The same comfort May and Jamie had.

“So my Margie is pretty impressed with you, Joanna. Says you’re a natural at this baking stuff,” he nodded a yes to Marjorie as she offered him more coffee.

Joanna grinned at the compliment, “I love working here.”

“It seems more like volunteer work, or maybe slave labor,” Marjorie began.

Joanna stopped making her latte to interrupt, “Marjorie!”

“I wish you’d let me pay you, Joanna, you’ve become such a huge help to me...”

“I feel like I’m supposed to be here, it’s become like a second home,” she sipped her latte, “you can’t pay someone to be home.”

“The girl has a point,” said Hal.

“Oh shut up, Hal, you are not helping,” Marjorie swatted at him and he ducked to avoid the blow.

33

Joanna was excited to see Mark, it had been too long. But mostly she couldn't wait to see Mason, an adorable little mini-Mark with flaming red hair and eyes flecked with gold.

She hadn't told anyone about the bakery, not even May. It felt too private, like in an instant it could disappear and she would go back to her same boring life. She knew Mark was the person to tell, he would really understand what it meant to her. Mark was a different kind of confidant than May. Maybe it was because they had been intimate with each other for all those years that they had such a special closeness, whatever the reason, she was eager to share her new life.

She wound her car into the hills of Marin, where Mark and his family lived in an unassuming ranch-style house in a deeply wooded area. The location was equidistant from the University where Mark taught and Susan's veterinary clinic - and a wonderland for a small boy, with ample land to explore, streams to investigate and rock piles to navigate. Susan planted rows of neat vegetables;

tomatoes, lettuces and squash flourished in the full sun. A magnificent butterfly garden with bright orange marigold, swaying milkweed and curling purple passion vine climbed the backyard fence, turning their backyard into a wonderful and peaceful sanctuary.

Joanna grabbed the large basket of treats she had assembled, with something for everybody: peanut-butter chocolate-chip cookies for Mark, pistachio-anise biscotti for Susan, snickerdoodles for Mason, almond croissants, carrot muffins and baguette for everyone.

Mark emerged from the house, Larry curling around his ankles. He took the basket from Joanna with one hand and pulled her into a hug with the other. He kissed the top of her head, "I'm so happy to see beautiful you!" he murmured into her hair.

Joanna pulled back slightly to look at Mark's face, "I'm so happy to see beautiful you too."

"Joanna!" Susan materialized, wiping her hands on a chili-pepper kitchen-towel which she tossed over her shoulder. She kissed Joanna and pulled her into an embrace, "Look at you! You look terrific!"

"Jo, what the heck is in here? It weighs a ton," Mark complained, rifling through the basket, "Oh, dude, this is a basket of yumminess!"

"Enough of you adults already. Where's Mason?"

"He's out back," Mark was already munching on a muffin.

"Mark! We're about to eat lunch!" chastised Susan.

"Dude, it's carrot, it's totally healthy, right JoJo?"

Susan snapped the kitchen towel at his butt as they all went into the house. Mark and Susan had put tons of elbow-grease into the inside of their home as they had the backyard. They lay hardwood floors, painted every last wall and tiled the kitchen and bathrooms. Mark probably would have lived with the crackled yellow paint and lazed around on the old green carpet forever but Susan was a doer, so she threatened divorce to get him motivated.

Mason was playing with a half dozen trucks in a large sandbox in the shade of an oak tree, smashing them together with much fanfare. Joanna couldn't get over how much he looked liked Mark, the red curls an obvious match, but also the deep set of his eyes, the angular jaw, and his thoughtful gestures mimicked his old man. In particular, the way he reached around the back of his neck and rubbed his opposite ear.

"Yep, I know, he's like a teeny-tiny Mark. Hard-headed like him too," Susan teased, "Hey Mase, come over and say hi to Joanna."

Mason looked up to inspect Joanna thoughtfully, and then went back to playing with his trucks.

"Well, apparently you are just not that interesting. Can we eat?" Mark asked hopefully.

"Yes, my darling bottomless pit, we can eat," Susan started back towards the house.

"Let me help," Joanna insisted, following her through the sliding glass door into the living room, "I brought a few baguettes."

"Perfect, we're having a salmon salad so that will be great."

They gathered the salad, fruit, bread, wine and water and brought the feast out into the backyard. Mark had joined Mason in the sandbox and Mason was busily burying his dad's feet.

"Mason, please come eat some lunch," said Susan.

Mason dutifully came sniffing around the table. Mark unearthed his feet and lifted Mason onto one of the chairs. He handed him a chunk of salmon and a piece of peeled apple. Mason chewed happily and then said, "Cookie!"

Mark cracked up, "Yup, Joanna is the one who bakes the terrific cookies. And she brought some for *after* lunch."

Mason thought this over and then smiled a big fishy grin at Joanna.

"Yea! I got a smile!"

Mark ripped off a piece of baguette and passed the rest to Susan. He sunk his teeth into the bread, scattering bits of crunchy crust into his plate and lap. "Wow, this bread is incredible. So, Joanna, tell us what's new," he leaned over his plate to begin working on his salad.

"Well," Joanna finished chewing a bite of salmon, "I'm working at a bakery. I baked that baguette."

"No shit!" Mark corrected himself before Susan had a chance to shoot him a look, "I mean, no way! What about your job at blah blah and blah?"

Joanna giggled, nearly choked on a bite of salmon,

"I'm still working at that heck-hole. The bakery gig is more of an apprenticeship. I'm going in before work and on weekends. It's awesome. I'm working with this incredible woman. She's teaching me everything she knows, an entire pastry-school education. It's been a totally amazing experience."

"Wow, Jojo, you just lit up! Did you find your Nirvana?"

Joanna sighed, "Dude, I did."

34

May felt ridiculous, and surprisingly nervous, dating her own husband, but Linda suggested that part of re-building trust was to go back to the beginning of the relationship. Linda said this may help to recapture what she called that "new love feeling." Like that new car smell that was just so elusive, May sensed the "new love feeling" would be elusive as well. How could they go back to the beginning of this relationship? And honestly, May didn't know if they needed to. At least she didn't. She never stopped loving Jamie, even for the few months where she despised him and wanted him dead and contemplated who she knew with Mafia connections. And Jamie said he never stopped loving her, despite his confused dick leading him down the rabbit hole, as it were. Stuck in May's head all day was that old Righteous Brothers song: "Bring back, that loving feeling. Oh that loving feeling. Bring back that loving feeling cause it's gone, gone, gone, and I can't go on, No-oh-oh." But it wasn't gone. Just briefly M.I.A.

Joanna was Leo-sitting that night so May and Jamie could go out alone. Now she sat in the little loveseat in

May's closet, (May's closet was so large, it had furniture of its own), helping her decide on an outfit while Leo played with his Lincoln Logs just outside. Joanna continued to be amazed, as she watched May try on sweater after sweater, that even after a lifetime of knowing her, everything looked so tremendous on May.

Joanna could try on every item of clothing in her own doll-sized closet and find numerous faults with how she looked wearing each item. *This skirt makes my already ample butt look at least like a double-wide, if not a triple-wide, plus, my knees look knobby. This sweater makes me look like an unsuccessful porn-star. These pants make my legs look even shorter than they already are. This dress makes me look pregnant, and this one just makes me look morbidly obese.*

May began the fashion show with a rather sexy black number, but quickly determined sexy wasn't the look she was going for. The peach, May said, was way too springy and youthful. Again, not the look for this "not really first date." The orange was just too dramatic, she didn't want to stand out (an insane statement, thought Joanna, and proof this state of affairs had really kicked May's ego to the curb). The cream with the little roses, May thought, made her look pudgy.

"Pudgy?" said Joanna, incredulous. She studied her sister with a critical eye. One thing was for sure, May had probably put on a few pounds since Jamie had left. Maybe five pounds tops stretched over her long silhouette, and it was scarcely noticeable. Joanna hadn't mentioned the tiny gain, as she was sure May would be mortified, but frankly, she was secretly pleased. The few pounds just barely softened May's features, and proved May was human. But pudgy? Give me a break! "May, are you smoking crack?"

"Joanna!" May screeched at her, frantically jerking her head in Leo's direction. Leo, completely oblivious, was busily building a tower.

"Sorry, sorry. You do not look pudgy; I think the cream is a lovely choice."

"I had lunch with Mom yesterday," she slumped into an armchair.

"Well no wonder you think you look pudgy, May, what are you thinking having lunch with that woman when you are feeling so low?"

"I know, I know, it was idiotic of me. In any case, we ate lunch at Pancho's and I ate an entire chicken quesadilla while she stared at me, aghast."

Joanna smiled, "Wait, you ate a tortilla and cheese in the same sitting? Was there guacamole involved? Did you vomit? " Joanna was only half kidding.

"Ha ha."

"Welcome to my sad little world, May. The disdainful stares, the disappointment..." Joanna slung her arm across her forehead dramatically, "You'll get used to it."

The V-necked dark green wool which brought out the green-gold in May's eyes and complemented the red in her hair, probably Joanna's favorite, was also Jamie's favorite and May absolutely did not want to be wearing Jamie's favorite. "It will come across as too willing; I don't want him to think I'm so eager to take him back."

Joanna began to fold the sweater mountain accumulating on the dressing table. "But...you are taking him back, aren't you?"

May paused in her dressing frenzy and leaned against the door of her closet, pondering the question.

Joanna stopped folding and looked at her sister. She was luminous as ever, but you could definitely see she had taken a beating.

"May, are you thinking of not?"

May shook her head, "No, I am, I am. Not to sound all New-Agey, but almost losing him really has gotten me thinking about our relationship and my whole outlook on...everything." She paused then asked quietly, "Jo, have I always been so flipping shallow?"

Joanna was quiet, thinking about the best way to answer.

"I'm guessing that your silence means yes."

"No, I'm just thinking. May, I don't think you're shallow at all. I mean, yes, you are the best-dressed and best-coiffed and your house is meticulous and you drive the newest cars and all that. But that's not who you are, that's just the wrapping. Under your pretty hairdo your big brain is still there, May. I think maybe you are asking the wrong question. Maybe you are looking for more from your life than lunches and pedicures. Maybe you need a new project or a new passion and maybe that's what is making you feel superficial."

May squished next to Jo on the loveseat and put her arm around her chummily, "A new passion, huh? Not a bad idea. Hey Jo, maybe you need the same thing?"

Joanna laughed, "You think?" But inside, Joanna's stomach did a little flip, because she knew she had discovered her not so new passion. She felt like she was like falling in love, she felt giddy, she felt excited, she felt happy. She liked it. But unlike falling in love, she wasn't ready to sing it from the rooftops. It still felt personal and private. She'd tell May soon, but right now, it was all her own.

May finally decided on a sapphire cashmere. The sweater fit snugly and looked great with slender brown herringbone slacks and dark-brown high-heeled boots. The amber necklace Jamie had just given her for her birthday circled her slender neck and perfectly completed the outfit.

The doorbell rang.

"He's ringing the doorbell?"

"Well, it's supposed to be like a date, remember?" May gave her lipstick a final check in the mirror and started downstairs.

Leo beat her to the door.

"Daddy!!!!!!!!!!!!!!" Jamie swung Leo around.

"Hey buddy, how are you?" Jamie held Leo's little cheeks and kissed him.

"You are taking Mommy to dinner?" Leo asked.

"Yup."

"Can I come?"

"Nope, you are staying with Auntie Jo. But we can have dinner tomorrow, ok?" He looked up at May for approval, and she nodded.

"OK. Are you going to have tacos?"

"What? Would I ever have tacos without you? Not in a million years, don't be silly!" Jamie pretended to pout.

"OK. Want to see my tower?" Leo bounded up the stairs to retrieve his Lincoln Log tower.

"Of course I do," said Jamie to his son's retreating back. He turned his attention to May, "You look great," he said a little nervously. He leaned forward and kissed her on the cheek.

"How about me? Don't I look great?" Joanna teased coming down the stairs.

Jamie smiled and enveloped her in a bear-hug, "Best-lookin' sister-in-law around. So what's on your agenda tonight, Jo?" Jamie asked.

"Well, first Leo and I are going to make some cookies, big surprise, I know, and then we'll be playing with Lincoln Logs until my head explodes, and then we'll eat my fabulous fish-fingers and broccoli and then he goes to sleep and I watch TV and go through your medicine cabinets and talk on the phone with my boyfriend."

"That sounds fun," Jamie said, turning to May, "Maybe we should stay in?"

May punched him in the arm.

35

"Hi, what are you doing?"

For the second time in as many weeks, May looked down guiltily at her croissant and coffee breakfast (she had recently upgraded to 1% milk rather than skim, because really, in the scheme of things, how bad could 1% be? I mean, it's only 1 %!), and said, "Uh...nothing. Why, what's up?"

"I want to go to yoga."

May nearly gagged on the flaky pastry, "Joanna, you are freaking me out here. Didn't we go for that huge walk around the lake? Doesn't that meet your exercise quota for the decade?"

"Be nice, May, I'm trying to improve myself here. Anyway, I read somewhere it might help me sleep better, and I'm too self-conscious to go alone. Please come with me. Pretty please? With Equal on top and a fat-free maraschino cherry? Class begins in two hours..."

An hour and a half later May reluctantly met Joanna in front of the gym. Joanna was wearing an enormous Howard Jones t-shirt, old ripped sweats that looked like she had painted something in them, ah, her kitchen based on the brick red splotches, and flip flops.

"That is quite a look," said May dryly.

"Thanks," answered Joanna, oblivious to the sarcasm and eagerly accepting the mat May offered, "I'm super-excited."

Joanna bopped around the dressing room as May changed into organic cotton palazzo pants and matching camisole with tiny oms stitched up the side. The entered the studio together and laid out their mats.

"I'm going to go introduce myself to the teacher, so he knows I'm new," Joanna began walking towards the tall blonde instructor.

As if he can't tell from that outfit, May thought, shaking her head at her sweet Sis. And then she looked to see who was teaching the class and May grabbed Joanna's hand and yanked her back, "For crying out loud, Joanna" May stage-whispered, "Ted is the teacher so don't act like a total dork, ok?"

Joanna's eyes widened, she had completely forgotten about May's tryst. "Oh, sorry, I won't say anything to him."

May softened, "No, don't be silly. I'm being paranoid. He is very much an 'in the moment' kind of guy, so he's probably forgotten all about our moment anyway. So, you're right, let me introduce you."

Joanna and May approached Ted, sitting in a complicated-looking cross-legged pose.

"Excuse me, Ted," said May, "I want to introduce you to my sister, Joanna."

As many men had before, Ted blinked in confusion and Joanna said, "I know, I know, it's amazing I have such a plain frumpy sister. Anyway, I've never done yoga before so I thought you should know in case I passed out or imploded or something."

May cracked up and Ted merely stared up at the two of them from his cross-legged pose on the floor. Finally the fog surrounding him seemed to lift and he put his hands together and did a little bow, "Namaste," he said, "It's nice to meet you, Joanna. Welcome."

"Uh, Namaste," Joanna answered awkwardly.

"Thank you for telling me you are new to yoga," he smiled a serene smile at her, "Right now I am sitting in *Padmasana*, a Lotus Pose I am using to calm my brain before class," he smiled. "I'll be sure to keep an eye out for you, although you already have an excellent example to follow." He nodded and smiled warmly at May, "So nice to see you, May," he gave May a knowing smile and Joanna surmised he fondly recalled his "moment" with May. He turned back to Joanna, "Please let me know if you need any additional assistance during class, Joanna. Again, welcome."

Joanna bravely struggled with the poses, trying to emulate May and Ted's long lithe lines but more closely resembling a clumsy toddler learning to stand and finally walk without hanging on to someone's leg or the table. *If I can get through this without falling on my face or, more likely, my ass, it will be a miracle*, she thought. If nothing else, she figured she'd get some endorphins going from comic relief if not bona-fide exercise.

Now she was attempting *Trikonasana*, the Triangle pose. She concentrated hard on Ted's precise directions, "Lift your hips into the air for downward facing dog, stretch, breathe and relax there. Now slowly move your left foot forward about a foot."

OK, I'm there, Joanna thought, *what now? What now? Quick! Before I fall over?*

"Now," Ted revealed slowly, "Put your left hand beside your foot and raise the upper part of your body until the lower back is straight. Breathe and relax."

OK, I'm breathing, I'm relaxing...OK I'm not relaxing exactly but I'm definitely breathing.

"Press your left hand against your heel and twist your upper-back to the left. Be careful to not twist your hips, just your upper-back. Very nice. Then raise your arm into the air, twist your head to look up at your hand. Feel the lightness in your body."

Lightness? Joanna struggled to look up at her hand. *No, no lightness here...but I'm not falling either so we're going to consider it a success thus far!*

"Now move back into downward facing dog."

Joanna did a silent cheer.

"Now," Ted continued, "*Vrksasana*, Tree pose. Begin in Mountain and concentrate on your core, gather strength from it."

My core, my core, Joanna thought, *I'm sure there are muscles under there...*

"Exhale and move your foot up your leg to your groin, inhale as you stretch your arms to the sides and then exhale as you bring your hands together in prayer and raise your arms overhead," Ted intoned, exuding tranquility.

Joanna found the eerie music almost hypnotic and felt exhilarated and proud when she mastered Tree pose without tipping over.

Thirty sweaty minutes later they sat at the organic juice bar, a shot of wheatgrass for May and a carrot cantaloupe bee-pollen concoction for Joanna.

"So," May began, "what's with all the exercise, Jo? I mean," She expertly downed the end of her wheatgrass shot and shuddered a little, "I think it's terrific, but a wee out of character."

Joanna sipped her fluorescent orange smoothie thoughtfully, "I guess I'm trying to branch out a little, and take better care of myself, and I feel pretty damn proud of myself!"

"You should feel proud; you did an awesome job today."

Joanna was quiet, "Did I mention I have a date?"

May punched Joanna in the arm, "No, big sister, you most certainly did not mention you had a date. Who with?"

"Bookstore guy. His name's David."

"The cute one in the glasses? Sandy-colored hair? Sweet smile?"

"That's the one."

May punched her in the arm again, "Good for you!"

"Yeah, I'm excited. I like him. We'll see," Joanna pushed her smoothie aside, "This is rather gross."

"Healthy doesn't always mean yummy," May hopped off her barstool, "Let's go get a cup of coffee!"

"You are becoming quite the coffee whore, aren't you?" Joanna slid off her stool.

"Hmmm, whore seems like a harsh word for it but I'll say yes."

"Lead the way, trollop!"

36

When Marjorie arrived at the bakery she was surprised to see the lights and ovens on, coffee brewing and Joanna elbow-deep in cookie batter.

"Well, good morning, aren't you the early riser?" Marjorie tied her "kiss the cook" apron around her waist and poured herself a cup of coffee.

"Good morning," Joanna was tentative, "I had an idea and I couldn't sleep so I thought I'd just come in and try them out. I hope that's ok..."

"Hell, Joanna, you can use this kitchen for anything, anytime, got it? You're family!" She leaned over and kissed Joanna on the forehead.

Joanna felt a lump forming and cleared her throat. Croakily she said, "Here, try this," she handed Marjorie a lumpy looking cookie.

Marjorie took a bite, chewed thoughtfully. Swallowed. Took another. Joanna nervously shifted her weight from foot to foot while she waited for Marjorie's reaction, "So...what do you think?" Joanna felt confident she was able to change, build on, *grow* a recipe from something pretty good, into something divine; but she also knew Marjorie's standards were sky high. Marjorie could taste a perfect cookie and instinctively know how to transcend it from perfection...to ethereal.

Marjorie studied the cookie and took yet another bite, "Hot damn, Joanna, this is terrific. It has great complexity and an interesting chew. Not too sweet. Is that toasted coconut?"

Joanna hadn't realized she was holding her breath until it came out with a whoosh, "Yeah, I shaved it a little thicker and toasted it. It's something I used to make as a kid, my signature cookie I guess. I've been tinkering with the recipe quite a bit, especially the coconut. I used to use sweetened, and then unsweetened and finally started toasting my own fresh. I think it really makes a difference. So...what do you think? Do you like it?"

"Honey, it's delicious! Now, it's not the prettiest thing I ever saw but we could work on that. What do you call them?"

"Uh... oatmeal-coconut-chocolate chip cookies. Not much of a name. Anyway, it's a near and dear recipe and you don't have anything like them..."

"Oh, we're adding them to the lineup, no question. It's been awhile since we had a new cookie. Let's work on the shape though, they are a little bit blobby," Marjorie rolled up her sleeves, "Come on, Girl, let's get to work!"

Joanna hopped to attention and beamed with pleasure as she walked Marjorie through the recipe.

Marjorie, ever the chemist, studied the leavening,

suggesting a slight increase in baking soda and slight decrease in baking powder to help the funky shape. An addition of refrigeration prior to baking produced the results they were looking for, a round, slightly domed cookie, still bumpy with texture. They high-fived and *Joanna's Jumbles* made their debut at *Sweet*.

37

And then there was the sex part. She and Jamie had always had a healthy sex life. But now, May couldn't help but wonder, was her husband bisexual, and did she care? She brought it up during their Monday session with Linda, which she had begun to look forward to. She liked Linda, thought she was smart and insightful and May liked her wry sense of humor. Most importantly May felt she and Jamie were exploring deeper into their relationship and building their crumbled tower back to its former glory, but on a much sturdier foundation.

"So, I'd like to talk about sex today," said May bluntly. Without hesitation, Jamie reached into his pocket for his inhaler and inhaled deeply, his eyes closed.

Linda smiled, "OK, May. Jamie, are you ok with that?"

"I'm ready."

"May, was there somewhere you'd like to begin?" asked Linda.

"Yes. So, Jamie," she turned to face her husband, "Are you bisexual now?" Jamie exhaled but May did not give him a chance to answer before forging on, "And if yes, what does that mean for our relationship? I mean, are you going to mourn this new discovery? Are you going to feel trapped in this heterosexual and monogamous relationship? And make no mistake Mister, if this relationship is truly to continue, monogamy is not just going to be expected, it's going to be mandatory. And there will be consequences. Betray me once and apparently I can move on, get over it, regroup. Betray me twice and you are asking for your testicles in a jar on my bedside table. Literally." She took a breath, "So, are you bisexual now?"

Jamie looked from May to Linda and then back to May, "May," he took her hand, "Apparently I am attracted to women, and the odd occasional man, so call it what you will, bisexual, bi-curious? Human? And no, I will not mourn the loss of this discovery. What I got from this whole horrendous situation is a stronger sense of my sexuality as a part of me. Not all of me, just a part. And attraction has as much to do with personality and charisma as it has to do with a penis or a vagina. And regardless of who I may be attracted to in the future, I will never, under any circumstances act on it. I am humiliated I did it in the first place and I would expect you to keep my head in the jar next to my testicles if I betray you again."

May smiled and leaned in to kiss her husband lightly on the lips, "It's a deal."

They continued to go to couples therapy and continued

to date, but May hadn't allowed Jamie to move back into the house as yet, and she was having difficulty putting her finger on why. She loved him, she missed him, she wanted him home, but something was holding her back.

She told Elsa, "I feel like this was almost too easy. I mean, he cheated, we separated, he apologized, I forgave, and we're back together. I almost feel as if I need more time, but I don't know what I need the time for. And I don't want to waste any more time either." May shook her hair loose from its clip.

Elsa, in her Elsa way, said, "Well, maybe what you need time to do, is mourn."

"To mourn? To mourn what?" May asked, irritated, "There's nothing to mourn. Although it's funny you should use the word 'mourn,' because I asked Jamie if he was going to mourn the fact he made this new bisexual discovery and now he's stuck back in a boring old heterosexual relationship with me."

Elsa cocked her head to one side, "And what was his reply?"

"That he didn't like the bisexual label, that he was human. And more importantly, that he loves me and would still love me if I had a sex change or lost my vagina in some sort of bizarre accident."

"And do you believe him?"

"Yes. Yes, I do."

"So then let's get back to mourning."

May rolled her eyes, exasperated, "But nothing died, nothing ended. There's nothing to mourn."

"Of course something ended, May," said Elsa kindly.

"What? What ended? The relationship will continue. Our lives, basically uninterrupted will continue. Shit, my mother doesn't even know we ever separated and here we are essentially back together as if nothing happened. Nothing has ended!" May realized she was shouting, but she couldn't stop herself.

Elsa tucked her blonde hair behind her ear and leaned forward in her ergonomically correct chair, "May, I don't want to get off topic here, but I want to make sure I heard you correctly, did you just say Lily doesn't know you've separated?"

May took a deep breath and blew it out loudly, "Yeah, I haven't exactly told her."

"Haven't exactly told her, or haven't told her?"

"Uh, haven't told her," May rearranged her long legs, "but I told my dad!" She forged a smile, as if she was hoping for brownie points.

Now it was Elsa who took a deep breath, "OK, May, I want to talk about the mourning piece, but then we will talk about this Lily piece, got it?"

May nodded like a child, chastised for spilling her milk or killing the family cat.

"OK May, there is definitely something to mourn, as something has ended. Your relationship with Jamie, I have no doubt, will continue to grow stronger and stronger. But you are moving to a new chapter now. You are leaving that age of innocence, if you will, behind." she waited for May to look at her before she continued, "That's what there is to mourn, May, the end of this life you had been living with Jamie. You cannot begin to rejoice over the next chapter until you mourn the end of the last one."

"But how do I mourn the end of that chapter? I feel so done, Elsa, so tired of mulling it all over and talking about it to death. I'm just ready to be done," May leaned her head into her hands heavily, holding back tears, "I want my happy life back."

May drove to her lunch date with Daniel with her head spinning and her mood surly. She was sick of this whole situation, frankly. Sick of feeling unsettled, sick of the waiting and sick of the talking. She was ready to move forward, not mourn the backward.

Daniel noticed right away May was not herself, no joking about his cigarette-scent (the cigarettes had increased in direct proportion to the increased pain in his knee), no small talk about the world in general, just a distracted kiss hello and an "Is our table ready?" for the waitress. Once they were seated at their customary table, May was visibly anxious. Squirmy. Indecisive. Not that indecisive was anything unusual for May when it came to ordering lunch, but the squirmy was unusual. May was one of those rare women who just felt comfortable in their own skin so tended not to fidget or wring her hands or fuss with her clothes. Clearly she was not herself.

"May," Daniel asked quietly, "what's up?"

Tears immediately sprang to May's eyes and Daniel quickly came around the table to hug her, "Sweetie? What's going on? Talk to me," he turned her tear-streaked face up to face him and stroked her cheeks with his thumbs, just as he had countless times when she was a child with a scraped knee or a bruised ego.

May rubbed her eyes with her fists, "I'm sorry, Daddy. Jesus, how embarrassing." She accepted his outstretched handkerchief, threadbare and initialed, and blew her nose loudly. "I'm kind of a mess."

Daniel returned to his seat and waited.

May huffed just ever so slightly like a petulant child, "It's so hard to explain, Dad." And then she launched into what Elsa had said.

Daniel listened thoughtfully, "And...you didn't particularly like what she had to say, I'm reading."

May looked up at the ceiling, blinking rapidly to avoid the next barrage of tears, "No, it's not that, I respect what she has to say I suppose. I'm just so so tired of the whole thing. I'm just ready for my happy life to continue the way it was before, or not how it was before. I just want it to continue to move. I almost feel like I'm stuck here, stagnant, and this is what it's going to be like from here on out," she drank a sip of her iced tea, "Oh fuck, I don't know what I'm talking about, of course Elsa is right. Of course," she reached for a piece of bread, "per usual that bitch is always right. I just don't want to hear that I need to mourn something, I mean, Jesus Christ, haven't I suffered enough?" She took a bite out of the bread; it was bland and a little gummy and stuck to the roof of her mouth, like peanut butter on Wonder Bread. "All I know is, Jamie better be just as fucked up as I still am over this." She drank her tea, trying to dislodge the bread expanding in her throat.

Daniel laughed and raised his glass, "Here's to mourning the end of innocence and to hoping he is just as fucked up as you are."

"I'll drink to that," she choked back the bread ball. "Elsa brought up the fact that I haven't told Mom." May's eyes avoided her father.

Daniel was quiet. He understood both of his daughter's difficulties with their mother, at least as much as he could. He knew the mother-daughter relationship was something sacred, something messy, something requiring copious energy, therapy and chocolate. But he didn't really *understand it*, per se. He never really got why his daughters would often roll their eyes when Lily spoke, or shoot each other knowing glances.

Of course he remembered a number of things Lily had done throughout the years his girls considered mortifying, most of which he found frankly...entertaining. Once, he recalled, a date came to the house to bring May to a homecoming dance or prom or some such adolescent adventure. The boy: tall, smart enough and nice enough looking, although he had heard both of his girls and several of their friends use the word "hot" to describe him. In any case they made small talk while they waited for May to emerge from the inner sanctums of the house where Lily was assisting with hair and makeup and whatever the hell else they did in there. Where was he applying to college? What were his plans after graduation? That sort of thing.

Finally, his youngest daughter, a gorgeous vision in a blue floaty number, hair ridiculously piled on her head unleashing several fiery ringlets around her shoulders in an extravagant up-do befitting a visit from royalty, appeared in the kitchen doorway, beads and Lily clattering behind her. The date, Tom? Todd? Tyler? He had no recollection. Anyway, the T Boy had sucked in his breath so rapidly, it was as if he had been punched in the stomach rather than confronted with his exquisite companion for the evening and had stammered a "Jesus you look incredible, May."

Lily swept between the couple, draping her arm around the T Boy saying, "Oh May, this one is so cute, and strong too," she squeezed his biceps through his rented tux.

"Mom! Cut it out," May said through her clenched teeth.

"Oh, come on now, May, jealous of me handling your boy toy, are you? Nervous your old mom is gonna steal your date or something?" She smiled and stroked T's arm.

T tried to laugh casually, sweat beading on his forehead, "Your mom has definitely got it goin' on May!"

May gave the T Boy a withering look under which he appeared to actually wither, and she then turned on her mother.

"Mother, would you be so kind as to unhand my date so we may leave?" said May icily, a terse smile pasted on her heavily lacquered mouth.

Daniel remembered May the next day, pacing the living room floor as she waited for Lily to return from her yoga class and finally unleashing as she walked through the door, hands on hips and smoke streaming out of her ears as subtle as a tornado, "What the hell was that, exactly?"

"What the hell was what, May?" Lily asked, startled out of her endorphin calm, "Why are you yelling at me?"

"What the hell are you doing flirting with my boyfriend? Trying to recoup some lost youth, Mom? Pretty sick, going after your daughter's boyfriend!"

Lily had snorted with laughter, "Going after your boyfriend? May, calm down, I was just doing some innocent flirting. You are overreacting."

"I'm overreacting? I'm overreacting?" May crossed her arms in front of her chest, "Did you or did you not flirt with my boyfriend?"

"For crying out loud, May, ok, yes, I flirted with your boyfriend."

"And do you or do you not find that to be unbelievably inappropriate and inexcusable behavior?"

Lily put her yoga mat down on the couch, "May, Honey," Lily took May's hands and sat her down on the couch, "Please settle down. I really did not mean to upset you in any way," May huffed, shaking out her hair and keeping her eyes in the air, "I apologize if you felt like I crossed over a line. What line, I'm unsure, but I'm sorry just the same, ok, Pumpkin?" she leaned over and gave May a hug, effectively letting the air out of her sails.

"So, why exactly haven't you told your mother, May?" Daniel asked.

May sighed heavily, "Oh Dad, she'll want to hear everything and dissect everything. She'll want to know the whole 'he said, she said' mess," she idly poked at a lettuce leaf. May didn't tell her father the other reason, although Daniel already knew, that she couldn't stand for her mother to be disappointed in her, Lily's approval was something she craved.

"Of course she will, May. She's your mother and she loves you."

"I know. I know. But maybe she loves me too much. Maybe she loves me so much that all she'll be able to see is how Jamie did everything wrong and I did everything right. She'll bring up all of his faults, every teensy thing he's done over the years that pointed him in this direction, and then she'll say, 'I knew something like this would happen, remember last year when he said he thought Clinton was the most attractive president? Even better looking than Kennedy or Obama? I knew it then!'" She smacked her hands to the table in a perfect impersonation of her mother.

Daniel couldn't help but laugh, the imitation was uncanny, "I hear all of that, May, but I still think you need to tell her," he said quietly, "Especially now that it looks like you two are trying to work it out. She may be able to help you, you know."

May slumped a little in her chair, "But Dad, once I tell Mom, its real. The whole ugly mess will be out in the open. She'll make it too real."

"But May, it is real, regardless of whether you tell Lily or not, this whole ordeal is real. You can't pretend that it isn't. I think Elsa gave you excellent advice, it's happened and you need to mourn it in order to let it go."

May reached across the table for Daniel's burger and helped herself to a large bite, "This sucks," she said, wiping at the juice dripping down her chin.

"The situation or the burger?"

"The burger is delicious."

38

When Joanna's eyes blinked open on Saturday morning the sun was streaming in the window. She had forgotten to close the curtain when she fell, exhausted, into bed the night before. It was the first morning in many that she was able to sleep in, as *Sweet* was closed. It was Hal's fifty-fifth birthday and Marjorie had closed her shop so they could spend the day together, hanging a little sign on the door that read "Sorry, gone fishin'! See ya' tomorrow!" Joanna had offered to work extra so they wouldn't have to close but Marjorie had said, "Heck no! What's the point in ownin' your own business if you don't get to play hooky every once in a while?"

Joanna stretched and surveyed. She felt, surprisingly, awake. She swung her legs over the side of the bed and reached her toes for the floor, nudging aside a tower of books threatening to tumble. Grabbing her robe from its perch at the foot of her bed she straightened the tower to its former precarious glory and padded down the hall for coffee and breakfast and to contemplate the day. She felt as if she may have bit off more than she could chew.

First, she had a play date scheduled with Leo. They were planning on having a picnic at the park, feeding the ducks, swinging like monkeys and running around on the play structures like maniacs until they were exhausted. Next, they were going to Leo's to cook dinner for May and Jamie. Although they weren't married until June, the couple traditionally celebrated the date they *began* to date, the infamous tea and beer date, which momentously took place on March 15th. So, today was their 11th "anniversary" and as they were nervous and confused about their tentative status as dating couple, Joanna offered to make them a casual supper at home to celebrate. What she didn't tell them was she was actually re-creating their favorite honeymoon meal.

When May and Jamie returned from their honeymoon they gave a rapt Joanna a complete review of the amazing things they saw (and most importantly, the food they ate) all the while finishing each other's sentences and peppering the story with "That's what I was just about to say!" in a way that although began as charming, quickly became tiresome. For this particular meal she was treated to a complete play by play, their eyes twinkling as only newlyweds' eyes can as they described each course of the meal. Both May and Jamie often expressed a desire to return to Morocco just to eat this extravagant dinner again. So in her usual way, Joanna thoroughly researched Moroccan cuisine in order to re-create the feast of lamb tagine with honey, olives and dates, couscous, cucumber and mint salad, mint tea, pineapple and banana pudding and almond macaroons for dessert. After seating the Cohen's at their dining room table with a big "ta-da!" her plan was to race home to shower for her first date with David.

Joanna yawned and poured cream into her first cup of coffee, happily breathing in the fragrant steam. While she waited for her toast she ticked off the items she needed to get done before picking up Leo. The night before she had made the pudding and macaroons, marinated the lamb and prepped the rest of the ingredients for the tagine. She needed to pack everything up so she could bring it over to May's when she picked up Leo. She had already packed a picnic and just needed to add an ice pack to the perishables. She spread peanut butter on her toast. What else? She probably should pick out what she was going to wear tonight, so she wouldn't need to rip her closet apart like a deranged ape moments before David was due to arrive. They were going out to dinner so she needed something cute, but wine country casual. She would definitely wear jeans, but wasn't sure what else and was pretty sure she needed to wear a top of some sort; it was only their first date, after all.

She walked to her dismal closet and flung open the door. Staring at the mess and fearful of venturing inside alone, she grabbed the phone and called May, "Hi, what are you doing?"

"Mourning."

"Uh, did someone die?"

May explained, "I'm mourning, apparently, or rather I'm supposed to be mourning the loss of my relationship," May took a bite of her muffin.

Joanna sat on the floor in front of the closet, momentarily forgetting why she called May in the first place, "What do you mean the loss of your relationship? You haven't lost your relationship, May, it's just been temporarily on hold and now you will continue, like, a new chapter I guess," she studied her toes, trying to decide what she should do about her ancient, chipped pedicure. *When did she get this pedicure? Was it presentable enough for a night-time first date or did she need to figure out how to fit a pedi in on this already packed day?*

May's mouth was still full of muffin when she answered, "Have you been speaking with Elsa because that sounds a lot like what she said!" She finished chewing and swallowed, "She said I needed to mourn the loss of the first part of my relationship with Jamie in order to enter the next chapter and live happily ever after."

"I'll bet she charged a lot more for that advice than I just did."

May took another bite of muffin and laughed, "You betcha she did!"

"May, what the heck are you eating in my ear?" Joanna asked.

May stopped chewing, but having decided she would no longer feel guilty for indulging in baked goods said, "Uh, a carrot-ginger muffin and a cappuccino."

Joanna laughed, "A muffin, huh? Well, I for one applaud your new diet. OK, not that I don't want to talk about you and be supportive about your mourning and commiserate and all that but...can I talk about me now? Big first date, remember?"

"Check, what do you need?"

"What am I wearing?"

May didn't miss a beat, "Where are you going?"

"Dinner, Roadhouse."

"Yum. OK, jeans, the dark blue ones we bought, not those old tattered ones."

"Check."

"Rust colored button-up with the teeny shell buttons and that dark brown blazer."

"Button-up is rumpled in a ball at the bottom of the closet awaiting a trip to the cleaners, and what brown blazer?"

"Look on the left side of your closet, behind that hideous dress you wore to Mom's sixtieth birthday party,"

"Hey! I like that dress."

"That dress is horrendous. Makes your hips look like you're stuck in an inner tube. Anyway, you have a lovely walnut-brown blazer."

Joanna got off the floor and approached the closet, warily. She located the dress, pushing it aside and sure enough, there was a blazer. She tossed her robe onto the bed and slipped the blazer on and looked in the mirror. It fit perfectly, although looked ludicrous over her t-shirt and sweats ensemble. "I look great in this! When did I get it?"

May laughed, "We bought it when we went to the City that day. Anyway, wear the cream colored blouse with the cap sleeves. That looks great on you. And those brown peep-toes. And those big blue drop-earrings I gave you for your birthday."

Joanna lay each item on the bed as May directed, making a person. "Wow, I look terrific!"

"Of course you do," May answered.

"Can I wear the peep-toes with an old pedicure?"

"How old are we talking here?"

"I have absolutely no recollection."

"It's red?"

"Sort of red."

"And you can't get a pedi today?"

"No, no, I really can't."

"Only your big toe will show with those shoes, so I think you are ok. It's nighttime. Or better yet, take the polish off and go bare."

"OK, thanks. See you in ten minutes."

Joanna changed into the aforementioned tattered jeans and a Madonna-esque sweatshirt complete with itchy collar removed. She pulled her hair into a ponytail, packed the car with her supplies and was off to pick up Leo.

The park was crowded as house-weary families took advantage of the beautiful, not too cold day and dazzling blue sky full of thick cottony clouds. Couples strolled hand in hand and lounged on blankets on the vast green lawn. Joanna and Leo began their day by feeding the perpetually ravenous ducks handfuls of oatmeal. Leo laughed uproariously as they fought over each tiny disc-shaped morsel. Joanna distracted one particularly aggressive duck with a puffed up brown chest and white wings so Leo could feed the less pushy ducks.

Leo's wiry frame swung merrily on the monkey bars. Joanna, baffled by his upper-body strength and unable to keep up with him opted to hang upside down instead. Leo found this endlessly entertaining and proceeded to hop down and take her dangling hands, jumping up and down and cackling, "Auntie Jo! You're upsee down!" Joanna laughed, dizzy with the blood rushing into her face.

A familiar, albeit fuzzy and upside down face appeared above Leo's bouncing curls, "Joanna?"

Mortified as the face came into focus, "David, hi! Hey Leo, let go so I can get down, please," she reached up to grasp the monkey bars, swung her legs down and dropped onto the cushy rubber playground floor.

"Hey, I thought that was you," David smiled, "and not a monkey," he looked down at Leo, "so who's this?"

Joanna felt her hair to see if she could determine just how catawampus she looked, this was NOT the impression she was hoping to make today. "This is my nephew, Leo. Leo, this is my friend David."

"Hi there, Leo," David bent down to shake Leo's hand furiously, making Leo laugh.

Joanna noticed another boy lurking behind David, "And it looks like you have a friend here too."

"Yup, this is *my* nephew, Spiderman. Spidey, this is my friend, Joanna and my new friend, Leo."

Leo was wide-eyed, "Spiderman! Is that really your name?"

Spiderman narrowed his eyes, considering the question, "No, it's Justin. I'm four."

"I'm four!" Leo pointed to his chest, disbelieving his good fortune.

David laughed, "Wowie! Both of you are four! Maybe you should play?"

Leo and Justin dashed off together as if they'd been friends since birth, leaving Joanna and David laughing hilariously.

"So, babysitting I see." Joanna continued to smooth her rumpled hair and clothing, conscious of how red and sweaty and gross she probably was.

"Yep, for my sister. I think I saved Justin's life today; she was ready to kill him."

"Hey, why aren't you working today?"

"I take an occasional Saturday off. And why aren't you at the bookstore?

"I take the occasional Saturday off too, I guess."

"You do? I can't remember you missing a single Saturday."

"I'm sure I missed one or two along the way."

He continued to smile at her, "What a terrific, unexpected surprise to run into you," His smile was so bright and infectious, his whole face lit up. She couldn't help but smile back at him.

"I was hoping to look a little less rumpled for our first date," she indicated her scruffy ensemble, maybe even shower and all." He, she noticed, looked terrific, in a green and white flannel shirt, sleeves rolled up to reveal strong forearms peppered with light red hair. His hazel eyes sparkled under his practical glasses.

"I think you look great, all rumpled," he reached and tucked some hair behind her ear.

Joanna froze; the touch at her ear was, not to be cliché, electric. She shivered. Neither of them spoke, just looked at each other.

Finally Joanna said, "Thanks."

"Hey, those two seem to be getting along great," he indicated the two boys racing through the play-town, pretending to ride horses. Their audible exchange peppered with "Hee-haws!" and "Ride 'em cowboy!"

Joanna invited David and Spidey to share their lunch. David giggled when he saw the spread: baguette, an assortment of cheese, including brie, camembert and provolone, prosciutto, cubed cantaloupe and strawberries. "Where are the cheese sticks and juice boxes?"

She smiled, and took two apple juice boxes out of the cooler and handed one to Justin, "You can have mine, Justin." Justin took the gift appreciatively and both boys began the battle to shove the little straws into the boxes.

"What do you say, Justin?"

"Tanks!" Justin replied dutifully.

They ate their lunch, ravenous from running around all morning. Joanna showed Justin how to wrap the prosciutto around the melon and eat the two together.

"It's a melon sandwich!" Justin exclaimed. Leo laughed uproariously as if Justin had just told the funniest of jokes. David marveled as Justin happily scarfed down his lunch.

David whispered to Joanna, "At home all that kid will eat is Kraft macaroni and cheese and Taco Bell burritos!"

Joanna laughed, "I find kids can have pretty sophisticated tastes if you just introduce them to a variety of foods."

David's mobile began to ring and he looked at the number and told Joanna, "Excuse me for just a minute."

Joanna eavesdropped just a tad to the one sided conversation:

"Hi Joan. "

"Yes, that's fine; just give her a refund, please. Don't worry about the paperwork, I know her. Just leave a note to remind me tomorrow. Everything else going ok?" He paused to listen to Joan's response, "Great. Don't hesitate to call if you need help." He hung up, "Sorry about that, newish girl alone at the store today."

"No problem. Are you the manager?"

He smiled, "No. I'm the owner. *Book Nook* is my store. It's kind of my baby, if you will."

"The owner?" It had never occurred to Joanna he could actually own the store. She thought he was just... Bookstore Guy.

"What? I don't look like owner material?" He teased.

"No, not like that, it just never really occurred to me I guess."

David entertained the boys with an excellent Mickey Mouse impression. Joanna told David about her surprise for her sister that evening.

"Wait, you are planning on cooking this entire feast before our date tonight?"

"Well, yes, but I'm pretty organized. I can do it."

"Let me help."

"Really?"

"Really. I'm useful in the kitchen, and the boys can occupy each other."

She hesitated for only a split second, "OK, sure. That would be fun." She looked at her watch, "But we'll need to get going in order to get it all done."

David clapped his hands, "OK, boys, how do you feel about continuing this play date at Leo's house?"

The boys loudly proclaimed their satisfaction with this idea and they were off to the cars. Joanna was relieved to see that David's car, a blue Honda with an unsightly scratch down the length of it, was almost as old as her Volvo as he followed her to May's house.

"Wow," said David as they unloaded the kids, "This is quite a house. Is your sister some sort of politician or drug lord?"

"I know; it's huge. My baby sis is rather...well off."

They plunked the exhausted boys in front of Sesame Street and got to work.

David was an excellent sous chef, following directions quickly and precisely and soon the kitchen was permeated with the spicy scents of Morocco.

"Joanna, this is the nicest present you are giving your sister."

"Well, she deserves it, they both do. May and Jamie have been having a rough time."

"And will Leo eat this?"

She giggled, "Well, he better because it's all I'm making!"

David went to check on the suspiciously quiet boys and motioned for Joanna to come take a look at them fast asleep in front of the television, Leo softly snoring.

"Wow, look how cute they are, all sweaty and happy. Wouldn't it be nice to just crash like that in the middle of the day?" David commented. Joanna watched David watching the two boys, Leo snorted and rolled over and the adults darted back into the kitchen to suppress a giggle.

They finished preparing the feast and sat on the deck outside the kitchen, drinking tea and talking. They heard the front door open and May say "Oh my God, it smells incredible in here!" Joanna hurried to meet her so she wouldn't wake the boys and to warn her that a strange man was in her kitchen.

"He's here?" May stage-whispered, eyes wide, grasping Joanna's hands.

"Yes, I ran into him at the park and he offered to help."

"How nice is that?"

"Very nice! May, he's so, so nice!"

They walked into the kitchen and David rose from the deck to be introduced to May. She surveyed him closely. Cute, bookish looking, smart glasses, cute as she remembered. She shook David's extended hand and noticed his firm grip and powerful shake.

"It's good to meet you, May. Although I'm fairly certain I've seen you at the store, buying *Esquire* if I'm not mistaken," he said, and then he smiled and May couldn't help but smile back, his face was so open, his smile so generous.

"You would be correct. My husband's an *Esquire* junkie." She turned to Joanna, "Jo, it smells unbelievable in here, what are you making?"

"Not telling, it's supposed to be a surprise, remember?"

"Ok, ok, but maybe you and David would like to join us? I'm sure you made enough for a small army."

David laughed, "That is a wonderful invitation, May, but I understand that it's a special day for you and your husband. Also, I've been working for months to get Joanna to accept a date with me so I'm really hoping to get her alone. But I hope you'll extend a rain check?"

"Absolutely," said May, and looking into David's kind face she thought that this man just may be the one Joanna had been searching for.

39

Huddled on the tiny balcony drinking coffee, Joanna debriefed May with a play by play of the big date the night before.

"Wait, wait, slow down, I don't want to miss anything!" said May, green eyes wide and luminous over her coffee cup.

"OK, ok, so he ordered a spicy tomato soup with gruyere toast and this beautiful lamb dish and I had this incredible Chioggia beet salad, that's the one with those gorgeous rings of pink and white? Totally delicious. And for my entrée I had these unbelievable ravioli stuffed with artichokes and cheese and..." Joanna was interrupted by the ringing phone.

May jumped and her eyes widened, "Do you think that's him?"

As she ran into the kitchen for the phone Joanna hollered over her shoulder, "Nope, he already called!"

"No way!"

"Way!" Joanna was breathless when she picked up the phone, "Hello?"

It was Lily, "Hi Honey, it's me!"

"Oh, hi, Mom, I'm just sitting here drinking coffee with May."

"Coffee? She's drinking coffee now? And I thought you were quitting coffee? Anyway I'm so glad I caught both of you! I know its short notice but can you come to dinner tonight? Guess who showed up today? Nuncle Pete!" Her voice escalated, almost reaching shrill.

"Nuncle Pete! Wasn't he just here?" Joanna practically jumped up and down, "Yippee! Of course we'll be there!"

Jamie and Leo had a taco dinner date so Joanna and May eagerly made the trip south to see their favorite Nuncle, bringing a change of clothes with them just in case they were too "something" to drive home.

Lily was flitting around the kitchen when they arrived, stunning per usual in a purple caftan and espadrilles, preparing pizza with pesto and salad, humming as she chopped. "Where's Jamie?" she asked, "We haven't seen much of him lately."

Joanna shot May a look that said, "Uh-oh," and then extricated herself from the kitchen, tongue firmly clenched between her teeth, muttering, "I want to go say hi to Nuncle Pete."

May was not so easily rattled, "He's been super-busy these days, Mom. He's working on this big deal; hopefully it will be done soon. He's been working so hard. Tonight he and Leo had a taco date. I'll bring these outside," she grabbed the silverware and napkins to bring onto the back deck and get the hell out of the suddenly sweltering kitchen.

Daniel and Nuncle Pete had settled themselves comfortably into the creaking teak Adirondacks, companionably sharing a joint. Daniel rarely smoked anymore, but did with Pete. Pete took a long, deep drag and offered the joint to May as she hurried out the back door of the kitchen. May took a more feminine toke and handed the joint to Joanna who in turn took only a small puff. Joanna tended to become giggly and slightly paranoid when stoned. Her college room-mate still referred to her as "Suspicious Giggles." So she declined the next round in favor of her glass of chardonnay.

Nuncle Pete animatedly updated everyone on his life. Two of his grandchildren were entering Kindergarten in the fall, "Can you believe it, Daniel? I can remember when Michael and Ethan and your girls were in Kindergarten and now their kids are going! It's crazy talk!" His youngest son, Kevin was finally getting married to his long-time girlfriend, Stacey, "Expect invitations within a few weeks. They're getting married on some mountain top or somewhere so bring your hiking boots."

Daniel laughed, "Sounds like Kevin," he quieted his voice, "So, how is Pearl doing?"

Pete sighed, took another drag, "She's good, thank God." Pearl had a few fishy looking moles removed, one of which turned out to be cancerous. The doctors felt confident they removed it in time and there was no spreading evident thus far. Pete and Pearl did not take the news lightly and were inspecting Pearl's body daily for new or weird growths.

The conversation drifted and soon Daniel and Joanna were deep in discussion about a stew Daniel had made. Nuncle Pete leaned towards May and said quietly, under his breath, "So May Day, you seem, I dunno, not my bubbly baby today. Maybe a little lost. What's going on in your pretty little head?"

May choked on the harsh smoke, startled from her Nuncle's astute revelation, "Dad hasn't told you?"

Nuncle Pete looked over at Daniel and shook his head no, "Do you want to go for a walk?" Pete squeaked, holding smoke in his lungs.

So May and her Nuncle walked around the block. The night was warm and balmy and the sky was crammed full of stars. May laughed as Nuncle Pete pointed out the Big and Little Dippers as if she were still four and spellbound by the mysterious shapes in the sky. Now it was Leo who oohed and ahhhed when he was able to spot the elusive constellations.

They walked in companionable silence, enjoying the night air. Pete breathed in the smells of honeysuckle and said, "So what's up, May Day?"

So May started at the beginning, told him about the cheating, the separation, the apology, and brought him up to date with the possible, probable reconciliation. Oh, and the fact she hadn't bothered to tell her mother about any of it.

"Wow, May, and you're going to take him back after this?"

May was surprised; she thought of all people, her new-agey Nuncle Pete would be the most understanding of her decision to take Jamie back. "Yes, I miss him like crazy, and I do forgive him. He fucked up, he made a mistake and now he's bending over backwards to gain trust again and get me back into his good graces."

"But..." prompted Nuncle Pete.

"But what? There's no but."

"Oh come on, May, of course there's a but. If there wasn't a 'but' you wouldn't seem so, I don't know, so fucking unhappy."

May stopped walking. "I'm not unhappy."

Pete stopped too, "You're happy then?"

May looked at him, squinting to make out his features in the dim streetlight, "I guess I'm confused is what I am."

Pete sat down on the curb and patted the space next to him and May obediently sat.

"My therapist says I need to mourn. I need to mourn the loss of my 'age of innocence'" May made little quotation marks with her fingers, "in order to move on to the next phase of our relationship. But I'm just ready to stop looking backwards and get my happy life back."

"And are you buying that?"

"Am I buying what? That I need to mourn?"

"No, are you buying that you'll be able to get your happy life back?"

May blinked at him. It was an interesting question. It never remotely occurred to her she wouldn't be getting her happy life back. Wasn't that what therapy was for? To work through your shit so you could be happy again? Wasn't it her inalienable right to be happy again?

"I'm not saying that won't happen, May Day. But maybe you're focusing on the wrong problem." Pete began to pull up the weeds growing along the curb. "Maybe you need to think about what you want out of your life moving forward, maybe that's where you will find happiness again. But I think you're kidding yourself if you think you're going to have your *old* happy life back. I think your therapist has hit the nail on the head there, Sweetheart. That part is dead and gone. Shit, Jamie cheated on you, and you are a better person than I am if you can forgive him. But I'm thinking you need to remember how fragile happiness is, and that you need to work on it, cultivate it, nurture it for it to grow. It's love, baby. It takes work."

Despite the marijuana, May's head felt clearer than it had in weeks as she watched her Nuncle continue to pull the weeds, working his way down the curb. "Thanks, Nuncle Pete, I kind of feel like, I don't know, I feel kind of better. I didn't know I felt this bad, but I feel better."

Pete pushed his weeds into a neat little pile and brushed the dirt from his hands. "But there's also that other thing you mentioned."

"What other thing?"

"The thing about your mother."

"Oh that."

Pete stood up and extended his hand to help May to her feet and they began to walk towards home, "Look,

I'm not Daniel so I'm going to try to not act like him, but as your favorite Nuncle can I give you one final piece of advice?"

"Sure."

Nuncle Pete stopped walking again, "Tell your mother, May. I know Lily can be overbearing, I don't need to tell you that. But she loves you more than life itself, and she's your mother, and you should tell her."

May traced the edge of the sidewalk with her thonged toe, "OK, I will."

"You've got a rough road ahead of you, May. But you're a strong lady, always have been, and you'll find your way. And Jamie's a good man. But he's a dumb-ass to have done this. I'm sorry but that just had to be said."

May laughed, "You're right, he is a dumb-ass. But he's my dumb-ass and I love him. But I'm pretty pissed at him too."

"You should be pissed. But you'll get over it. Come on, I'm starving!" Pete put his arm around May's slender shoulders and gave her a squeeze as they made their way back.

40

The phone rang at the bakery and Joanna picked up, "*Sweet*, this is Joanna, how can I help you?"

"Hey Joanna, its Hal. Is Marjorie there? I uh, know it's busy there but I kind of need to talk to her."

"Sure Hal, hang on." Holding the phone between her ear and shoulder, Joanna wiped her floury hands on her apron and walked to the front of the shop where a line snaked out the front door. "Marjorie, Hal's on the phone, I'll help out here."

Marjorie rolled her eyes and took the phone, "What's up, Buttercup I'm kind of busy here!" she leaned into her case to box up a half dozen *pain au chocolat*, "You did what?" She stood straight up and Joanna's head whipped in her direction. "Are you ok?" Marjorie and Joanna stood stock still, awaiting Hal's reply. "Ok, I'm on my way." She took off her apron and leaned in to Joanna to whisper at her, "Joanna, Hal wrapped his truck around a tree, I've got to go."

"Is he ok?"

"Well, he's talking so he can't be too bad off."

"Well hurry and go and call me later. I'll finish up here."

"Are you sure? Don't you have to work today? We could just close."

"Don't worry, just go!"

Joanna worked the line like an old pro, barely stopping to breathe until the line ended with a familiar face. It was Dan, who she had met on her first visit to *Sweet*, reading the paper while he patiently waited for his morning addiction and looking dapper in his work attire rather than the ripped jeans and t-shirt he'd worn on that first day, "Hi there, Dan, I'll bet Marjorie has a bag stashed under here for you somewhere." She began searching through the mass of pastry bags on a low shelf under the counter.

He cocked his head and looked at her quizzically, "I know you. You're an angel from heaven."

Joanna laughed, "Actually, I'm Joanna, now where's your bag?"

"Nice to meet you Joanna. And so are you the one responsible for this new addition to the lineup?" he waggled his finger at the one lone *Joanna's Jumbles* left in the case.

"Uh, yes, those ugly yet delicious *Jumbles* would be my concoction. Perhaps you'd like to try one today? Oh, here's your bag, right under my nose." She peered inside to see what to ring him up for, "Two almond tea-cakes, oh, and two *Joanna's Jumbles*! I guess you've tried them already!"

He leaned over the counter to hand her a twenty,

"Joanna, they are my new favorites and wholly responsible for this unsightly bulge I am developing in my middle," he indicated his washboard stomach.

Joanna laughed, "Well, sorry about that, although I see not an iota of a bulge," she smiled at him, "And I'm glad you like them." She handed him back his change.

"Like them? Like them?" Dan brought his hand to his forehead dramatically, "Don't you understand? They are my new obsession! Bravo, my Dear!" He sauntered out the door with a little wave.

After Dan left, Joanna called Helen to let her know what had happened and she'd consequently be a tad late, "Oh! I hope he's ok!" said Helen, her voice filled with trepidation. Helen was one of these rare beings who felt everyone else's pain, a quality she shared with Joanna. "Do you need to take the day off, Joanna? It's quiet in here today; remember all the lawyers are at their retreat?"

Joanna had forgotten, "Are you sure, Helen? It won't be too much trouble?" Strangely, Helen was the only person besides Mark that Joanna had told about *Sweet*. She figured it was the least she could do to confess her own secret after Helen had divulged her meditatethebigO obsession.

"No trouble at all, I was going to send everyone home after lunch anyway! Keep me posted about your friend though!"

Joanna began to close up the shop, seeing as there were only half a dozen items left. The phone rang. "Sweet, this is Joanna, how may I help you?"

"Hey Jo, its Marje."

"Marjorie! How's Hal?"

"Well, he's just fine. A little shook up and very bruised and sore but they already released him, told him to go home and rest for a few days and he should be good as new. The truck, well, we'll be buying a new truck but that's better than buying a new husband I suppose!"

"I'm so relieved."

"Yeah, he's a tough old bird, just needs to keep his eyes on the road."

Joanna assured Marjorie there was no reason for her to come in, she should stay with poor Hal. Anita and Esteban had already begun the prep for the next day and Joanna jumped in to join them. The trio worked through the rest of the morning, quiet and methodic. Joanna found she worked so intently at the bakery; it was as if the rest of the world melted away. She didn't think about men, or May. She didn't make lists in her head. She didn't think about Leo and what he was up to, or her parents. She didn't think about her actual job that she was missing, or even that she was going to miss a fun lunch with Delia and Bruno today (now that Bruno and Roger were moving in together a number of new dramas had ensued, including a particularly nasty brawl about whose couch they would be using in their living room). She certainly didn't think about the laundry she desperately needed to do, as she was nearly out of clean underwear. She instead lost herself in the work, kneading and mixing and tasting and stirring. The only items of importance that required her undivided attention were her closest compadres: flour, butter, and chocolate, eggs, vanilla and leavening. The hours flew by without her noticing, and when she was done she felt exhausted and happy and calm and exhilarated all at once.

It was a high she couldn't get enough of and one she didn't want to come down from.

41

May was officially a wee bit chubby. Well, maybe chubby was too strong of a word. Plump? May was just getting a little meat on her bones.

Surprisingly, it wasn't as devastating as she thought it would be. She felt good. She was just slightly more curvaceous then she had been. It was refreshing, or something.

She and Jamie had taken the sex step. How bizarre, as a married couple, to be nervous as sixteen year old virgins. "Does that hurt? Is that ok? How about there? Ouch!" As if they didn't know each nook and cranny of each other. But with May's new teeny extra layer of flesh, Jamie commented she was deliciously...chewy. And it felt nice to be gnawed on. She had missed her husband.

So she really didn't complain too much when she realized a shopping spree was in her future. Because her pants were just a little, well...snug.

So May was trying on jeans a size larger than she ever had. Last night over dinner (where Joanna had witnessed May's consumption of both cheese and bread AND wine, in one sitting), Joanna had been less than sympathetic.

"You are still skinnier than your average anorexic, May. The average woman in America," she pointed down at her soft, fleshy body, "is a size 12. Yours truly? A voluptuous size 14. And smokin' hot, I might add."

May was sidetracked in her quest, because she couldn't help but overhear the bullshit the woman in the next dressing room was being fed by the overzealous saleswoman. She had heard the poor woman, clearly out of her element, explain to the obviously incompetent saleswoman that she just earned a promotion and needed a power outfit for her first major presentation which didn't necessarily involve a suit. So far she'd been told a fuchsia blouse was so becoming on her and that the black slacks were slimming. May struggled back into her slightly snug jeans; she felt it was her duty to intercede. This woman should not be wearing fuchsia; she was obviously a Spring from the glimpse May had gotten and a Spring shouldn't be caught dead in fuchsia. And in what way was fuchsia and black a "power outfit?" Was this 1985? And why did she need slimming pants? She was already slim! May was shocked this saleswoman was actually being paid for doing this job. Especially here, one of the best boutiques in town, one should expect a higher caliber of service.

May exited her dressing room and knocked on the one next door. The woman opened the door wearing the offensive blouse.

"Hello," said May.

"Hi," said the woman, obviously puzzled, "may I help you with something?"

"I'm sorry" said May, suddenly realizing she may be slightly overstepping, but continued to overstep just the same, "I just could tell from the conversation you were having you could use some real help and that salesperson is completely useless. I mean she has you wearing fuchsia! Of course it's terrible on you. She's an idiot. Let me help you. Please."

The woman narrowed her pale, almost teal colored eyes at May; she was clearly perplexed as to what May was doing there, "I'm sorry, do you work here?"

"No, I don't, and I know this is weird, but I'm good at this, so let me help you. I'm May." She extended her hand.

"I'm Melanie, and you're right. This color is hideous. How come it makes me look gray? I didn't know it was possible for a person to be gray," she shook the outstretched hand.

"Because you're a Spring. A Spring shouldn't ever wear fuchsia. I'm going to find you a terrific outfit. Give me ten minutes ok? What size are you? About an 8?" Melanie nodded, "That's what I thought. I'll be back."

Clearly in her element, May rifled through racks of clothing, blouses, sweaters, slacks and skirts until she had an armful. A saleswoman approached her.

"I'm sorry, did you need some help?"

"No thank you. I'm just fine," May continued to look through the racks. *Spring, Spring, Spring, she thought. This color is good, but I don't like this cut...*

"May I start a room for you?"

"Oh, these aren't for me. They're for the blonde in the dressing room. You could bring these to her and tell her

I'm on my way," She transferred the load into the saleswoman's outstretched arms.

"I'm sorry, are you assisting this customer?" The saleswoman was clearly confused but trying to remain professional.

"Uh, yeah. She needs some help so I'm helping. Call it charity work." May smiled.

"We are certainly capable of assisting her, if you'd like to return to your own shopping," the saleswoman smiled at her, trying to disguise the claws emerging.

"Well, your help over there," she indicated Melanie's saleswoman with a tip of her head "has no business helping anyone, so I'm stepping in. Excuse me," May smiled sweetly and moved on.

It took a measly ten minutes for Melanie's transformation. May had chosen a simple lilac cashmere sweater set and paired it with soft camel-colored slacks.

"See how the lilac picks up the honey-tones in your hair? It's feminine, still reminds people that you are a woman, but sleek and professional. And see, you can wear a color like lilac and not look too girly because it complements you so well. You need some gold near your face; do you have a chunky gold necklace you can wear? That would help complete the look. And these slacks just look great on you; they hang beautifully and really elongate your leg. I own these slacks in three colors, although I'm going to need an upgrade. You can also get away with a moderate heel with these slacks, since I see you prefer a flatter footwear. They do have coordinating jackets which are very smart. I know you said you didn't want a suit but I can't help but think you would wear the jacket at some point. It would be a good investment." May finally paused and smiled, "So what do you think? Do you like it?"

Melanie turned to May, "I look terrific!" She twirled in the mirror like a girl in a prom dress, "Have you thought about becoming a personal shopper?"

May smiled, "Well, no, but that's sweet of you. You look great, don't you think?"

Melanie persisted, "May, I'm not kidding. I just met you but I'm ready to hire you. What do you think?"

May was flabbergasted, "Like a job? Are you offering me a job? I haven't worked in over a decade. I wouldn't even know how."

Melanie laughed, "Of course you would. This is what I need: Someone to keep my wardrobe current. Shoes, purses, jewelry, the whole shebang. I hate this stuff and I'm not good at it and you clearly are. Really, will you think about it?" May was dazed as Melanie handed her a business card, "And do you have time to help me buy shoes and jewelry to go with this outfit...right now?"

"Well," May began, "Sure, I have some more time. And I'm so glad to hear you say shoes because you really need to update those. You know, you do need a bag too. No offense intended and that Coach *was* a classic, but it's ready for retirement," she put her hand on Melanie's shoulder, "let's go put that puppy out of its misery."

42

David turned out to be such a wonderful companion; it was a little petrifying. The eeriest thing about their dates was that he asked her all sorts of questions, actually listened to her answers and then asked *another* question based on her answer. He also remembered their conversations, remembered what she liked and didn't like. He even remembered what she wore...

"Remember last Saturday when you came into the bookstore, you were wearing that green cardigan sweater and your hair was in a ponytail? I love that color green on you. Anyway, you mentioned you were interested in robotics and I found this article I thought you'd enjoy."

Then he'd smile at her or ask her about robotic limb movement or whatever it was on that particular day. She couldn't remember when she had been listened to so intently, so intensely. As if everything she said and thought were incredibly interesting and creative. Or maybe not so creative, but important. As if everything she said really mattered to him.

The weirdest part was she realized Delia had been

right at the get-go, she hadn't given David the time of day. Joanna had been in that bookstore hundreds of times. She could tell you the color of the worn sofas, where to sit to get the perfect slice of sun directly on your page, where the floor creaked while walking from the self-help section to photography. How could she not have noticed this adorable man right under her nose? A man who, she had come to realize, was doing everything he could to get her attention aside from waving a flag in front of her face or smacking her sharply across the jaw with an open hand.

He was right under her nose, and now that he was directly in front of her she was scared scared scared. And she didn't want to get her hopes up. And she didn't want to be disappointed. But she was ready to take the plunge. To close her eyes and dive in.

Their dates were fun and varied. He took her bowling, to a piano concerto in the park and surprised her with a romantic dinner at the bookstore.

For their fifth date she invited him to her apartment for dinner.

She agonized over the menu. Delia tried to alleviate her fears, "Joanna, you are an excellent cook, and David will love whatever you make. But if I were you I'd make that fried chicken you made for the pot-luck because *never* have I eaten anything so delicious. And then you could bring me the leftovers. See how that works?"

Joanna shook her head, "No, fried chicken is not going to work for this potentially romantic evening. One that will definitely involve kissing, and hopefully lots of it. That's picnic food."

"Oh yeah, well, good point, you want something sexier. Well, your lasagna is mind-boggling terrific, but that's a lot of garlic. And those Indian pastries you make? Samosas? Is that what they are called? They are delicious; they'd be a great appetizer. Oh! Oh! Make that coconut curried soup with the shrimp, oh my God that is so good! Or maybe rack of lamb, remember when you made that with the rosemary and the mustard?" Delia was off in her own world, salivating down memory lane.

She finally decided to go simple: roast chicken with potatoes and carrots. She had just finished setting the table when her phone rang.

"Hey there Jelly Jo. What are you up to?"

"Hi Daddy. What a nice surprise, how are you?" She took the bottle of chardonnay she had been chilling in the fridge out and screwed the corkscrew into the cork, pulling it out with a soft pop.

"I'm good, I'm good. I just wanted to say hi, I was missing you."

"Dad, I saw you like three days ago." She poured herself a glass.

"I know, I know. So," he paused.

Joanna sat down on her couch and took off her flats, putting her feet up on her scuffed coffee table, letting her dad take his time with whatever was on his mind while she sipped her wine.

"So, May tells me you had a date?"

Joanna smiled to herself, "May tells the truth. Yes, I've actually had several dates with this really super-duper nice guy. His name is David."

"David huh."

"Yes, you'll like him and I suspect you'll get to meet him. Hey, but there's another thing going on for me that is also super-cool…"

And she told him all about *Sweet*. She told him about Marjorie and *Joanna's Jumbles* (which were proving so popular they had tripled their production), and about how she finally felt as if she had found her destiny, the place she had been looking for. She told him she didn't feel empty anymore, that she felt happy and whole. And then the doorbell rang.

"Daddy, I have to go, that's David at the door now. I made him dinner."

"Wait, what did you make?"

"Roast chicken, potatoes and carrots."

"Dessert?"

"Devils-food cupcakes with vanilla-bean icing."

"Yum. I'm drooling! Ok, Sweetie, have fun tonight. I love you."

"I love you too." Joanna hung up and smoothed her hair before answering the door.

She opened the door to find David mostly hidden behind an exorbitantly large bouquet of flowers which he handed her and said "Oh my God, Joanna, it smells like heaven in here."

43

They had gotten to know each other quite well. Joanna knew Marjorie was originally from Butte, Montana of all places, and she was the only girl in a family of five children. Marjorie itched to get out of Butte from a very young age, "The most interesting thing in Butte is that it's Evel Knievel's home town. And the second most interesting thing is it's the home of the oldest running brothel in the US. Neither of these facts was ever much interest, or use to me!" Marjorie conceded that Butte is beautiful, but "Snow and I just don't get along." Marjorie was rather an odd duck in this town of copper mines and outdoorsmen. She was interested in food, and especially baking. Her home ec teacher, a French expat, saw the spark in Marjorie and arranged for her to study with a colleague in France. So at seventeen, not knowing a word of French, she moved to Paris to study pastry. She spent the next five years learning to bake with some of the best pastry chefs in the world, and the following five working as a pastry chef all over France.

Three of Marjorie's four brothers had also fled

from Butte, scattering across the U.S. from California to Florida. Paul, the brother who stayed, worked for the Anaconda Mining Company just as their father did until Paul learned that strip-mining was causing an environmental disaster. He quit his job and began working for the EPA with a specialty in Superfund sites, consequently targeting the very companies he and his buddies growing up had worked for, making him one of the most hated men in Butte. Ben was a real estate broker in Florida and Jess lived and worked on a dairy farm in Georgia. Ralph, her favorite sibling, nine years her senior, landed in Santa Rosa, California. Ralph worked his way up into owning a vineyard company and described Northern California as the home Marjorie had always yearned for. "Marge, its agriculture and wineries and restaurants and educated folks, it's homey and beautiful. It's just your style!" He encouraged her to move back to the states to live near him and his new growing family. Although she created a full life for herself in France, a lovely home, a varied and interesting group of friends, Marjorie never felt quite at home. An odd duck in Butte, Marjorie really was a fish out of water in Paris.

Plus, she was lonely for her brothers and wanted to see her new nieces and nephews grow up so she gave notice and made the leap to California.

"And the rest, as they say, is history. When I first arrived here I worked in bakeries from Healdsburg to Marin, some really great places. But I wanted to have my own place so I scrimped and saved and finally came up with the dough to open my own spot. Ha! Get it? Dough!" she slapped her thigh. "Anyway, best decision I ever made was to move here. I met my husband here, had Emily here. Made a life for myself here. It's really my fairy-tale come true; just what I always wanted."

Joanna felt a guilty stab of green envy. Marjorie had the life she was craving, that she was itching for and that she suspected was finally within reach.

One Sunday morning, after the shop had closed at 9:45, having run out of every last item, the two women sat and sipped coffee in companionable silence.

"So," Marjorie began, "I don't believe in fate or any of that new-agy foolishness, but something brought you into my shop in the first place and I sure want to know what it was."

Joanna smiled, "I can't believe I haven't told you. A guy brought me one of your *pain au chocolats* and I was hooked. I agreed to go on a date with him if he told me where he bought it."

"Are you kidding me?"

"Nope. Not kidding."

Marjorie paused to sip, "Was it David?"

Joanna almost spit out her coffee, startled, although she rapidly recognized Marjorie knew the bulk of her customers, Dan being an obvious example of just how well Marjorie knew them.

Marjorie began to smile, "He owns the book store?"

Joanna nodded

"And are you still dating him?"

"Uh, yes..." Joanna answered, confused by the third degree.

Marjorie threw back her head and let out a whoop of laughter, "That sly little devil! Well, I've got to give it to him; he picked himself a good one this time. My Dear, David is my nephew."

The little bell rang as the door opened to reveal May. Per usual, she was already speaking as she walked through the door, "Marjorie, please tell me there's a cookie here with my name on it." Noticing Joanna, she continued, puzzled "Jo, what are you doing here?"

"Well this explains your expanding waistline," answered Joanna.

"You two know each other, I gather?" Marjorie reached under the counter for a pastry bag with May's two oatmeal-raisin cookies inside.

"Uh, yeah," Joanna answered, and the sisters laughed.

44

May begged Joanna to come to the park with her and Leo. "I just cannot stand those mothers who want to talk to me! I need you! Please oh please! I'll buy you lunch. Anywhere you want to go."

Joanna had been sitting on her balcony, reading her book and happily enjoying a croissant with her coffee. She was home from the bakery already; they ran out of product even earlier than usual today, partly due to a panicked father who forgot to order cupcakes for his daughter's party ("The ONE thing I asked you to do," growled his disgruntled wife). Joanna wasn't sure if she wanted to disturb the blissful plan she had of doing nothing but this until her movie date that evening with David.

"Please oh please! Leo, get on the phone and tell your Auntie to get off her bottom and come to the park with us."

"Hi Auntie Jo." Leo was on the phone, sounding rather sullen, "Can you get off your bottom and come to the park with us please?"

"Hi Leo, ok, ok, I'll come."

“Yippee! She’ll come,” Leo screamed, tearing Joanna’s eardrum in two.

May was back on the phone, “OK, we’re turning on your street! See you in 2 secs!”

Joanna jumped up, “What! You’ve already here? Jeez May I’m not even wearing a bra yet for crying out loud!”

“Well, get those boulders under wraps, Girl because here I am!”

Joanna heard a honk and saw the minivan with May waving out the window. She rolled her eyes and reluctantly went inside to put on some clothes.

Once at the park, Joanna was happy to be out. It was a beautiful sunny day, and unlike May, Joanna did love going to the park with Leo, an excellent excuse to get in touch with her inner child. She enjoyed the rush she got chasing him along the play structure, pushing him on the swings as he giggled with glee. Leo was freakishly strong for a young boy; he had already mastered the monkey-bars and could deftly climb the huge scary spider climber Joanna wouldn’t have touched with a ten-foot pole as a child his age. Even now it made her wary.

“C’mon, guys, don’t poop out on me, puh-lease!” Leo complained as the two women sat heavily on a bench.

“Leo, I’ve been chasing you around this park like a deranged puppy for an hour and I’m old old old! So give your old Auntie a break to catch her breath and I’ll be back on your tail shortly, okey doke?” Joanna took a sip from Leo’s discarded juice box.

"Oy vey!" Leo exclaimed theatrically, tromping away towards the spider climber.

May and Joanna laughed. "He is just like you," said May, furtively reaching for Leo's discarded goldfish crackers.

"Dude," said Joanna, "you're eating carbs? And they're not even low-sodium. Think of the swelling!" she shook her finger at May, "tsk, tsk!"

"Shut up, would you?" May elbowed her in the ribs.

Leo was already halfway up the giant climber, spry as a monkey.

"Be careful, Leo!" shouted May.

Leo gave her the thumbs-up, international kid's sign of "its ok, Mom, just chill."

Joanna and May ate the goldfish crackers. Joanna was people-watching, fascinated by a homely boy in a "Mr. Happy" tee-shirt and red shorts who kept digging in his butt. His cranky grandmother did not approve and kept admonishing, "Xander! Stop that immediately!" To which Xander would simply ignore her and dig some more.

A perky mother wearing a matching sweat suit and a ponytail paused next to the sisters, "Is that one yours?" She pointed at Leo.

"He's hers," Joanna gestured to May.

"He's an excellent climber. That one is mine." She pointed to a burly-looking boy struggling up the spider. "He's not so nimble," she smiled and left them.

"See how they always want to talk?" said May.

"Oh for crying out loud, May, she was just making

friendly conversation, not trying to sell you a pyramid scheme or something."

"So anyway, I wanted to tell you, apparently I have a job," May began.

Joanna worked her hair back into a shabby ponytail, "A job? I didn't know you were looking for a job."

May expertly tossed a goldfish into the air and caught it in her mouth. "I didn't know I was either," she crunched the cracker, "it just sort-of fell in my lap."

May told Joanna about the boutique and meeting Melanie. Melanie, despite her inability to dress herself properly, was actually a real muckety-muck, a new partner in a prestigious fancy-pants law firm. After their shopping spree they had gone to lunch and defined the terms of their new working agreement. May told Joanna how unbelievably satisfying it was to shop for an acre of beautiful clothing with someone else's charge card, and even better to see Melanie's confidence explode as she modeled her new up-to-the-minute stylish attire. Now that Melanie's closet was in decent shape, at least until the Fall, she was ready to tackle Melanie's husband next. Bruce was a COO for a small but impressive group of boutique wineries, so jeans and flannels were his outfit of choice. May pointed out to Bruce that jeans should be stylish too, and it was time to update his "butch lesbian from the 80's" look. Luckily, Bruce and Melanie shared May's wry sense of humor, and Bruce had cracked up at May's comment.

Plus, and perhaps the pièce de résistance, the couple had a five year old daughter, Madeleine, so May finally found another mother she could truly dish about parenthood with, while still discussing events of the world over a mani/pedi. Bliss!

"I'm totally loving it," she caught another fish, "who knew I'd go back to work?"

"Back to work? Don't you have to work in the first place to go back to work? Anyway, May, how cool!" Joanna smacked her sis on the knee, "I'm super proud of you!"

"I'm getting to do special-occasion stuff too. They went to a formal wedding last weekend so I got to shop for a couture gown and tux. It's fun. Maybe now that I'm a professional you'll let me tackle your pathetic closet. "

"Well, that would be easy; you could just haul the whole mess to the dump, or just light a match and run. May I'm so freakin' excited for..."

The scream was ear-splitting and unmistakably Leo, even from 30 feet away.

In seconds they were on their feet and running towards the little heap under the spider.

It wasn't that the fall was so enormous; Leo was a tough little man and he was making his way down the spider when he lost his footing and fell, so he was maybe a third of the way up the 40 foot climber. Like a cat, Leo generally landed on his feet and his daddy had taught him how to fall properly, how to protect his head and tuck his body into a ball and roll to a stop so he wouldn't hurt himself too badly. If it weren't for some unbelievable moron, some cruel hater of children, some stoned, mindless teenager who had left a broken beer bottle underneath the play structure, partially camouflaged in the wood chips so even the most anal of mothers or park maintenance crew had easily missed it, he may have only been bruised. But Leo landed and rolled hard, directly on top of the broken glass.

The sisters reached him in seconds; May lifted him in her strong arms to reveal the large chunk of glass well-wedged into Leo's little arm, jutting out of a gush of blood. Leo was crying hysterically and trying to shake the glass free, but was only able to feebly flop his arm about.

"It's ok, Sweetie, we're going to take you to the doctor...he'll make it all better..." May murmured into his hair and rocked her little one, calm as possible.

Joanna ran like a chicken with her head cut off with May's keys to get the car. Within minutes they were speeding towards the hospital, May rocking Leo in the backseat, and trying to not look at the blood seeping out, definitely more slowly now, around the glass. She knew enough about first aid to know not to remove the glass, which was acting as a painful plug in Leo's arm. But she couldn't look at it and tried to get Leo to look at her instead, "Look at Mommy's eyes, Sweetie, look at Mommy, Leo the Lion." She also knew she had to try to keep him awake and not lose consciousness. She was also nervous that in addition to the gash, his arm may be broken, she was fairly certain it had to be what with the odd, disgusting angle and the flopping motion.

"Sorry!" yelled Joanna, as she swerved to avoid hitting a pothole and jostled the minivan.

"Please don't get us pulled over, Joanna," May said as calmly as she could, "that would not be good."

Joanna hustled the car into the parking lot and braked abruptly in front of the Emergency Room. May gently pulled the now whimpering Leo up into her arms, carrying him like a baby. Before sprinting inside the double doors she turned and called to Joanna, "Call Jamie!"

Joanna lurched the car into a parking space and fumbled for her mobile, her hands were shaking uncontrollably. She left a message on Jamie's cell, letting him know she'd call as soon as she knew something, and then she left a message for David, telling him she needed to cancel their movie date, and sped inside, muttering to herself, "Please oh please oh please."

The tiny waiting room was empty except for a sleeping man in a postal uniform and a teenager, glassy eyes glued to Judge Judy on the silent TV. Joanna paced for what seemed like an eternity while she waited and before May finally came rushing through the double white doors.

May explained Leo's arm had needed to be x-rayed before they could remove the glass. Now the glass was out, stitches were in and they would be able to set the broken ulna shortly.

"The ulna?" Joanna asked idiotically.

"Yes, the ulna, this bone right here," May pointed to the bone that ran from her pinky up to her elbow. "It's broken, but it's not too bad apparently. He's ok, Jo." May set her hands on Joanna's shoulders firmly and looked into her eyes, trying to ground her, "He really is going to be ok. You're as pale as a ghost; do you need to sit down?"

Joanna nodded and sat down right where she was on the floor, "No, I'm ok, he's ok. I'll calm down now."

"OK, good. No passing out on me now."

Joanna was startled by her ringing mobile. It was David, and Joanna couldn't help but smile when she saw his sweet mug. She quickly filled him in on Leo, telling him she'd call him later on. She had barely hung up when the phone rang again, Jamie this time, and she handed the phone to May, listening to the one-sided conversation.

"Hi," now May paced as she talked.

"He's ok. He was very lucky, but he's ok."

"Yes, it's broken."

"I love you too, baby. When are you coming home?"

"No, home. Our house, home. It's time for you to come home."

Joanna looked at her hands in her lap and smiled.

"Luckily for little Leo," the ER doctor, an enormous Asian man with an unruly mustache explained, the glass that punctured the poor guys arm narrowly missed the blah-blah-blah artery; which could have caused him to lose an excessive amount of blood which could have meant the need for a blood transfusion. May and Joanna blinked at him.

"So, what you're telling me is he's lucky that didn't happen and his arm will be fine?" May asked impatiently. She continually smoothed and then rearranged the hair on Leo's forehead while he slept. She wasn't sure whether it was the shock and the following exhaustion or the pain killers had knocked him out, but she was grateful he was resting. Leo looked peaceful as he quietly snored, clutching a teddy bear in one sweaty fist the nurse had given him on arrival at the hospital. His new cast lay heavily across his chest; his powerful little legs splayed out as he slept.

"Oh yes, yes," said the doc, fingering the mustache. "His arm will be fine, although he'll be in that cast for a month or so, and that wound may scar. He's a very lucky little boy!"

"He's a tough little man, he'll be fine." May heavily lay her head next to her sleeping child's. Tears finally seeped out of the corners of her eyes.

Joanna rubbed May's back as her baby sis quietly cried.

45

May tried to contrive a reason to invite her mother to lunch. She knew she needed to tell her what was going on, what had gone on, the guilt over not telling her was overwhelming any desire she had of keeping it from her so she decided to bite the bullet, to take the bull by the horns, to put it all on the line and tell her. She tried to be blasé, keeping her tone light and airy, saying, "Hey Mom, how about I take you to lunch on Friday, just you and me?"

But of course, Lily, first-rate bullshit spotter that she was, saw right through May's contrived tone and said, "What's going on, May? Is something wrong? I knew something was going on! Are you finally telling me that you are pregnant?"

May couldn't help it. The laugh tickled at her throat and burst forward until she dropped the phone onto the counter and was rolling with laughter, tears streaming down her face. She could hear Lily screaming into the phone: "What? What? What is so God-damned funny? I do not appreciate this, May!" May could only rock back and forth, trying to catch her breath.

Finally calmer, she picked the phone back up and pressed to it her ear, "No Mom, no, I'm not pregnant. Jamie and I have been separated, that's all, but we're back together now, it's all going to be fine..."

"What? Are you kidding me? What?"

"Really Mom, I'll start at the beginning and tell you everything but first of all everything is going to be fine..."

46

Joanna had been dating David for two months when he invited her to his Cousin Emily's wedding. "I hear you'll know a few people there," he said nonchalantly, with his gentle smile, just the corners slightly turned up. She hadn't yet mentioned to him she knew he was Marjorie's nephew, but apparently Marjorie had. She told him of course she would love to go with him.

Joanna and Marjorie spent the weeks prior to the wedding in a cake and candy-making frenzy. They made delicate almond and apricot petit fours for the bride's wedding shower, dark-chocolate toffee for the groomsmen and petite caramel and champagne filled truffles for the wedding favors. Joanna's back ached as never before from leaning over rows of perfect little gumdrop-shaped chocolates as she sprinkled the final dusting of cocoa powder onto each one.

The morning of the wedding, Joanna rose before dawn to help Marjorie put the finishing touches on the cake. When she arrived at the bakery, Marjorie had already made her a latte and they ate muffins with their coffee to fortify them for the busy morning. The cake was dazzling, alternating layers of lemon chiffon and devils food, generously frosted with creamy vanilla-bean buttercream and decorated with tiny edible silver stars. It was so elegant, the most ambitious thing Joanna had ever helped to create. She was bursting with pride.

Hal showed up to transport the goods to the wedding site and Marjorie practically pushed Joanna out of the bakery, insisting "Go! I don't want to be blamed if you look like hell, all ragged and tired tonight at the wedding!" So she finally went home to nap.

Joanna lay down to nap on her couch, closing her eyes and willing herself to sleep but soon gave up. She was too restless and excited to sleep. Sitting up, she reached for the remote and idly flipped channels on the TV, settling on a cooking show. The host was making some sort of butter-soaked thing aptly called a *Gooey Butter Cake*. Bored, Joanna went into her own kitchen, surveyed the blackening bunch of bananas on the counter and snapped on the oven to preheat. She reached into her cabinets to gather muffin tins and her tiny pantry for ingredients.

The gentle banana aroma filled her apartment, and half an hour later, she pulled the banana-bran muffins from the oven. She placed the warm, fragrant muffins on a rack to cool and then split one open, spreading butter inside, watching it instantly melt from the heat of the steaming muffin. She took a bite, her taste-buds exploding with banana and she immediately felt peaceful and centered. "Ah," she thought, "there's my core strength."

Finally, it was time to get ready for the wedding. May arrived to help with the transformation and brought Leo to survey the results. She began with hair. The night before, May had rolled it into big wide waves which Joanna had tucked under a scarf like an old Russian woman while she worked at the bakery. Now it bobbed prettily as she swept it back over her ears. She liked the effect of it gently curling around her dangly earrings. Next, May carefully applied Joanna's makeup, blending and swirling and using a delicate hand with the mascara wand. Joanna cautiously slipped the graphic black and white dress over her head ("A bold choice," said the saleswoman. "Not many women can wear such a dramatic print, but it suits you.") being careful not to smudge her sister's meticulous work. The dress swirled around her rather bumpy middle with ease, "tricking the eye" into thinking she had a slender waist. Although Joanna had been slightly offended by the "tricking the eye" comment, the effect really was miraculous. The dress made her look curvaceous and sexy, a far cry from the dumpy girl she had felt like for the past months. Joanna stepped carefully into sparkly high-heeled sandals (Easy Spirits, but no one needed to know), stood up tall and inspected herself in the mirror. She hardly recognized herself. She looked good, really good. Bordering on "hot" good. And not only that, she could even walk.

Joanna grabbed her pashmina and clutch (both borrowed from May), snapping her newly purchased *dare to be red* lipstick inside. Taking a deep breath, she confidently ventured down the hall and into the living room, ready to present herself for May and Leo's critique.

"Oh, Auntie Jo!" exclaimed Leo, smiling hugely and flapping his arm, still in its cast, "You look like a big beautiful cow!"

Joanna stopped on a dime and couldn't help but draw in her breath. She made an audible "ooof," like she had been punched in the stomach. May's eyes bugged out and she looked like she was choking, as if she had swallowed something way too big, like a potato, or maybe a cantaloupe. Leo's little face, on the other hand, was quizzical; clearly he was confused as to how his super-excellent compliment hadn't brought an enormous grin to his Auntie's face.

Joanna finally cracked a smile which turned into a giggle and finally a full-on belly laugh. She gave him an enormous hug and a *dare to be red* kiss on his mouth, "Thank you, Leo, that's the best compliment I've heard all day!"

She slowly drove to meet David. Her window was open wide, letting in the warm summer breeze which blew her nicely coiffed "do" around a bit. Down the median of the road grew a tangle of vibrant wildflowers, weeds. A big beautiful intertwine of eye-popping color growing unattended and free. They were magnificent and Joanna smiled contentedly. She breathed in the balmy night air and looked up at the comic-strip moon, glittering brightly in the receding light. She was excited about what the evening may bring.

The End

Joanna's Jumbles

Ingredients:

1 cup shredded unsweetened coconut
6 ¼ ounces unbleached all-purpose flour (approx 1 1/3 cup)
½ teaspoon baking powder
1 teaspoon baking soda
1 teaspoon salt
1 ¼ cups old-fashioned rolled oats (Quick oats will yield a less chewy cookie)
4 ounces bittersweet chocolate (60-70% cocoa) chopped into chip-size (½ cup)
4 ounces semi-sweet chips (½ cup)
1 stick softened butter
1 ½ cups packed dark brown sugar (light is ok, dark is better)
1 large egg
2 teaspoons vanilla extract
½ cup coconut milk, well shaken

Preparation:

1. Set oven to 250 degrees. Spread coconut on a jelly-roll pan or cookie sheet. Toast for 5-10 minutes, stirring coconut occasionally (it may stick), until lightly browned. Remove from oven to cool. Keep an eye on it, coconut can burn in a flash!
2. Increase heat on oven to 350 degrees. Line two large (18 by 12 inch) cookie sheets with parchment paper or silpats.
3. Whisk flour, baking powder and soda and salt together. In second bowl mix oats, coconut and chocolate.
4. Fit standing mixer with flat beater. Beat butter and sugar at medium speed until the sugar lumps are gone. Scrape sides of bowl and add egg, vanilla and coconut milk. Beat 30 seconds. Scrape down bowl. Turn mixer to low, add flour for 30 seconds until incorporated. Do not overmix!
5. Turn off mixer and add oats/chocolate. Mix by hand until incorporated. Refrigerate mixture (will be wet) 15 minutes or longer. Overnight is ok too.
6. For big bakery-style cookies: divide dough into 16 equal portions (¼ cup each), roll into balls. Place 2 inches apart on baking sheets. Gently press balls with palm to ½ inch (may want to wet palms first, batter is very sticky). Bake 8 minutes, rotate pans front to back and top to bottom, then bake an additional 8 minutes, until edges begin

to brown and middles begin to set. They will still look wet! Cool on baking sheet 2 minutes before removing to rack to cool. For smaller, lunch-box sized cookies: divide dough into 24 portions, about 2 ½ tablespoons each. Reduce baking time to 12 minutes total.

Enjoy!

Acknowledgements

A huge thank you to my very first reader and dear friend, Jodi Litman who replied to my query of whether I should keep writing with "yes please – I need to know what happens!" Thank you also to Amy Grams, Robin Rosenzweig, Wendy Welling, Stephanie Hughes and Cat Canto for reading early drafts and offering suggestions, reinforcements and encouragements – plus wine and chocolate.

Thank you to Amy Grams for helping me to develop the Joanna's Jumbles recipe. To Jackie Winquist for website and cover design and execution. And to Kirstin Dill for her beautiful cow artwork.

Thank you to my parents for instilling a love of reading; encouraging me to read anything and everything at probably "*too young an age*".

Finally, thank you to my wonderful husband, Ed and amazing children, Lucas and Willa for their love and support as I pursue my own passion and figure out what I want to be when I grow up.